PR ... VELS

"Jaci Burton's stories are full of heat and heart."
— Maya Banks, #1 *New York Times* bestselling author

"A wild ride." — Lora Leigh, #1 *New York Times* bestselling author

"Passionate, inventive, sexually explicit." — USAToday.com

"A captivating and satisfying mix of physical and emotional passions . . . The deft characterization, snappy dialogue and sizzling love scenes will keep the pages turning." — *Publishers Weekly* (starred review)

"One of the strongest sports romance series available."
— Dear Author

"Endearing characters, a strong romance and an engaging plot all wrapped up in one sexy package." — Romance Novel News

"Both sensual and raw . . . Plenty of romance, sexy men, hot steamy loving and humor." — Smexy Books

"Hot, hot, hot! . . . Romance at its best! Highly recommended! Very steamy." — Coffee Table Reviews

"Burton knocks it out of the park . . . With snappy back-and-forth dialogue as well as hot, sweaty and utterly engaging bedroom play, readers will not be able to race through this book fast enough!"
— *RT Book Review*

Titles by Jaci Burton

Play-by-Play Series

THE PERFECT PLAY
CHANGING THE GAME
TAKING A SHOT
PLAYING TO WIN
THROWN BY A CURVE
ONE SWEET RIDE
HOLIDAY GAMES
(an eNovella)
MELTING THE ICE
STRADDLING THE LINE

HOLIDAY ON ICE
(an eNovella)
QUARTERBACK DRAW
ALL WOUND UP
HOT HOLIDAY NIGHTS
(an eNovella)
UNEXPECTED RUSH
RULES OF CONTACT
THE FINAL SCORE

Hope Series

HOPE SMOLDERS
(an eNovella)
HOPE FLAMES
HOPE IGNITES
HOPE BURNS

LOVE AFTER ALL
MAKE ME STAY
DON'T LET GO
LOVE ME AGAIN

Wild Rider Series

RIDING WILD
RIDING TEMPTATION

RIDING ON INSTINCT
RIDING THE NIGHT

Stand-Alone Novels

WILD, WICKED, & WANTON
BOUND, BRANDED, & BRAZEN

Anthologies

UNLACED
(with Jasmine Haynes, Joey W. Hill, and Denise Rossetti)
EXCLUSIVE
(with Eden Bradley and Lisa Renee Jones)
LACED WITH DESIRE
(with Jasmine Haynes, Joey W. Hill, and Denise Rossetti)
NAUTI AND WILD
(with Lora Leigh)
NAUTIER AND WILDER
(with Lora Leigh)
HOT SUMMER NIGHTS
(with Carly Phillips, Erin McCarthy, and Jessica Clare)
MISTLETOE GAMES
(*Holiday Games*, *Holiday on Ice*, and *Hot Holiday Nights* in one volume)

eNovellas

THE TIES THAT BIND
NO STRINGS ATTACHED

WILD NIGHT

THE FINAL SCORE

JACI BURTON

BERKLEY SENSATION
New York

BERKLEY SENSATION
Published by Berkley
An imprint of Penguin Random House LLC
375 Hudson Street, New York, New York 10014

Library of Congress Cataloging-in-Publication Data

Names: Burton, Jaci, author.
Title: The final score / Jaci Burton.
Description: First edition. | New York : Berkley Sensation, 2017. |
Series: A play-by-play novel ; 13
Identifiers: LCCN 2017018302 (print) | LCCN 2017024102 (ebook) |
ISBN 9780399585159 (ebook) | ISBN 9780399585142 (paperback)
Subjects: | BISAC: FICTION / Romance / Contemporary. | FICTION /
Contemporary Women. | GSAFD: Love stories.
Classification: LCC PS3602.U776 (ebook) | LCC PS3602.U776 F56 2017 (print) |
DDC 813/.6—dc23
LC record available at https://lccn.loc.gov/2017018302

First Edition: September 2017

Printed in the United States of America
1 3 5 7 9 10 8 6 4 2

Cover photo by Claudio Marinesco
Cover design by Rita Frangie
Book design by Kristin del Rosario

To all the readers who have loved the Play-by-Play series.
This one's for you.

ACKNOWLEDGMENTS

Huge thanks to my bestie, Shannon Stacey, for coming up with the title of this book and saving me hours and days and months (okay I exaggerate—a little) of anxious brain cell usage. You saved my life, as always, and I love you.

ONE

"SO, HERE WE ARE, ONCE AGAIN LIVING IN THE SAME city." Mia Cassidy took a sip of her green tea and looked over at Nathan Riley. "How did that happen?"

Nathan, the epitome of tall, dark, well-muscled and absolutely hot, leaned back in his chair and grinned at her. "Easy. You're obsessed with me so you followed me."

She laughed. "I don't think so. You knew I was thinking of starting a business here so you decided you had to get drafted by the San Francisco Sabers."

Nathan took a swallow of his iced tea and set the glass down. Mia tracked the movement of his hands. He had really big hands. She remembered that night several years ago in college when he'd used his hands to touch her—all over. They'd only had that one night together, but it sure had been memorable.

Yeah, the guy had magnificent hands.

"I've been here a year already, Mia. You just got here. So like I said, you followed me."

Her lips quirked. "And aren't you happy to have me here?"

"Actually, I am. Although who would have thought this kind of major shit would go down for both of us? You were going to get your PhD, and instead, you've got a start-up sports management company. I thought I'd end up in Cleveland or maybe in L.A., but not here in San Francisco, taking over as the Sabers quarterback now that my dad has retired."

Mia clutched her glass, feeling the cloud of anxiety rain down over her. Which was why she'd asked Nathan to have lunch. His charm and humor had always been a distraction for her, and oh how she needed it today. "Big changes for both of us for sure. How is your dad? Is he okay with the decision he made to retire?"

"He seems fine with it. The Sabers won the championship last year, and he had the knee issue that plagued him at the tail end of the season. He's thirty-seven, so he felt like it was the right time for him to step away."

"And you don't think he did that for you, to give you a chance to play?"

"I asked him that—more than once. He said no. Knowing my dad, he'd never walk away from football if he wasn't ready. He loves the game too much."

Mia nodded. "Since I have three brothers who play football, I believe that. You should believe him, too."

She knew Nathan had been worried when his dad announced his retirement at the end of last season. She also knew it added some pressure for Nathan, because he'd take over as starting quarterback this season for the Sabers. He'd had all last season to learn from him, but succeeding someone as high profile as Mick Riley wasn't going to be easy. Plus, Mick was his dad.

Now she was doubly happy she'd made the decision to launch

her company here in San Francisco. Besides being a prime location for her, she and Nathan had always been close in college. Despite their one night together—which had definitely been a mistake—they'd remained friends. It was a bonus that now they would be in the same city.

"How's your company coming along?" Nathan asked.

"Just getting things rolling. I told you Monique Parker came on board as my executive manager, didn't I?"

He grinned. "Yeah. She'll make sure nothing falls through the cracks."

"I know. She's incredibly organized, even more than me."

"If that's possible. I've never known anyone as anal as you."

"Hey, I'm good at everything I do."

He waggled his brows at her. "Don't I know it."

She laughed. "We promised we wouldn't bring up that mistaken, drunken night ever again."

"No, *you* made *me* promise it wouldn't happen again. I thought it was amazing."

Her body heated at his words. "It was amazing. But we're friends, Nathan."

"And friends can't have sex?"

"I don't know. Do you have sex with your friends?"

He cocked his head to the side. "You know what I mean, Mia."

"I do. But we agreed after that night it wouldn't happen again."

"You made me agree. I wanted to keep you in bed with me the next day."

She laughed. "We were drunk. It was a mistake. And I'd much rather have you as a friend than a lover."

"Oh, so now you're implying the sex wasn't good enough?" He leaned over and grasped her hand, the contact instantly electrifying. "Because if that's the case, I'm calling you out for faulty drunken memory loss. If I recall, you came three times that night."

At least he whispered that last part. And if he kept talking that way she was going to have an orgasm right there in her chair. So much for pushing those memories aside. She snatched her hand away. "That is not what I meant and you know it."

"Fine. We're friends."

"You need me as your friend, Nathan. Who will get you past all your training camp anxiety?"

He frowned. "Who says I have training camp anxiety?"

She twirled the stirrer around in her tea glass. "Don't you?"

He leaned back in his chair again. "Maybe. Don't you have a little anxiety, too, miss big-shot business owner?"

"Yes, I have anxiety. Like you would not believe. Which is why I'm glad we're friends. I need you, Nathan. As my friend."

He glared at her. "Shit. Fine. You know I'm always going to be here for you."

He had no idea how much his friendship and counsel meant to her. "Good. Now let's order lunch because I have to get back to work."

"You're a tough woman, Mia Cassidy."

"But I'm also your best friend, Nathan Riley. And don't ever forget it."

These next few months were going to be critical—for both of them. They were going to need each other more than ever.

As friends. And nothing else.

TWO

AFTER HAVING LUNCH WITH MIA, NATHAN DROVE TO the Sabers stadium. He felt calmer after spending some time with her.

In many ways, Mia was right. Having her as his friend was one of the best things that had ever happened to him. They both came from sports families, so when they met in college in Texas they'd formed an instant bond. It had been a little weird for Nathan to have a female friend at first, but Mia was smart, funny and absolutely beautiful. And since she hadn't seemed at all attracted to him, she was the one he'd gone to with girlfriend issues.

She'd always been straightforward with her advice, and it had always been helpful. When his girlfriend Sonja had broken up with him his junior year, he'd been a wreck. It was Mia who'd been there to help him pick up the pieces and move on. She'd kept him focused on football while soothing his ego about the breakup, reminding him that college romances rarely lasted anyway. After that he'd played the field without getting emotionally attached.

Until that one night he and Mia had been at his apartment, drinking and watching one of her brothers and his dad play a game against each other on TV. They'd ordered pizza and drank a lot. After the game they'd talked sports and family and careers and what they wanted to do with their futures. It was a heavy conversation. He didn't know how it happened, but suddenly they were on the couch making out.

Damn it had been good. He was pretty sure it had surprised both of them, but neither of them stopped once they'd started.

Mia had been soft and pliant and the sounds she'd made had driven him crazy. She'd been receptive to his touch, and they'd moved things into the bedroom.

They'd spent all night together, and it had been a damn good night.

Until the next morning when Mia had told him it couldn't happen again because she valued his friendship more than anything.

He could still remember the way her body had moved under his, could still feel the softness of her lips when they kissed, could still hear the sounds of her breathing as he moved inside of her. And now, goddammit, he had a hard-on as he sat in his car in the stadium parking lot.

He cranked the music up loud and focused on the playbook to get Mia out of his head. When he finally got his shit together, he got out of the car.

He bypassed the locker room and stepped onto the Sabers field. It felt like the first time. Hell, he'd been there countless times before with his dad, the famous Mick Riley. He'd watched him play the game, learned under his tutelage, picked his brain after every play, good and bad.

Now his dad was retired and the Sabers was his team to lead. It wasn't his first time on the field as a Sabers player, of course, since he'd been drafted by the team last year, but back then he'd been nothing more than a benchwarmer. This was the first time Nathan walked the field as the Sabers starting quarterback.

Christ, how had all this happened? It had been a goddamned whirlwind starting with his dad announcing his retirement. These past several months had been some kind of otherworldly dream, like he'd been asleep all this time and it wasn't real.

But as his feet crunched into the turf, it all felt solid. Real. As if he belonged here, like he'd always belonged here.

He could still remember the first time he'd walked out onto the field, after seeing his dad play. His mom and dad had just gotten together. Nathan had been fifteen at the time, and being around professional football had been new to him. This stadium seemed enormous, out of reach to a scrawny kid who had only dreamed of someday walking in shoes as big as Mick Riley's.

And then his mom had fallen in love with and married Mick, and Mick had adopted him. He'd been one lucky sonofabitch to end up with a father who loved him as much as his dad did. He'd taught Nathan everything he knew about football. How to love and respect the game, and how to respect himself in the process.

Nathan couldn't have asked for a better role model. And he was going to do everything he could to make his father proud of him.

He sucked in a deep breath and walked from one end of the field to the other, cognizant of the weight that now lay on his shoulders. When the Sabers had drafted him, he'd been excited to learn the game under Mick Riley. But he didn't think he would play right away.

In college, he had worked hard, played hard, and he'd been a damn good quarterback.

Now he was going to have to be better.

"Hey, Riley."

He turned to see the coach walking onto the field. He cracked a smile and reached out to shake Tom Butterfield's hand. Tom had been hired on as head coach three years ago, and had been doing a kickass job. Nathan couldn't wait to work with him as the starting quarterback.

"Hey, Coach."

"Getting a feel for your turf?"

His turf. The crush of expectation already weighed on him. "Yeah. Feels good."

"We expect great things from you this season."

Nathan felt that squeeze of pressure in his chest. He shook it off. This was what he'd waited his whole life for. "I'll give you everything I've got."

Coach slapped him on the back. "You sound just like your dad. We're going to miss him around here." Dad had retired. He understood the reasons for it. The Sabers had won the championship last season. His dad was thirty-seven and he wanted to go out on top, plus he had the knee issue that had cropped up. He'd fought through it all season, and the docs said he needed surgery.

Sure, he could have rehabbed and come back. Mom and Dad had discussed it. Dad had even talked to Nathan about it, but in the end, it was his father's decision to make. Man, Nathan was going to miss watching him play.

And now to step into his shoes, for this team, on this field?

Yeah, that was the reason for the tight knot in his chest.

One of many.

"Let's go talk over the new season," coach said.

Nathan pushed all those pressures aside and tried to remember to breathe. He plastered on his signature grin, the one that said "I've got this," even when he didn't.

"Yeah, Coach. Let's do that."

THREE

MIA LIVED FOR HER PLANNER AND HER CHECKLISTS. At this moment she needed them more than anything, because she had a million things to do. The movers were supposed to be here an hour ago and they were late. She had a separate furniture delivery that was supposed to be here this morning, and it was almost noon and so far no one had showed up. She had a client coming in at three. If stuff didn't show up soon, she and her client were going to be sitting on the damn floor.

Not good. Not good at all. Her heart beat like a jackhammer in her chest.

She stopped and remembered her breathing. Falling to pieces wasn't going to do anyone any good.

She pivoted and headed down the hall of her very spacious and very empty offices.

"Monique, are you in here?"

Monique, her best friend from college and her absolute life-saver, was on the phone, so she held up a finger to silence Mia.

"You need to be here yesterday," Monique said, obvious impatience in her voice. "We had a guaranteed eight a.m. delivery time and it's now eleven thirty and no one is here. So get it done and if you can't, then transfer me to the manager."

Monique listened for a few seconds, then smiled, shooting Mia that look, the one that said she had it all under control. And when she nodded at Mia, Mia exhaled.

This was why she'd begged and cajoled and pushed Monique into moving from Texas to San Francisco to be her executive manager. No one had better organizational skills or the take-no-shit demeanor that Monique did. When Mia had decided to start up her company, she knew she wouldn't be able to do this without having Monique on board.

Monique finally hung up. "The movers are on the way. They got hung up in traffic, then thought they could stop for lunch. I made sure to let them know their movers could have lunch *after* they delivered our furniture."

Mia exhaled. "That's why you're the best."

"Now I'm about to crawl up the ass of the supply delivery people."

"Monique Parker, will you marry me?"

Monique laughed. "You are pretty and all, but I like dick. Thanks for the offer, though."

Mia laughed. "Fine, then. Don't marry me. Just continue to be awesome."

"Girl, I'm always awesome. Now go away and let me work my magic."

Mia walked away and wandered through the new offices, still unable to believe she'd managed to get all this up and running just as she'd envisioned. She had her brothers and her parents to thank for a lot of it, especially her brother Flynn. She'd been so hesitant at first to set up her company in the same city as one of her brothers, but Flynn had been instrumental in helping her. He had contacts everywhere, and he'd hooked her up with an amazing real estate agent who'd found the perfect office space in the Embarcadero Center, right in the heart of the Financial District.

The location and the space were ideal. They'd had the office re-carpeted and painted, and it looked fresh and new. Now all she needed was furniture.

Her phone buzzed with a text. She smiled when she saw Nathan's name come up.

How's it going?

She typed back: Insanity here. How about you?

He replied with: Intense. But cool.

She could well imagine. She was as excited for Nathan's new beginnings as she was for her own.

She typed back. Let's decompress together. Dinner tonight?

Yup.

She grinned. How does 7 work? Going to be crazy here.

It took him a few minutes to reply: Sounds good. Later.

She was still thinking about their lunch yesterday, and her response to his touch. It had been brief, but she had been surprised by the intensity of it. It was probably just her heightened nerves. She'd been wired lately because of all of . . . this. That had to be it.

Because good friends were hard to come by, so she didn't want to screw it up with sex. Sex could ruin a great friendship, and she never wanted to lose Nathan.

And if that hot spark of attraction still remained between them, they were adults and they could handle it.

She shook it off and went in search of Monique to check on the status of those deliveries.

FOUR

AFTER TALKING TO BOTH HIS PARENTS ON THE PHONE, as well as his little brother, Sam, who never missed an opportunity to FaceTime, Nathan got to work. He'd leased a town house in Santa Clara, near the stadium. When he'd first moved here last season, his parents offered up their house for his use, but he knew they'd come and stay there as well, and while he loved his family, he craved independence. And privacy. God he'd really wanted some privacy.

He'd shared plenty of apartments in college, sometimes with several guys. There was nothing worse than three guys sharing one bathroom. This was his time to be alone. As he walked into his bedroom and bathroom, for the first time in his life he actually felt like an adult. It was about damn time. He'd stayed the extra year in college, not only to finish up his dual degrees in finance and mathematics, but to win the national championship again.

He'd been offered the chance to enter the draft in his junior year at Texas, but his mom wouldn't have it. Education had been more important to her than football. His coach had told him it wasn't a good year for quarterbacks in the draft that year anyway.

It turned out they were both right. He'd finished up his degrees, and he'd been drafted in the second round by his dad's team.

It was all good now.

His phone buzzed. He grinned when he saw Jamal's name.

"Sup?"

Jamal laughed. "Chillin'. You?"

"Doing some paperwork. Hey, I went to the stadium today. Talked to coach."

"You did, huh? That's cuz you're the hot-shit new quarterback, so you're special as fuck."

Nathan laughed. "Yeah, baby, that's me. And you can't wait for me to throw you a pass since you're the hot-shit wide receiver."

"You know it. And now that the other hot-shit receiver is gone, it's my time to shine."

"'Bout damn time, isn't it?"

"Yeah. And I've been waitin' on you for a year now. You as good as your dad?"

That was the million-dollar question, wasn't it? Or the multi-million-dollar one. "You caught passes from me for three years in Texas. What do you think? You've seen my awesome rocket arm."

He heard Jamal's infectious laugh. "We're gonna blow it up this year, Riley."

Jamal was exactly what he needed right now. He was so damn glad his best friend was on the same team. "Hell yes we are."

"Now get your ass over here and let's play some games."

He looked down at his phone. He had a few hours to kill before he met Mia. He looked over at his computer and the bills he needed to pay. Yeah, that could wait.

"Be right there."

* * *

MIA WAS WIPED OUT. THE FURNITURE HAD BEEN PUT
in place just in time for her three o'clock appointment with one of
the hottest new cornerbacks in the league. She left all the details
about office stuff to Monique, and brought Clyde Motts into their
"Oh my God we finished setting this up thirty minutes ago" fantastic conference room. And then she sold him on how amazing her
company was and what they could do for him from a management
standpoint. That part, at least, she had together, from financial to
contractual to promotion. She already had Clyde's agent as part of
her company, so she sat with them. Mia brought in her finance and
marketing team to do one hell of a presentation, and thank God
the tech team had managed to hook everything up, because the
video was a knock-you-right-out-of-your-cleats demonstration.

She name-dropped a high-profile basketball player and hockey
player who they'd already signed, along with an award-winning
pitcher. Then she added on the tight end she'd signed, also a huge
name. She could tell Clyde was trying to play it cool, but he was
impressed. By the time he left the office, she knew he'd sign with
MHC Management.

She still smiled whenever she looked at the letterhead with
those initials. MHC. Mia Helene Cassidy. It was her. Her baby.
Her company. She sucked in a breath. So much pressure to succeed.

She could do this. She *would* do this.

She found Monique in her office, and leaned against the open
doorway.

Monique looked up and pulled off her tortoise-frame glasses.
"Well?"

"He didn't commit, but he will."

"If he's smart he will. And that boy is smart as hell. What did
Victoria say?"

"I haven't heard back from her yet. I'm sure she'll text me after she has a chat with Clyde."

"He'll sign with us. Why wouldn't he?"

"And yet another reason I need you with me, Monique. That positive attitude."

"I'm just a ray of sunshine and utter beauty in your life, Mia."

Mia laughed. "That you are."

"Hey, do you want to have dinner tonight? I have a date and he has a really gorgeous friend. We're going to try out this new Korean place that everyone's talking about."

She shook her head. "Thanks, but I already have plans."

"Ooh, a hot date?"

"No. Dinner with Nathan Riley."

Monique arched a perfect brow. "So it is a hot date."

The only person she'd ever told about her onetime hookup with Nathan was Monique, because she was the only person Mia trusted with all her secrets. "Not ever going to happen again."

Monique leaned back in her chair and shoved her pen into her gorgeous afro. "I don't know why. The man is delicious."

"The why is because we're friends."

"Oh, and you can't fuck a friend?"

Fortunately, Monique's office was at the other end of the hall, away from everyone else, so no one could hear them. "No, I can't. My friendship with Nathan means too much to me."

"Pff. Bullshit. You're just afraid it was too hot for you and you might fall in love with him."

"I am not afraid, and falling in love with Nathan is the last thing on my mind." She walked in and slid into the chair across from Monique's desk. "Though it was very hot sex. But love? I don't have time for love. I'm building a dynasty here."

"Uh-huh. You can build all the dynasties you want. But you can still jump on Nathan Riley."

She shook her head. "What if I want to bring him on board MHC?"

"Do you?"

"I don't know. The thought just popped into my head. But if I did, I can't have sex with him and then sign him as a client, too."

"Why not? Wouldn't that be just an added incentive, like a fringe benefit?"

She rolled her eyes. "Monique. You have like . . . zero boundaries."

Monique grinned. "I know. Isn't it great? How do you think I landed a date with third-floor hottie?"

Mia arched a brow. "Your date tonight is with elevator guy?"

Monique nodded. "Yes. Hot business-suit elevator guy."

"He is extremely sexy."

"Yes he is, in that buttoned-up, tie-wearing, you want to take all his clothes off kind of way."

Mia laughed. "Been thinking about that, have you?"

"I have. I intend to explore him in depth after dinner tonight. Maybe loosen up that designer necktie he wears, along with some of his other clothes."

Mia shook her head. "I can't wait for the details."

She got up and went back to her office. She finished up for the day, and she and Monique locked up the office. They took the elevator downstairs and walked outside.

"You sure you don't want me and elevator guy to come to dinner with you? I could point out Nathan's fine ass and remind you of how great he was in the sack."

Mia turned Monique in the opposite direction. "Oh my God no. Enjoy dinner alone with hot elevator guy. Try to call him by his real name."

"Are you sure?" Monique asked as she started to walk away. "I can recall you damn near reciting poetry about all of Nathan's fine attributes. Don't forget about his enormous—"

Fortunately, whatever Monique said was drowned out by traffic sounds.

Mia slid into her jacket, loving the feel of the cool, crisp July evening breeze. Having grown up in Texas, summers were always hot and humid. San Francisco summers were entirely different. She loved everything about it. She could get out and walk, and there were always people around. There was a pulse to this city like it was a living, breathing thing, and she enjoyed all of it, from the clanging of the trolleys whisking their way down the street to the honking of the boats in the bay to the fast hustle of people going to and from their jobs. It was high energy while somehow also being laid-back.

The first time she'd visited Flynn several years ago, he'd taken her sightseeing through the city and she'd known she had to live here someday. She just fit here.

She got on the train at the BART station, rode a couple of stops and got off, then walked the block to her town house, a charming Victorian she'd fallen madly in love with on first sight.

The location was perfect, near Dolores Park, with a variety of restaurants and plenty of shops nearby. She adored everything about it, from the original brick steps to the gorgeous forest green front door with its stained-glass inserts. Inside was a beautiful original oak floor and plenty of living space. The owners had renovated the place so it was fresh and modern while still retaining its eighteen hundreds charm. She had fallen instantly in love with the bay window in the living room that let in so much light, the lovely stone fireplace and the small garden out back. San Francisco was tight on space, so to get even a smidgen of an outdoor area was a bonus.

She walked up the stairs to her bedroom and kicked off her

shoes, then lay back on her bed, taking a few minutes to re-center herself. It had been a long, fairly stressful day, so breathing was important. She laid her hands over her stomach and closed her eyes, focusing on the ceiling as she inhaled, then exhaled. If she had more time she'd go into her spare bedroom and do yoga, but she had to get ready for dinner, so she did about ten minutes of focused breathing, then got up and went into the bathroom. She washed her face, redid her makeup and changed clothes. By the time she went downstairs she felt immensely calmer. She had Monique to thank for getting her into yoga.

When they'd first met, Mia was all about school and studying, and Monique had told her she was a ball of nervous energy and anxiety. Then she'd dragged her to a yoga class and changed her life. Mia changed her diet and exercise routine and had slept better than ever before in those months following.

Of course, she'd like to think she taught calm, centered and all-about-Zen Monique how to cut loose and party. Reluctant at first, Monique had eventually taken partying to a new level and the two of them had been inseparable all through college. And now Monique was here with her as her right hand. Mia smiled. Sometimes the fates worked in your favor.

The doorbell rang and she went to answer it. It was Nathan, looking entirely too delectable in his relaxed jeans and a gray Henley, his muscles straining against the dark cotton of his shirt.

Friend zone, Mia, remember?

Yeah, yeah. With all the work she'd been doing over the past year, she hadn't made time for fun. Fun being sex. Which was why she was ogling Nathan like she was sex starved.

Because she was.

"Hey," she said. "Come on in."

He wandered in and started looking around. "Nice place. If you like old shit."

She punched him in the shoulder. "Shut up. My place is amazing."

"Yeah. If you like old shit. How old is this place anyway?"

"It was built in the eighteen hundreds. But you know, it's been modernized since then, asshole."

He stopped and turned to face her. "You mean you can actually use the bathroom indoors?"

She laughed. "You are such a dick."

He shot her a grin. "That's why you like me. Because of my dick."

"No. I do not."

He gave her that look, the one where his chin came down, and he slanted a heavy-lidded gaze at her. It was sexy as hell and it made her quiver.

"Come on," he said, "show me your awesome old place."

"Vintage, Nathan."

"Sure. Vintage."

She took him on the tour and she had to admit he at least acted like he was interested as she pointed out crown moldings and arched doorways.

They had worked their way upstairs. He stopped in the doorway of her bedroom. He glanced at her bed, then looked over at her.

"Nice big bed. Expecting nice, big company?"

"No. I just like to stretch out."

He leaned in closer to her. "Uh-huh. Hiding a boyfriend you haven't told me about?"

"No." He smelled entirely too good so she stepped away. "Let me show you the bathroom."

She caught his smirk and wanted to slap it off his face. The problem with having a friend who knew you so well, and having said friend be someone you'd once slept with, was he also knew you well enough to know when you were thinking sex things about him.

And now that they were living in the same city again, this was going to be a constant problem. At least until she got laid again and she stopped thinking about Nathan in a sexual way.

She'd have to put "Have Sex" on the top of the To-Do list in her planner.

"Okay, so it's kind of cool, in a girlie way."

She rolled her eyes. "There isn't a single spot of pink in the entire place. It's not girlie. It's just not all black and white and chrome like your place. Which, by the way, is decorated like a garage."

He laughed. "Is not."

"Seriously, Nathan. You need an interior designer to put some color in that place. It's so stark."

He shrugged. "It's fine. It's not like I spend a lot of time there anyway."

They had worked their way back downstairs. She grabbed her purse. "You spend enough time there. And besides, now that I live here, I might just come visit you and I'd like to not think I'm in jail when I'm at your place."

"Fine. Whatever. Bring me a purple vase or pillow to add some color or something."

She laughed. "You know I'm going to do exactly that, don't you?"

He put his arm around her waist and tugged her against him. "Why do you think I suggested it? You don't think I can pick out stuff like that, do you?"

She shook her head and they walked out the door. She lived close enough to several restaurants, so they walked to Delfina.

"There's a line," he said.

She nodded. "There always is. But I made a reservation."

He looked down at her. "Because you're so smart."

She grinned. "Exactly."

They went inside and she gave her name.

"It'll be a few minutes," the hostess said. "Would you like to wait in the bar?"

"Sounds good to me," Nathan said.

The restaurant was sleek and modern, but also felt charming and cozy. Mia had eaten here with Flynn and his girlfriend, Amelia, and loved it.

The bartender made his way over, so Nathan looked at her. "What would you like?"

"A pinot noir."

Nathan nodded. "I'll have a beer."

After the bartender gave them their drinks, Nathan took a pull of his beer, then slid around on the cushioned bar stool to face her. "How did it go today at work?"

She had taken a sip or two of wine, so she set the glass on the bar top. "Good. Hectic. More than hectic. We barely got the place set up when a prospective client came in."

"Yeah? Who was it?"

She slanted a look at him. "You know I can't tell you until I sign him."

"Oh. Confidentiality shit, huh?"

"Yes."

"Fine. I can respect that." He picked up his beer and took a drink. "Anyone I know?"

She laughed. "Nathan. I can't tell you."

He pointed his bottle at her. "You're good at this."

"At what?"

"Keeping secrets."

"It's not a secret. It's my job. And I take it very seriously."

"Relax, Mia. I won't make you divulge your client info."

She lifted her chin. "You couldn't make me."

He studied her. "You're wound up tight."

She realized he'd been teasing her, and she'd taken it too seriously. She picked up her glass and took a few sips, hoping the wine would relax her. Nathan wasn't some stranger. He was her friend and he'd never put her in an awkward position. She was just being bitchy and that wasn't like her—most days.

"You're right. Sorry. It's been a stressful few months."

He smoothed his hand over her shoulder, then down her back. "I know you've been stressed and I've been wrapped up in my own shit and haven't been here for you. So I'm sorry for that."

"Hey, don't worry about it. Like you said, you have your own things to worry about."

"Which doesn't mean you couldn't pick up the phone and call me so we can talk. If I can't fuck you, I can listen to you, ya know. That was the deal, right?"

She laughed. "Yes, that was the deal."

"So . . . talk. What's got you stressed?"

She inhaled a deep breath, then let it out. "Have I bitten off more than I can chew? Do I really have what it takes to make this business a success? Will people in this industry take me seriously even though I'm so young? Are they going to think that I'm using the Cassidy family name to climb the ladder without the smarts to back it up? I'm asking athletes to put their entire careers in my hands, and that's a big deal. And I'm asking the people who've come on board my company to trust that I'm going to make them successful as well. So, you know . . . everything has me stressed right now."

He put his beer down and took her hands in his. "Mia, I've never known anyone as loaded with self-confidence and drive as you. While other people our age were content with living off their parents or staying in school for as long as possible, you've been determined to forge a career for yourself. You came up with this amazing idea, and despite how daunting it was, you ran like hell with it. And not only did you run like hell with it, you spent a year putting it all together. So you didn't rush into anything.

"You got your financing in order, you've surrounded yourself with all the best people in the business and you took your time to make sure you did it all right. So it's not like you just pulled this idea out of your ass in a day and decided to give it a try without thinking about it.

"Is it scary? Hell yes it is. But if I were going to have someone manage my career for me from top to bottom, I can't think of anyone I'd trust more than you."

Her heart squeezed. That meant more to her than anything, because she knew Nathan's career was everything to him.

"Would you let me?"

He frowned at her. "Would I let you what?"

"Manage your career."

"You mean would I consider going with MHC?"

"Yes."

"I don't know, Mia. Not that I don't think MHC is the shit, because I do. But you and I being friends, and then in business together? Don't you think that would muddy the waters?"

"I have account managers, Nathan. You wouldn't even have to deal directly with me."

He cocked a brow. "So this is a sales dinner?"

"No. Of course not. And I'm insulted to think you'd actually believe that. Even though I do think we can manage your career more effectively than anyone else."

He laughed and took a long swallow of his beer. "You just can't turn it off, can you?"

She lifted her shoulders, the tension a constant knot there. "I'm sorry. Again. I can't seem to tell these days when you're teasing and when you're serious. I'm out of sync."

"You probably need to get laid."

She lifted her glass and took a long, deep drink this time. "There's no 'probably' about it. I definitely need to get laid."

Their name was called, so they were seated at their table. It was an intimate place, with loud chatter going on and tables strung close together.

"Great place," Nathan said. "And crowded."

"I know, right? You're going to love the food."

Their waiter brought menus, so they perused those and ordered food, along with refills on their drinks.

"So you're going to come to the games and watch me play, right?"

She gave him a look. "You do realize my brother plays for the Sabers, too."

"Yes, I'm aware. But I mean to watch *me* play."

She laughed. "Yes, I'll come watch you play. Flynn got me season tickets when he found out I was moving here. And Amelia has tickets as well so we'll both be going."

"That's his girlfriend?"

"Yes."

"She's the chef at his restaurant, right?"

Mia nodded. "The head chef. She's amazing."

"You should take me there to eat sometime."

"Sure. You'd like it. Amelia makes some incredible and unique dishes."

"Sounds good. How about tomorrow?"

She shook her head. "All you think about is food."

He slanted a smoldering look in her direction. "That's not all I think about."

"Okay. Food and sex."

"Correction. Food, sex and football. Not always in that order."

She laughed. "That sounds about right for you. Speaking of sex—"

"Now we're getting to the good stuff."

She rolled her eyes. "Speaking of sex, are you seeing anyone?"

He shook his head. "Nah. Too much going on right now. Plus the press is all up my ass about succeeding my dad, and the last thing I need to do is bring a woman into all that bullshit. You know how it is."

"I definitely know how it is."

"So that means *you're* not seeing anyone?"

"You remember the discussion we had at the bar about me needing to get laid?"

"Yeah?"

"That means I'm not currently seeing anyone."

"Right."

Their food arrived. Nathan had ordered the hangar steak and fries, while Mia opted for the spaghetti with plum tomatoes. She reached over with her fork and snagged a slice of his steak.

"Hey," he said. "Don't you know every bite of protein counts?"

"Oh, you poor baby. You'll just have to go without this one tiny morsel."

"You're a mean woman, Mia Cassidy."

"Uh-huh. You're what—six four?"

"Yeah."

"And I'm five four. So I think if you wanted to, you could eat your meal and mine and there wouldn't be much I could do about it. So spare me your sob story about how mean I am."

"You are mean. You know I have to be nice to you."

"Or what? It's not like I'm your girlfriend and I'm withholding sex."

He gave her a shocked look. "Women do that?"

"I don't, but some do."

"What kind of bullshit is that?"

"Obviously none of your women have ever done that."

"Of course not. I'm so good at it the last thing they'd want to do is deny themselves."

She rolled her eyes, then went back to eating, deciding that boosting Nathan's already overly healthy ego wasn't on her agenda tonight.

"So how many clients—the ones you can talk about—do you have now?"

She thought about it. "Six."

"That's good considering you just started."

She nodded. "I wanted to make sure to bring some on board beforehand. The Cassidy name definitely helped, and I'm not above using it to entice people in the door. And my brothers definitely helped me out by pushing some people in my direction so I could pitch to them. It's what MHC can do for them once they get in the door that makes all the difference."

He'd finished his steak, so he leaned back in his chair. "Okay, tell me."

"Tell you what?"

"What MHC can do for me."

She looked around. The restaurant was packed with people, and the ones nearest to them were only a couple of feet away. "I'm not going to do that here. It's too noisy."

"Fine. We'll go back to my place."

"The jail? No thanks. We'll go to my place, have some wine and not talk business. I'm not giving you a sales pitch unless you come to my office."

He studied her. "So you're going to make MHC seem so enticing I won't be able to help myself until I go there and hear what you have to say."

"Exactly."

"You know I'm immune to your considerable charm, Miss Cassidy."

She batted her lashes at him. "Are you?"

He leveled a smirk at her. "At least business-wise."

"Hmm. We'll see." She wasn't sure why she was pushing this. It wasn't like she wanted so desperately to have Nathan as a client. Having him at MHC could get sticky. Not that it wasn't doable. Anything was doable. It would just be—complicated.

Once they finished eating, and they both declined dessert, their waiter brought the bill. Nathan started to grab the check but Mia insisted they split it.

"We're not dating, remember?" she said. "So you don't get to pay for my dinner."

He shook his head. "Does everything have to be an argument with you?"

"We're not arguing. We're splitting the check."

"Fine. Split the check."

They each paid their portion, then they took the walk back to her town house. It had gotten cooler out. She was glad she'd brought a cardigan, which she pulled tighter around herself.

"Cold?" Nathan asked.

"A little."

He put his arm around her and tugged her close to his body as they walked. She was instantly warmer.

"Your body is like a furnace," she said.

"Hey, I'm hot. Everyone knows that."

She lifted her gaze to his. "Everyone? Hyperbole much, Nathan?"

"Everyone who has gotten naked with me knows that."

"Better. And I've been naked with you."

He arched a brow. "See how getting naked with me is always on your mind? It's probably making you warmer just thinking about it."

If she didn't know Nathan so well, she'd think he was some asshole, always thinking about sex. But she was well aware of his teasing. She did the same to him. The one thing she liked so much about Nathan was his blatant honesty. Even if said honesty often included sex banter. It was when she *didn't* know what was on his mind that she became concerned. Nathan had always been an open book with her. That's why they'd become such close friends.

She dug her keys out of her clutch and opened the door, then flipped on the light.

"If I remember, there's a bathroom downstairs, right?" he asked.

"Down the hallway to your right."

"Okay."

"I'm going to grab a glass of wine. Do you want a beer?"

"Yeah, thanks."

She went into the kitchen and turned on the lights, dropped her clutch on the kitchen island and pulled a wineglass from the cabinet. She reached for the wine bottle and set that on the island, then went to the fridge to grab a beer for Nathan. By the time he came out of the bathroom she was opening the bottle.

Nathan took his beer and opened it, then wandered into the living room. Mia poured her wine and followed him, taking a seat on the sofa next to him.

She had a game of solitaire on the table that she'd started, and Nathan had picked it up and continued it so she joined in. They played the game for a while, chatting while they did.

"Oh, you know what?" she said as they paused to refill their drinks. "Amy Mackenfield broke up with her boyfriend."

Nathan feigned shock. "What? The couple that was going to be together until the end of time?"

Mia laughed. "That was my thought, too. I guess 'until the end of time' didn't last very long past college graduation."

Nathan braced a hip against the kitchen island. "So what happened?"

"She got a job offer in Houston and Bill wouldn't make the move with her. He said his job in Austin was going so well that he didn't want to lose it. They tried the long distance thing for about six months. Amy realized it wasn't going to work any longer, so she broke up with him."

"Ah. I always thought they were mismatched anyway."

She tilted her head at Nathan as they made their way back into the living room and resumed their seats on the couch. "Really? How so?"

"She's very ambitious. He was content with the status quo and wasn't the motivated type. Seems that didn't change much after college."

"You're right about that." She swirled her wine around in the glass, then took a sip. "I don't know of many relationships that last through the tumultuous years of college."

"Ours did."

She laughed. "We're not in a relationship, Nathan. We're friends."

"Is there a difference?"

She leaned back and kicked off her shoes. "Of course there is. I'm friends with several people from college."

"Close friends?"

"Maybe not. I'd say I'm closest to you and to Monique. You're the two people I tell all my secrets to."

"I'm glad I know all the dirt. At least the non-sex dirt."

She laughed. "That's true. You don't get to hear about my sex life."

"Why is that?"

"Because that would be weird."

"In what way?"

She shrugged. "I don't know. I guess maybe because we've been intimate before. Or maybe because you're a guy. I don't know."

"Now you're being sexist. Just because I'm a guy doesn't mean I can't hear the dirty details of your sex life."

"Oh, right. Like you share the details of your sex life with me."

"True. I don't. I wouldn't want to make you weep about what you're missing out on."

She rolled her eyes. "Please."

"See? Now you've resorted to begging. I knew this would happen." He stood and reached for the zipper of his jeans. "Okay, give me a second to lose my pants and we'll get down to it."

She was laughing so hard she had to put her glass down. "Oh, my God, Nathan. Stop."

He stilled and turned to face her. "This is not the reaction I typically get when I'm about to drop my pants, Mia."

She wiped her eyes. "Well, I'm not your typical woman, am I?"

He took a seat and picked up his beer. "No, you're not. I can't figure out why you're so immune to me."

She leaned into him. "I wouldn't say I'm exactly immune to you. I find you immensely hot. It's just that I love our friendship more than I love your penis."

He sighed and tugged her close. "Dammit. Maybe I should be meaner to you."

"Oh, please don't do that. Then who would give me those awesome shoulder rubs when I'm tense?"

"Was that a hint?"

"Not even a hint." She pulled herself forward. "I've had a rough day."

He sighed. "Come on and sit between my legs."

She got up, then nestled her butt in between his thighs, spreading her fingers over all that delicious hard muscle.

Keep it in the friend zone, Mia, she reminded herself. Ignoring her body's reaction to being cradled against him, she decided it would be more prudent to keep the touching to a minimum. She removed her hands and placed them in her lap and focused on the way his hands moved over the tight muscles of her shoulders. He knew exactly where the knots of tension were located. In a matter of minutes all those muscles were relaxed as his fingers glided over her skin.

But as he moved his hands over her body, that tension was replaced with something else. For some reason, she was aware of Nathan like never before. The way it felt to be caged between his thighs, the sound of his breathing as he leaned forward to dig deeper into her muscles, and his cool, clean scent whenever she took a deep breath.

What was wrong with her? This wasn't the first time he'd given her a massage. But for some reason, tonight she was vibing off him in a distinctly sexual way.

She found it very disturbing. After that one night a few years ago, she'd shut those feelings down completely. Other than having a penis, he'd been no different than one of her girlfriends.

Something had definitely changed, though. It had to be the unmet sexual need on her part that had surfaced with all the stress she was under.

She really needed to take care of it so that whenever Nathan put his hands on her or looked at her or breathed near her she'd stop feeling achy and aroused.

And stop feeling this overwhelming need to ask him to strip her down and lick her all over.

Oh, God, her body throbbed as she visualized him doing just that.

NATHAN NOTICED RIGHT AWAY THAT MIA WAS TENSE. More edgy than usual. He chalked it up to being wound up tight about the new business. She probably had a lot on her mind and wasn't sleeping well. He knew all about pressure and what it could do to your body.

Maybe the wine tonight and the back rub would relax her. Though if she continued to wiggle against his crotch, he was going to get a hard-on. She might be all "let's be BFFs" about him, but ever since that one night in college, Nathan wanted Mia and that hadn't changed.

He'd sucked it up and toed the line on the friendship side because he cared about her happiness and that's what it was going to take to stay in her life, but if it was up to him she'd be in his bed.

Unfortunately, it wasn't up to him, and he respected her wishes. Though right now what she wanted was making it damned uncomfortable for his dick. With her moaning about the back rub and wriggling her butt between his legs, it was all he could do not to join in on the moaning. Instead, he gritted his teeth and did his best to make her feel good.

"You know what you really need?" he asked as he slid his fingers into her hair.

"Mmm. What's that?"

"A good screaming orgasm."

She stilled. "Isn't that a cocktail?"

He laughed. "No. Well, it might be. But that's not the orgasm I'm talking about."

"Oh. Yeah, you're right about that. I do need an orgasm. Or five. Or ten. It's been a long dry spell for me."

Great. He could already envision making her come—with his hands, his mouth and his cock. Why had he even brought it up?

Because you enjoy self-torture, Nathan?

"So why don't you have one? You can do it yourself, right?"

"I can. And I do. But you know it's not the same as having someone do it for you—or with you."

He slid back on the sofa so Mia couldn't feel his boner. This was a really idiotic topic of conversation and he had no one to blame for it but himself.

But now a thought entered his head. A really great one, too. "I have an idea."

She half turned. "You do?"

"Yeah. Let's have sex."

She laughed. "Nathan. No."

He turned her so she sat on one of his thighs. "No, listen, Mia. This is a really great idea. You and I are friends, right?"

"Yes."

"Neither one of us is looking for a relationship right now. At least I'm not."

"You know I'm not, either."

"So it's perfect. We both have high-pressure jobs, and what's a better pressure reliever than sex?"

"Okay, that's true, but, Nathan, we're friends."

"Exactly. We know each other. We trust each other. And we're not looking for anything permanent. So let's have sex. A friends with benefits thing. No strings."

She opened her mouth and he knew she was going to object. But then she paused. "Okay, say we have sex."

He grinned. "Yeah, say we do."

"And say one of us gets . . . emotionally involved."

"That won't be me."

"It won't be me, either, Nathan. Honestly, I just have too many other things going on in my life."

"Then what's the problem?"

"What happens when one of us wants to have a relationship with someone else?"

He shrugged. "Then we're done. We'll still be friends, just not sex friends."

She frowned. "You make it sound so simple and I don't think it is."

"Why isn't it that easy? We've been friends for years, Mia. I don't plan on changing that. Do you?"

"Of course not. I trust you."

"Same. But you obviously need to get off. So do I. And the dating thing right now is full of complications that I don't need or want."

"And what if tomorrow you meet the woman of your dreams and fall madly in love?"

His lips curved. "Not gonna happen. I don't have time for the woman of my dreams."

Her lips flattened and she gave him that look she always gave him when bullshit fell out of his mouth. "Say all the guys who will fall in love tomorrow."

"Fine. But I'm not one of those guys. And if you meet the man of your dreams tomorrow, then you and I go back to being best friends who don't have sex with each other."

She sighed. "It kind of sounds too good to be true. And I don't believe in too good to be true. I value our friendship and I don't want to lose it."

"If we do this the right way, and keep emotions out of it, we'll stay friends. I can handle it. Can you?"

"Of course I can."

He knew Mia was competitive. And even though this wasn't a contest, he knew if he'd told her he could keep emotion out of this and handle their relationship, she'd step up and say she could, too.

He *could* handle it. He liked Mia. He wanted to keep her in his life. And there was no way in hell he was going to get emotionally attached to her. He wasn't going to fall in love with any woman.

This was going to be easy for him. And he knew Mia was in love with her company, so despite her reservations, he knew she could handle this, too.

"You wanna think about it?" he asked.

She shook her head. "No. What I want is some relief from this constant stress."

He swept his hand over her thigh. "Then let me take care of it for you. In a purely clinical, non-emotional way."

She laughed. "Sounds so romantic."

"That's the key, isn't it? To keep the romance out of it?"

She looked at him for the longest time. But that's what Mia did. She considered things before jumping in.

Finally, she nodded. "You're right. Let's do this. Let's fuck."

His lips curved. Music to his ears.

He moved and lifted her off his lap, then stood and held out his hand.

"Okay, Miss Cassidy. Let's get you off."

FIVE

MIA LED NATHAN UPSTAIRS TO HER BEDROOM. SHE flipped on the light, then turned to face him.

"Now I feel weird."

He smiled at her. "Change your mind?"

"No. I just feel weird. Like this isn't spontaneous, you know?"

He stepped up to her and put his hands on her shoulders. "Want me to take you back downstairs and ply you with more wine?"

Her lips curved. "No. I want to be mostly sober for this. I'm just . . . tense, I guess."

"Yeah, I know. That's your whole problem. And don't feel weird. It's me, Mia. I'm not some stranger that you picked up in a bar and brought home to get naked with."

"I realize that. Still, this wasn't something that was on my To-Do list for tonight."

"What? You didn't put 'Have Sex with Nathan' in your planner?"

"Shockingly, no. I'll have to add it in retroactively."

"With stickers? And what do those look like? Are there planner stickers for sex? With penises and vaginas?"

"You are not funny."

"Yes, I am. That's why you like me. I lighten your mood and make you laugh."

"Right now you need to make me come. So drop your pants."

He arched a brow. "Oh, so it's going to be like that, huh?"

"It is."

He stepped toward her. "You know what your problem is, Mia?"

She frowned. "No, but I'm sure you're going to tell me."

"You're tense. And when you're tense, you're cranky. I can fix that. But we're not going to make sex all clinical."

"We're not?"

He swept his hand from her shoulder down her arm, feeling that slight shudder as her body responded. "No. We're going to make it sexy and fun. But with no emotion, of course."

"Of course."

He reached for the button on her cardigan, popped the button open and slid it off her shoulders. "Let's make you comfortable. Relax you."

Mia was anything but relaxed. She couldn't believe she'd even agreed to this. That after all these years, she and Nathan were going to do this again.

Back in college, it had been a wild, drunken tumble. Now she was sober and going into this wide-eyed and with all her faculties intact. Tomorrow there'd be no taking it back, no making a pact to be just friends.

Was she making an incredible mistake? She and Nathan had developed an amazing friendship over the past few years. Was she sacrificing that in the name of sex? Was losing their friendship worth it?

She lost sight of all those questions when Nathan smoothed his hands over her body, rubbing her back in that oh-so-familiar way that was suddenly something way more sensual. She melted into his touch, into the way he seemed to know her body with such ease, such familiarity.

"That's it," he said, turning her so her back was to him. "I like touching you, Mia. I like putting my hands on you. Even when it isn't sexual between us, there's something about the softness of your skin that just gets to me. You feel like melted butter against my fingers."

She sighed at his words, got lost in the deep, husky sound of his voice. She leaned back against him and he brought his arms around to pull her closer. She felt his erection and it made her damp with desire. This was what she needed, what she wanted, but she couldn't turn off that warning bell that told her if she took this step with him, it would irrevocably change their friendship forever.

She pivoted to face him. "I can't do this."

He took a step back immediately. "Okay."

"I'm sorry."

"You don't need to be sorry. If you're not into this I totally get it."

"Oh, my God, Nathan. It's not that. I'm into it. Like, way into it. I want you. I just . . . We're friends. And that means more to me than anything. More than sex."

He nodded. "I get it. I really do."

"Do you? I don't want to hurt you."

He cracked a smile, that easy smile of his that always made her feel good. "You couldn't hurt me if you tried, Mia."

"So we're good?"

"We're good. Though I think I need a cold shower."

She looked down at his jeans, at his, oh, God, mouthwatering erection that she so wanted to get her hands and her mouth on. But she knew she couldn't do it. "I'm so sorry."

He laughed. "Don't be sorry. I'll take care of it when I get home."

"Oh, no, don't give me mental visuals of you whacking off. That is not making me feel better."

He slung his arm around her shoulder. "Really? Aww, too bad."

"Jerk."

They went downstairs and Nathan stopped at the door. "I'm heading out."

"Are you sure we're okay?"

"You know what I think?"

"What?"

"I think you worry too much. We're fine. I'll call you tomorrow."

"All right."

He leaned over and brushed his lips against her cheek. She couldn't resist shuddering at the contact. When he pulled back, she saw nothing on his face other than his signature friendly smile. No disappointment, no anger, just . . . Nathan. Her friend, Nathan.

"Night, Mia."

"Night, Nathan."

He walked out and she closed the door, feeling a mixture of relief and utter disappointment. She locked the door and went into the kitchen, contemplating pouring herself another glass of wine. Second-guessing that idea, she made herself a cup of tea instead and grabbed a book to read.

After an hour of reading, she realized she had no idea what the book was about.

She knew what she needed. She grabbed her phone and texted Monique.

U available?

Monique texted her right away.

Yeah. What's up?

She paused, almost pulling back from telling Monique what happened. But she trusted her as much as she trusted Nathan. And she had to talk to someone about this.

I almost had sex with Nathan tonight.

Just as she suspected, her phone rang right away. She pushed the answer button.

"What do you mean, you almost had sex with Nathan?"

"We went out to dinner. We talked. A lot. About tension and sex. He offered up his services."

"You mean as sex stud?"

"Something like that. More like a friends with bennies arrangement."

"And you turned him down?"

"Not at first."

"Okay. Hang on, I need to refill my wineglass for this."

She waited for Monique, trying to get tonight's events straight in her own head. She knew she'd made the right decision, but it didn't hurt to get her best friend's agreement on it.

"Okay I'm back. Now tell me everything."

She took a deep breath. "We had dinner. It was fun. Then we walked back to my place for some drinks. Nathan knows me so well and he picked up on my tension, so he gave me a shoulder rub. We talked and he suggested I needed sex."

"Which you do."

"Yes, I do. Then he came up with this wild idea that we should go down the friends with benefits rabbit hole."

"And you said no."

"Not at first. Well, actually, we discussed it at length."

"Of course you did."

She could picture Monique rolling her eyes. "You're rolling your eyes at me, aren't you?"

"You know it. Why not just get him naked, hop on his amazing magic penis and get yourself off, then throw him out the door?"

Theoretically, that sounded like exactly what she needed. It was exactly what Nathan had suggested. But this was the reality of her friendship with Nathan, and that made it a lot less than simply sex.

"That was the plan, but then I got scared."

"Scared of Nathan? Why? What did he do?"

"Not scared of Nathan. I was afraid of screwing up our friendship."

"Oh, honey. I totally understand. That was your freak-out in college after that night you two had together. But you're not the same people you were back then. You're adults now."

"I know, Monique. But we're even closer now than we were all those years ago. I don't want to do anything to mess that up. Is no-strings sex really worth it?"

"I can't answer that. Only you can."

"I don't know, Monique. I keep coming back to friendship being more important than sex."

"That's true. It is. But don't discount the fact you still need to get laid. And if Nathan is offering that to you, do you really want to turn him down?"

She sighed. "I don't know. I'm conflicted."

"I can tell. You're also under a huge amount of pressure with the business. A little release wouldn't be a bad thing."

"Says the woman who can get it anytime she wants."

Monique laughed. "I can and I do. Not that I'm not picky with the men I choose, because I am. That's why I'm giving you advice. You don't want to date right now, you don't want a relationship of any kind, so you might want to give some serious consideration to the benefits of having a good friend who's offering you exactly what you need. Sex with someone you know and trust. Without all those dating distractions and the emotional nonsense."

Monique had a point. She knew Nathan better than any guy. She trusted him. "I have some thinking to do. Thanks for letting me vent, and as always for your invaluable advice."

"That's what I'm here for, honey."

"Oh, how did it go with elevator guy?"

"All looks, no substance. Sadly, there won't be a second date."

Mia wrinkled her nose. "That's disappointing."

"Tell me about it. I had high hopes for that stud. I thought about having steamy sex with him anyway, but since he works in the building I tossed that idea since I'd have to see his face in the elevator every day."

"Good call. Okay, thanks for the talk."

"Anytime, honey."

"Good night, Monique."

"Night, Mia."

She clicked off and tossed her phone on the table next to the sofa. She thought about doing some work, then decided maybe some relaxing yoga would be more beneficial to a good night's sleep. She went upstairs, changed out of her clothes and pulled up one of her favorite calming yoga workouts on her netbook. The thirty minutes of breathing and stretching put her in a relaxed state, and when she was finished she felt immensely more at ease.

It might not be as good as a couple of screaming orgasms, but after she washed her face and brushed her teeth, she climbed into bed and turned off the light, keeping her breathing as normal as possible.

She stared out the window, trying to clear her head of the day's events. But Nathan kept popping in there and she couldn't shake loose of the feel of his hands on her body.

She flopped over onto her back in disgust, feeling the tension return to her shoulders. What she really needed was those great hands of Nathan to give her a back massage.

While she was naked. She could already imagine him sliding his hands over her body, starting with her back and then roaming ever lower. She loved his hands, the way he moved his fingers slowly over her skin, as if he wanted to take his time getting to know every inch of her. Then his mouth would replace his fingers and he'd—

She rolled over onto her stomach and pulled the pillow over her head, willing the images to go away.

The thirty minutes of yoga had been totally wasted.

Giving up, she threw the pillow off her head, got out of bed and went downstairs to do some work.

SIX

AFTER LAST NIGHT, WHEN HE GOT ZERO SLEEP BE-
cause he tossed and turned with a hard-on thinking about what might
have happened with Mia but didn't, Nathan got up early and hit the
gym, hoping to relieve some frustration with a pounding workout.

Unfortunately, he used the same gym as Mia's big brother
Flynn, who he ran into in the parking lot.

"Good to see our new quarterback at it early," Flynn said as
they walked to the front door together.

"Yeah. I've got big shoes to fill."

"You'll do it. But if you need me to push you around some and
toughen you up, feel free to ask."

Nathan laughed. As a defensive lineman for the Sabers, Flynn
was as hard-hitting as they came. "Thanks. I'll keep that in mind."

They went inside and stored their bags. Flynn grabbed his
phone and his earbuds. "Going for a run. Wanna join me?"

Since the track was exactly where Nathan was headed, he nodded. "Sure."

Nathan followed Flynn onto the track and shoved his earbuds in, flipped on his running music and started his pace. He tuned in to the music, paying no attention to Flynn, who ran ahead of him. Nathan stayed in his own head, marking his mileage, checking his heart rate and counting his steps as he ran. He dove into the beat of the tunes, picking up the pace as the music revved up along with his heart rate, pushing it like he always did right at the high point of the music tracks, then taking it down slow at the end, walking off the last two laps during the cooldown.

"Get a few miles in?" Flynn asked, walking up beside him.

Nathan's lips curved. "Yeah. How about you? Manage a mile?"

Flynn laughed. "Something like that. Ready to pound some weights?"

"Ready."

They walked off the track and stopped at the juice bar. Nathan grabbed an energy drink and Flynn went for water.

"You seen Mia lately?" Flynn asked.

Nathan put the cap on his drink, trying to play it cool. Flynn knew Nathan and Mia were friends. And that's all he knew about them. "Yeah. We had dinner together last night."

"How's she doing? I've been trying to stay out of her business because she doesn't want the family interfering. But I'd like to know how she's handling it all."

"She's a little frazzled, which is understandable given all she's got going on. But honestly, Flynn, she's managing it great. I'd tell you if she was having trouble."

Which he wouldn't, because his first loyalty was to Mia and always would be. Flynn didn't need to know that, though.

"Good. I'm glad to hear it. Why don't you ask her to bring you to the restaurant soon? That way I can check up on her without really checking up on her."

Divided loyalties. He could see that was going to be an issue. "We talked about that recently. I'll see what I can do about it."

"Thanks. Now come on. I'm gonna kick your ass on bench press."

Nathan laughed. "I don't doubt it."

He did, too. Nathan was no slouch on the bench, but Flynn could press some serious weight. He decided it was good to work out with someone much stronger than he was, though, because it pushed him to be better. And he always wanted to be better.

While they worked out, Jamal and a few of the other guys from the team showed up, so Nathan got a great workout in. Flynn moved over to some of the other machines with a few guys from the defense, and Nathan and Jamal worked on some upper-body free weights.

"So I've been out on a couple of dates with this really cool woman."

Nathan finished up the last of his chest flies, then sat up to look at Jamal. "Yeah? Who?"

"You remember Wendy?"

He frowned. "Is that the woman we met at the club last month? Smokin' hot, long legs, beautiful hazel eyes?"

Jamal nodded.

"She's in finance, right? Super smart, too."

"Yeah."

Nathan picked up the weights and leaned back. "I can't believe she agreed to go out with you."

"Hey, screw you."

Nathan did his next set then got up so Jamal could take his turn. When he finished Jamal looked up at him. "I like this woman."

Nathan arched a brow. "So not just a random, huh?"

"Nah. She's smart, she's funny, obviously hot as hell, too. She's not into me as a football player. We've had several dates. And we spend a lot of time just talking. We just click, man, ya know?"

He had as tight a friendship with Jamal as he did with Mia. Jamal knew he could always be honest with him, that they could leave the bullshit elsewhere. "Hey, that's good, Jamal. I hope it works out for you."

"I wasn't looking for a relationship, but I wanna see her all the time. I wanna talk to her all the time. That's weird, right?"

"Nothing weird about it. Sometimes you just find that person and it all seems right."

"Oh, yeah, like you'd know all about that."

Nathan shot him a look. "Hey, I had a relationship in college. I was in love once."

"Right. Sorry."

Nathan shrugged. "It was a long time ago. But I still remember what it was like. And it's good. Just take your time with it."

"Yeah, I know. Anyway, I was wondering if you'd like to go out with us. Maybe we could double-date."

"I'm not seeing anyone right now."

"So? Grab Mia. She's not seeing anyone, either, is she?"

"No."

"Good. Grab Mia and we'll all do something fun together."

"Sure."

"Okay, then. Let's do something this weekend. Wendy said there's a wine festival in Napa."

"Sounds fun. I know Mia would enjoy that."

Jamal held out his fist and Nathan bumped.

He'd text Mia about it and see if she was on board.

"In the meantime, training camp starts damn soon," Jamal said. "You've been workin' hard and it shows. You ready to lead this team?"

Was he? He wasn't sure. Every time he thought about it he felt a weight on his chest. And a little nauseous, too. But he'd never admit that even to his best friend. Or to anyone else on the Sabers. This team was counting on him.

"You bet your ass I am."

Jamal leaned back and grinned. "We are gonna kick some ass this year, Nathan. You're gonna lead us just like your dad."

Just like his dad. Mick Riley was a legend. He'd broken records that no one would touch for years.

Nathan had tried his best to follow in his footsteps, to do everything right, but he wasn't Mick Riley. He wasn't even Mick Riley's blood, so he didn't have the genetics going for him, either. All he had was drive and ambition and the hope that he could someday be half as good as his father had been.

But all the sports commentators and his teammates saw was the Riley name, and the expectations were high.

Jamal got up. "Your turn."

Yeah, it was his turn all right. And every day that passed it came closer and closer to the first day of the season, and he hoped like hell he didn't fuck this up. There were too many people counting on him, and if he failed, not only would he disappoint his team, he'd disappoint his father.

And he never wanted to do that.

SEVEN

MIA CHECKED HER PLANNER. IT WAS FRIDAY AFTER-
noon and so far today she'd hustled through three player meetings
and two internal staff meetings. It was two thirty and she almost
had things wrapped up. One more hour and she'd be out of here.

She knew—had hoped, actually, that her business would take
off like a rocket. But she had no idea they'd be this incredibly busy.
They'd signed cornerback Clyde Motts at the beginning of the
week, and he'd recommended one of his friends, a defensive back
from Philadelphia, so they'd made a presentation to him on
Wednesday. He'd accepted, and he'd made a recommendation for
one of his basketball friends from Los Angeles, who they met with
this morning. At the same time they signed a deal with a Texas
shortstop and also made a presentation to one of the San Francisco
Sabers running backs.

Mia was exhilarated—and exhausted—as she walked into her
staff meeting.

"Wow," she said as she stepped to the front of the conference room. "Busy week, huh?"

"Stellar week, Mia," John, her finance guy, said, bringing up numbers on the screen. "Better than we anticipated. I don't know how you managed to get this many people on board so quickly."

She stared at the numbers and blinked. Holy crap. They had budgeted for a heavy push the first six months, allowing for small or no gains in the first three considering start-up time.

They'd already surpassed their first six months' projections.

"These numbers are amazing. I wish I had a magic answer, but I can't take credit for it. Much of the success has to do with client word of mouth."

"Which means they like what they're seeing during the presentations," Monique said.

Mia nodded. "So kudos to our presentation team. What you're all doing is working, and I thank you for that. Now we need to make sure to deliver on our promises to these athletes. Let's wrap up early today and talk it all out on Monday morning. I don't know about the rest of you, but this has been a whirlwind week and I'm wiped. I need a drink."

They all laughed, but, as she suspected, no one was going to argue with her about getting out early. They'd all put in late hours the past week hustling to get presentations put together at the last minute. Her team deserved to hightail it out of there early on a Friday.

"Got a hot date tonight?" Monique asked.

"Not a hot date. Nathan's friend Jamal is seeing someone, so he wanted Nathan to double-date with him for this wine trip to Napa. Since he isn't dating anyone at the moment, I'm going with him."

"Oooh. That sounds so fun. And relaxing. Maybe while you're there you'll get a second chance to ease some of this week's tension." Monique waggled her brows.

Mia rolled her eyes. "No, there will be none of that."

"Shame. You're very tense."

Mia frowned. "Who said I'm tense?"

Monique grasped Mia's hand and leaned in close. "Your best friend. Me. You're working very hard. You're tense. Go have a great weekend—and some sex."

Monique made it sound so simple when it was anything but. Fortunately, she'd been so slammed with work this week she'd had no time to think about her lack-of-sex dilemma, which had suited her just fine.

She went into her office, packed up a few contracts and PR items she wanted to review over the weekend, then headed out the door. She answered some e-mails on the train, and by the time she got home she realized she was hungry. Since it was going to be a while before Nathan picked her up, she grabbed a snack from the fridge and sat at the counter to eat it while she finished answering her e-mails.

While she worked, a text popped up from her mom. She smiled at that and called her.

"Hi, Mia," her mother said. "I didn't expect you to call. I figured you were busy."

"Actually, I let everyone go early today."

"Really? Was it a slow day?"

Mia laughed. "No, we just had a very intense week and I wanted to give everyone the rest of the day off to enjoy a kick start to their weekend."

"You're such a good boss, Mia."

"I try to be."

"Tell me how it's going. You said you had a busy week. Does that mean it's going well?"

She grabbed her glass of iced tea and moved to the living room so she could sit on the sofa and put her feet up. "It's going shockingly well."

She filled her in on the week's events since she knew her mom would want details.

"I don't know why you're so surprised, Mia. You showed your business plan to your father and me. We were very impressed with how detailed it was. I'm not at all surprised that you're growing already."

"We're still in the initial few months. I had budgeted for almost nothing in the way of growth this fast."

"That just means you're doing it all right. You should be proud of yourself."

Panicked was more like it, but she wouldn't tell her mother that. "Yes, it's great. So how's Dad doing?"

Her mother launched into a discussion about her dad and the ranch, and Mia was happy to have the topic off herself and the new business. They talked for about twenty minutes, then hung up.

Mia breathed deep, deciding she needed a good workout to ease some of the stress from this week. She changed clothes and walked to the gym. She saw there was a yoga class starting in about an hour, so she warmed up on the elliptical for twenty minutes, then went to work on the equipment for a while. When she was done, she took some time to get a drink in the lounge before heading upstairs where the classes were located.

She was glad to see Cheyenne was leading the class. She'd taken a few yoga classes from her since she'd moved out here and liked her style of teaching. She'd also found a yoga studio nearby that she enjoyed as well.

It was always good to have options.

This class was great. After an hour she was a hot sweaty mess, but she was also calm and relaxed and totally de-stressed. She'd worked all the tension and kinks out of her body and she was ready for the weekend. She thanked Cheyenne for the great workout and walked back home.

She brewed some green tea, checked her phone, saw she'd missed a few key e-mails, so she answered those, then stripped out of her clothes and decided to soak in the tub for a while and read a book. She took her tea upstairs with her, ran the tub and climbed in.

It was steamy hot and perfect. She grabbed her book, read and relaxed, needing this so much after this week. Her phone buzzed so she picked it up. It was a text from Monique.

What are U doing?

She typed back: Did some yoga. Taking a hot bath now. U?

Watching Netflix. Have a fantastic date set up for tonight.

Mia laughed and typed: Lucky you.

Monique typed back shortly after with: Super smart guy and he's gorgeous. Should be fun. What are you packing for the weekend?

She hadn't even thought about it. No clue.

Monique replied. Be sure to pack that short dress you bought last week. It's sexy.

Mia rolled her eyes. I'll think about it.

Monique typed back: Pack the damn dress and have some fun!

Mia laughed and tossed her phone on the bathroom counter, then picked up her book and continued to read. When the water in the tub went lukewarm, she got out and dried off, then went into her bedroom. She had time yet, so she climbed onto her bed with her book. She was still warm from her bath so she slid under the sheets and started flipping pages. She was at a really good point in the book. It was a suspense novel from one of her favorite authors and it was right at the good part.

She didn't know when she fell asleep, but she woke with a start. The nap had felt great.

She went into the bathroom to grab her phone to check the time. She had about an hour until Nathan was coming to pick her up.

Plenty of time to get ready and pack. She pulled out her overnight bag and looked in her closet.

Despite Monique's suggestion, she was most definitely not packing the short black dress. This wasn't a hot getaway weekend, it was something fun to do together. Nathan explained Jamal and his date had invited him and he didn't want to third wheel it, so he wanted her to come along to balance things out.

Perfectly understandable since she'd been put in that kind of situation before and it tended to be uncomfortable as hell. She was happy to go along. Plus, there'd be a wine tour, which sounded so fun.

She packed a pair of capris, a sundress, and then figured they'd go somewhere nice to eat. She pursed her lips and stared into the closet.

Well, damn. She grabbed the black dress and packed that, too. Just in case.

She did her makeup and her hair, then got dressed and carried her bag downstairs and laid it by the front door.

She gathered up her planner and her phone and charger and put those in her tote bag just as the doorbell rang. She opened it and Nathan stood there, wearing his signature boyish grin.

"Ready?" he asked.

"Yes." She nodded and picked up her bag. He took it from her. "I've got this."

She followed him out to his SUV, surprised to see they were alone.

"Where's Jamal and his girlfriend?"

"Wendy had a client meeting that went longer than she planned, so they're going to meet us there."

"Oh. Okay."

He put her bag in the back of the SUV. Mia climbed into the passenger seat and buckled up. Since they waited until after six to leave, they should miss most of the traffic leaving the city. Or that was their hope when they planned this out.

They did hit some traffic in the city, but once they got over the bridge, it wasn't too bad. Mia still couldn't believe she lived here. It was so beautiful and as she looked out over the Golden Gate Bridge and the San Francisco Bay, she took a deep breath and reminded herself how lucky she was to be living her dream.

"What are you thinking about over there?" Nathan asked.

She turned her attention toward Nathan. "I was thinking about how lucky I am to live here, and to realize my dream of starting up MHC. The past several months I've gotten bogged down in all the stress of the start-up and I've forgotten how much this all means to me and how fortunate I am to have the opportunity to do it."

He nodded. "Yeah, we're both lucky."

"No, you're talented. I'm lucky."

He changed lanes and moved into the carpool lane. "Bullshit. You think you'd be able to do what you're doing if you didn't have the smarts and the talent? Come on, Mia. Give yourself some credit. You worked hard for this. No one hit the books in school more than you did. You were always focused and driven. It's one of the things I admire most about you."

She looked down at her hands, feeling her face warm from the compliment. "Thank you, Nathan. But I wasn't fishing for compliments. What I meant was, it took a lot of good timing and things to fall into place for me to be able to start up this company. For you, that athletic ability was either there or not. You've had it your entire life. And look what you've done with it. You want to talk about drive and ambition? That's you. You knew what you wanted to do and you made it happen."

"I don't know. I think we're both talking about the same thing. We both have talent. It just manifests itself in different ways. I could never do what you do."

"Oh, come on. You have the book smarts. You could have gone into the draft after your junior year. Instead, you stayed and got your degrees. And they aren't fluff degrees, either. They are in finance and math."

"That's only so I could pick up the smart chicks. Like you."

She rolled her eyes. "Was not and I know it. Though it was fortunate that you and I met in Differential Calculus. I saved your ass in that class."

"That you did. And then I saved yours in Geometrical Statistics."

She wrinkled her nose. "I hated that class."

He laughed. "I remember."

"Then how about we never revisit it again? How did your day go today?"

"It was fine. I worked out and met with some PR people."

Her ears perked up. "PR people?"

"Yeah. Some new team that wants to hire me now that I'm going to be the starting quarterback. They had some marketing ideas about how to get me more exposure, commercials, shit like that."

"That sounds . . . vague."

"It was. I don't think I'll use them. They didn't have anything concrete to offer."

"Do you have other people to talk to? Other companies in mind?"

He shrugged. "I don't know. I haven't thought much about it."

She sighed. She didn't want to do this, but she was more concerned about Nathan's career than crossing that line between friendship and business. "You should let MHC do a presentation for you."

He gave her a quick glance before turning his attention back on the road. "You mean have your company manage me?"

"At least see what we have to offer. We're very good and now that you're going to be the starting quarterback, you need a company that will handle you right, from your public relations to brand strategies to your financial future. I know you have a great agent and he's worked with our team with some of our other clients and prospective clients. He could sit in on the presentation."

"I know you've mentioned it before, but I'm still wary about mixing business and our friendship."

"I understand your concern, but I think we could make it work without any trouble. You need good representation, and I believe we're the best. So . . . think about it."

"I'll do that."

"Okay. Enough work talk."

His lips curved. "And I was just going to ask about your day."

She laughed. "It was hectic."

"Tell me why it was hectic."

"I thought we were done talking about work?"

"We're done talking about your work as it relates to me, not as it relates to you. Tell me why your day was hectic."

She told him about her entire week and when she was finished, that tension she'd worked so hard to dissolve was back.

"You're a badass, Mia. Maybe I will consider letting MHC present to me."

She couldn't resist the satisfied smile that crept onto her face. "Take the weekend and think about it. But I told you, we're good."

"*You're* good."

"It's not just me. I've got a really good team and they're the ones who would be taking care of you. Not me."

He looked over at her again and the look he gave her didn't have anything to do with business. "What if I want you to take care of me?"

She felt a rush of heat, of need and desire mixed with the memory of his mouth on hers. All of those feelings were very bad. "Nathan. We aren't going there."

"What? I meant it in an entirely professional way."

"Did you?"

"Of course. What did you think I meant?"

Maybe she'd read him wrong and it had been entirely in her own mind. "Nothing."

"Not nothing. You were thinking about you and me, weren't you?"

It didn't surprise her he'd pick up on that. "Yes."

"You already made it clear that wasn't gonna happen, so I really was talking about you taking care of me from a business point of view."

"Okay. But no, I don't deal with the athletes once they're on board. Everyone has their own point person. My function is overall management of the company. I'm there in the beginning, during the presentation and signing of the contracts, to be sure it all runs smoothly. After that, I hand you off to your designated managers."

"I see. Sounds very well organized."

She smiled. "Of course it is. I totally have my shit together."

Professionally, anyway.

The drive to Napa Valley took a couple of hours. It was always enjoyable to spend time with Nathan, because their interests were similar, even down to liking the same music. They sang together in the car, though Nathan sang off-key. Not that he cared much, which made Mia laugh. They talked current events and families. She'd known Nathan long enough to know everything about his, and he knew all about hers. Of course, he already knew one of her brothers personally since they played on the same team.

"So my Aunt Jenna is pregnant."

Mia blinked. "She is? Really? That's fantastic. I know you told me she and Tyler were talking about having kids, but she was focused on her music and the club so they couldn't decide when."

"Yeah. I guess it was kind of a surprise, but they're both really happy about it."

"Aww. That's great. When's the baby due?"

He shrugged. "Uhh, no idea. I know my mom told me, but I forgot. I think it's during hockey season, so Tyler will probably miss some games."

She rolled her eyes. "Well, that's not at all specific since hockey season runs from October until next April."

"Hey, you can text my mom. She'll tell you."

"I might just do that." She'd never met Jenna or Tyler, but from conversations she'd had with Nathan she felt as if she knew them. She had met Nathan's mom, Tara, though, along with Nathan's dad, Mick. They were wonderful people.

"How's Sam?"

Nathan grinned. "Feisty. He's doing great. Loves school."

She shook her head. "They grow up fast."

He laughed. "That's what my mom said about me."

"She did space you and your little brother out quite a bit."

"Yeah. It took her a long time to find the right guy to fall in love with. Then she found my dad."

"You have a great family, Nathan."

"Thanks. I think so, too."

Mia smiled and leaned back in her seat. She loved the story of how Nathan's parents met and fell in love. Even though Mick Riley wasn't Nathan's biological father, Mick and Tara had met and fallen in love when Nathan was fifteen. Nathan's biological father wasn't in the picture and had never been, so Mia was happy that Nathan had such a strong father figure in Mick Riley, who had adopted Nathan after Mick and Tara got married. And then Nathan's little brother, Sam, came along.

There was nothing better than a real-life happily ever after.

Nathan adored his little brother. She'd met Sam one family weekend at college, where she'd also met his parents. Seeing the way Nathan doted on Sam reminded her of the way her big brothers had treated her when she was little. There was a lot of teasing, but also genuine love and tenderness.

It was one of the reasons she had kept Nathan in her life. A man who wasn't afraid to show that kind of love to both his parents and his brother was a man worth keeping as a friend.

They rolled up to the lodge and Nathan parked out front.

"Let's go get checked in," he said.

She was more than ready to get out and stretch her legs. They went inside to the reception desk.

"You still have time to attend the wine hour," the person at the reception desk said. "Complimentary wine from our vineyard, along with snacks. We also have information there about our wine tours."

Nathan smiled and nodded. "We'll be sure to check that out, thanks."

"I do want to attend," Mia said as he grabbed their bags.

"Then let's drop the bags and go."

Their rooms were right next to each other, so Mia keyed into her room and put her bags inside, then met Nathan outside his.

The wine reception was great. There were several varieties to choose from, and she was happy to see there were snacks left, because she was hungry. She ended up choosing a cabernet and filled her plate with a few hors d'oeuvres. Nathan grabbed a glass of wine and then went back and filled two plates.

"Hungry?" she asked as she found them a place to sit on the outside patio.

"Starving."

"We could have stopped someplace to eat along the way."

He shrugged. "I figured we'd eat when we got here. This will do for now."

His phone buzzed so he pulled it out of his pocket and looked at the message. "It's from Jamal. They're on their way. He said don't wait on them to eat because it'll take them a while to get here."

"Okay. What would you like to do about dinner?"

"I think there's a restaurant here. Or we could go exploring."

"I'm all about exploring."

"Okay. We'll have our wine and snack, then we'll drive around and see what's for dinner."

"Sounds great. But I'm going to go to my room and change clothes."

He nodded. "You do that."

Since he was wearing jeans and a button-down shirt, he looked fine for dinner. She'd thrown on capris and a T-shirt, so she finished nibbling on her snack and drank her wine, then dashed upstairs. She unpacked and hung up her dress and some of her clothes, then put on a pair of black pants, a black tank and red button-down silk top. She slid into her flats and brushed out her hair, fixed her makeup and added some lip gloss and jewelry, then went back downstairs.

"You look hot," he said with a smile.

She couldn't resist smiling back at him. "Thanks."

They got into his SUV and he took off down the highway. Mia got out her phone and looked up some places where they could stop and eat.

"What are you in the mood for?" she asked Nathan.

"A beer."

She laughed. "Food-wise."

"Don't care. I'm just hungry."

"Okay." She scanned the list. "We could do fancy, like French food, or something simpler like pizza."

"What are you in the mood for?"

She thought about it. "Actually, I don't want to eat anything super rich and heavy since we had those snacks. How does pizza sound to you?"

"I love pizza."

Her lips curved. "I know you do. One night in college I watched you polish off two large pizzas by yourself after a game."

"That was the night our O-line wasn't playing their best and I spent most of the game running for my life. I burned a lot of calories so I was starving."

"Oh, please. You could eat an entire pizza by yourself even without having played a game."

"True. So we're having pizza?"

"Yes, we are." She gave him directions to the Italian restaurant, which fortunately wasn't far, because now that they'd started talking about pizza, she was really hungry, too.

She wasn't sure how busy they'd be, so she made an online reservation, which they had available.

They pulled up and parked, then went inside.

"Busy place," Nathan said as they gave their name and hustled over to the side to wait to be called.

Mia looked the place over, from the concrete floor to the wood-fired pizza oven to the giant copper bell that lit up the place. It was quaint and beautiful, and waiters hustled back and forth to serve their customers.

It wasn't long before their name was called and they were seated at a small table near the back. They looked over the menu and a waiter came over to take their drink orders. Nathan ordered a beer and Mia decided on a glass of wine.

"You should probably order your own pizza," Mia said as she put her menu to the side.

"I can share, you know."

"Oh, I know. But I'm having spaghetti."

"Fair enough."

They put in their food order when the waiter came back with their drinks. Mia had ordered a glass of Syrah, which was delicious and just what she needed to cap off the night.

"Good?" Nathan asked.

"Perfect."

He lifted his beer. "To a fantastic weekend."

She tipped her glass against his beer. "I'll definitely drink to that. I feel like it's been nonstop frantic for the past six months. This is the first weekend I've taken off in . . . I don't know how long."

"Then you're overdue and I'm going to make sure you party your ass off this weekend."

She smiled at him. "I'm so ready for that."

When their food arrived, Mia realized she was hungrier than she thought. She dove into her plate of spaghetti, while also ogling Nathan's sausage pizza, which looked amazing.

"Want a slice?" Nathan asked.

"Definitely." She ended up scooping some of her spaghetti onto his plate, but in the end, it was Nathan who finished off all of the pizza and the majority of her spaghetti. She had another glass of wine, though, which was heavenly.

"Are you sure you had enough food?" he asked.

"More than enough." She sat back in her chair, feeling entirely relaxed for the first time in months. This weekend was a brilliant idea. If she'd stayed home she'd likely be on her laptop about now, going through financial projections and staffing, and reading proposals for next week's meetings.

This was so much better.

When the waiter came and asked if they were having dessert, she fully expected Nathan to say yes, so she was surprised he declined.

"No dessert?"

He shook his head. "Nah. I'm good for now."

When the waiter laid the check on the table, she grabbed it and took out her credit card.

Nathan frowned. "I can get that."

"Or I can get this one, and you'll get the next one."

He nodded. "Okay."

She liked that he respected her enough to let her pay and that he wasn't one of those guys whose ego got out of joint when a woman paid the tab.

They left the restaurant. It was a nice night. The air was crisp but the stars were amazing. Nathan headed for the car, but Mia grabbed his hand.

"I'm so full. Let's take a walk."

"Sure."

The grounds of the hotel the restaurant was located in were amazing, with places to sit by the pool and waterfall. There were walking paths so they traversed those while Mia occasionally looked up to gape at the night sky. As they wandered, she caught sight of some of the rooms. What she could see of them anyway. They were shrouded in privacy with tall walls and shrubbery.

"I did a little reading on this place on the way over. They have both indoor and outdoor showers. Plus a massage table in every room."

Nathan's brows rose. "Yeah? We should stay here next trip up."

"I thought so, too. I love a good massage."

"You should book one while we're here."

"I've considered it. I need to work out the kinks."

They made their way to a fire pit, and since she was chilled and no one was there, she led Nathan to a cozy bench in front of it so they could sit.

"This is awesome," Mia said as she warmed her body in front of the fire. "I need a fire pit."

"Where? In your living room?"

She laughed. "No. It's a someday thing. When I have a house and a backyard."

"Why didn't you buy a house?"

"I had enough going on trying to find the space for MHC, getting the company up and running and hiring staff, plus moving here. The last thing I wanted to do was go house hunting. Leasing the town house was enough for now. Eventually, though, I do want to buy."

Nathan leaned forward, closer to the fire pit. "We'll have to go house hunting."

She lifted a brow. "Oh, we will, huh?"

"You'd buy a house without my input?"

"Of course not. You being such an expert on house things."

"Hey. I know house things."

She gave him a skeptical look. "You do, huh? Like what?"

"You might be surprised to know I've learned a few important details about home ownership over the years from my dad and my uncles."

"Which means they used you as free labor."

"You got that right. But if you do go house hunting, you might want to bring me along. I have mad skills and can tell you if plumbing is crap or if an A/C unit is a piece of shit."

"I'll definitely keep that in mind. But it's going to be a while, so cool your house-hunting jets. I have enough on my agenda to keep me busy."

"Yeah, I get it. You're in building-an-empire mode right now."

"I don't know about building an empire, but not having my company sink in the first year is a good start."

He scooted closer to her and put his arm around her. "Babe. You're not gonna sink. Look at how busy you are right now. You've already said you've gotten more business than you thought you would right out of the gate."

"True." She turned her attention from the fire and focused on Nathan. "But can I keep the momentum going?"

"Of course you can. Word of mouth is what breeds success in a business like yours. And the more clients you bring on board, the more they'll talk about your company, and that means other athletes will want to know about you."

She inhaled a deep breath, then let it out. "I hope you're right."

"I'm always right."

She laughed. "I'm going to bring you into my Monday morning meetings as a motivational speaker."

"Uh-huh."

"Are you Nathan Riley?"

Mia looked over to see a guy with a camera. And not just a random fan, either.

"I am."

"Okay, thanks." He took a quick photo. "Is this your girlfriend?"

Nathan frowned, stood and took Mia's hand. "Let's go."

They started walking back, the guy following them. Mia heard the click of the camera as they walked along. They got into their car and drove off.

"Who is that guy?" Mia asked.

"Paparazzi would be my guess."

"I thought those guys only took photos of famous people, like TV and movie stars."

He shrugged. "They take pictures of anyone they think will earn them a buck."

Nathan parked and they made their way inside the hotel.

"Nathan, that was so weird. I mean, I'm no stranger to cameras. My brothers have had their photos taken by fans and press photographers before. But not in the middle of dinner or on the street."

"I'm sure it's because the season is starting soon and there's this whole idea of me stepping into my dad's shoes. This guy's thinking he's got a story to tell, and he got a lucky shot of me out in public, that's all."

"I guess." But still, it worried her. For a lot of different reasons.

"Come on, let's step into the bar," he said. "I need a beer."

They grabbed a table and a waitress came over. Mia ordered a glass of cabernet and Nathan ordered a beer.

Mia sat and pondered the run-in with the photographer. What did he want and how had he found Nathan up in Napa?

The waitress brought their drinks, and Mia sipped hers, lost in thought.

"Hey," Nathan said, laying his hand over hers. "What's going on in your head?"

"Oh. Thinking about that photographer. I mean, how did he even find you?"

Nathan laughed. "I don't think he was specifically looking for me. He probably trolls all the hotels and restaurants hoping to spot someone he can photograph. Likely he knows sports, so he recognized me. That's all."

She took another sip of her wine. "You're probably right."

"Don't worry about it, okay?"

"What? Me worry?"

He laughed. "It is kind of your middle name, isn't it?"

Her lips curved and she felt the tension begin to dissolve. "At least three people mentioned that to me in meetings at work this week."

"Hey, you're just organized. That means you worry about every detail. Nothing wrong with that."

"I do tend to get a little obsessive, but that means I'm doing the best for my clients. You should see me in meetings. I'm very good at my job."

"I know you are." He quirked a smile at her and swallowed the last of his beer. Then he stood and held out his hand for her, pulling her to stand. "I could think of a lot of fun things to do with you, Mia, but biz meetings isn't one of them."

Maybe it was the wine buzz, but she moved in closer to him. "Is that right? What kind of fun things?"

He put his arm around her and tugged her close. "Depends. If it's friends only, then it's hanging out. If it's friends with benefits, I could show you."

She'd had a rough week, and the thought of Nathan helping her release all that pent-up tension sounded very appealing. She laid her palms on his chest. "Well, since you mentioned it . . ."

His phone buzzed. He ignored it and she lost herself in the depth of his gaze. But his phone continued to buzz.

"Shouldn't you get that?"

With a sigh, he removed his hand from around her back and took a step back. "It's probably Jamal."

He answered the call and she took a minute to breathe and recover her senses. If that call hadn't come in, she might have told Nathan she wanted to have sex.

Which she did, of course. But not with Nathan.

She really needed to get over this desire for him.

Nathan hung up and slid his phone in his pocket. "Jamal and Wendy checked in, but Wendy's wiped out so they're going to meet us for breakfast in the morning."

Mia nodded. "Sounds good. I'm a little tired myself."

He gave her a look that told her he knew she'd had an abrupt change of mind from their conversation before the phone call. "Sure. Let's head upstairs."

She appreciated that he didn't push her about it, and on the ride up in the elevator he was quiet. But he didn't seem upset. They got off on their floor and headed to their rooms. Nathan waited until she slid her key card in and opened her door. Then he smiled at her.

"See you in the morning, Mia."

"Good night, Nathan."

She closed and locked her door, wishing she could be brave enough to take what she wanted without worrying about the repercussions. But that was just too big a risk to take.

EIGHT

NATHAN MET JAMAL IN THE GYM EARLY THE NEXT
morning. They did a solid workout for a good hour and a half, and
by the time they finished, the buffet was open, so Nathan was
ready for a tall glass of juice and a large coffee.

"That was a hell of a tough session," Jamal said as they settled
down at a table.

Nathan took several swallows of orange juice before he answered. "Yeah, it was. But not as brutal as training camp's gonna
be when that starts up."

"Gettin' anxious?" Jamal asked.

"More like excited. I'm ready for this season to start."

"You and me both. I can't wait to get out on that field and catch
some balls. And with you as QB? We're gonna kill it this season."

Just talking about it made Nathan's stomach knot up. This was
his shot, the one he'd dreamed about his whole life. He was ready

and he knew it, but this team? This was his dad's team. This hadn't been the way he wanted to do it.

His ultimate dream had been to someday play against his dad. Him on one team, his dad on the Sabers.

But that wasn't how it happened. So he was just going to have to live with it going down like it had.

Jamal nudged him. "What's going on over there? Workout kick your ass?"

He jerked his head toward Jamal. "Huh?"

Jamal laughed. "You asleep? I'm talking to myself over here, man."

"Sorry. Just thinking about the season, ya know? For sure we're gonna kill it."

"That's what I'm talkin' about."

Nathan noticed Mia and Wendy rounding the corner from the elevator banks at the same time.

"Our ladies have arrived."

Jamal stood and turned around. "Good morning. I didn't know you two knew each other."

Mia stopped and looked at Wendy, surprise evident on her face. "We don't, actually. But we rode down in the elevator together. We said good morning."

Wendy laughed. "And then both of us buried our noses in our phones." Wendy extended her hand. "I'm Wendy."

"And I'm Mia. Nice to officially meet you."

"Since the guys started without us, let's have some coffee. And I need an omelet."

Mia nodded. "I'm all over that."

Jamal got up. "I'm hungry, too."

Nathan got up and followed the group over to the buffet. After a hard workout he was more than ready to fuel up and the buffet had plenty to offer. He loaded up on eggs, sausages and pancakes, along with a separate plate of fruit.

Mia raised a brow as she eyed his plates. "I'm surprised you could carry those without some help."

"Somehow I managed it."

Mia dug into her omelet. "I'm taking bets on whether he goes in for seconds."

"If he's anything like Jamal, I say yes," Wendy said.

"Oh, you think you know me so well?"

Wendy batted her lashes, then leaned over and rubbed Jamal's arm. "You know you're having two plates so don't even try to deny it."

Nathan laughed. "And so will I. Who knows when we'll eat again."

"Yes," Mia said. "Because it's such a wasteland out here. You poor starving athletes."

Nathan shot her a look. "Hey, we get hungry. We burn a lot of calories. Quit giving us shit."

Mia laughed. "You invited me this weekend. Get used to me giving you shit."

"You two aren't a couple, right?" Wendy asked.

"No, we're like best friends," Mia said. "Just think of me as one of the guys. Only I have a vagina, so that makes me smarter."

Wendy laughed. "Oh, we're going to get along great, Mia. In fact, we should plan the wine tour day today. God knows Jamal is only interested in what we drink, not where we go."

Jamal was lifting his fork to his mouth, but stopped and nodded. "True that."

"We should plan a beer tour day," Nathan said.

"We should. Invite the guys."

Wendy turned. "Oh, because women don't like beer?"

Jamal started to say something, closed his mouth, then said, "I should shut up now."

"You should," Nathan said.

Jamal shot him a look. "Hey, aren't you on my side?"

"I'm on the side of keeping you alive. Which is why you should shut up."

Wendy laughed. "Your best friend keeps you on your toes, Jamal."

"Yeah, yeah."

Mia was enjoying this group. And she really liked Wendy. As Nathan and Jamal ate and talked about their team, she and Wendy outlined their day.

"I booked us a limo service for the day," Wendy said. "They'll take us to several wineries, plus we'll have lunch. Everyone can enjoy the day without worrying about who's going to drive."

"That sounds amazing. I can't wait."

"They'll pick us up here at ten and have us back here by six."

Mia grinned. "Perfect time for cocktail hour and then dinner."

Wendy laughed. "Yes, it's going to be that kind of day. Which I need after the hellish week I've had."

"I'll definitely drink to that."

After they finished breakfast, they headed up to their rooms. Mia took a shower and dried her hair. She did her makeup, then put on a pair of capris and a sleeveless top and slid into her sandals.

She took another look at social media as she'd done when she'd gone to bed last night, and again when she'd awakened this morning, convinced she was going to see a photo of Nathan and her that the photographer had taken last night.

But she'd found nothing. She'd even typed in Nathan's name in several search engines. Relieved, she grabbed a cardigan and her purse just as Nathan knocked on her door.

As always, Nathan looked hot. He wore dark jeans and a white T-shirt. How could such a simple outfit make a man look so sexy? His sunglasses rested on top of his head and she wanted to take them off so she could run her fingers through the thick mass of his hair.

Whoa. Rein it in, Mia.

Instead, she smiled. "I'm so ready for this. How about you?"

He devastated her with the curve of his lips. "Yeah. Should be fun today."

They met Wendy and Jamal downstairs. Wendy wore a red and yellow polka dot sundress and silver sandals, along with an antique-looking silver necklace that complemented the beauty of her tawny skin perfectly.

"I absolutely love your necklace."

Wendy fingered the dangling chain. "Oh, thank you. Actually, I made it."

Mia's brows rose. "You did? That's amazing."

"Thanks. It relaxes me. My job is high stress, and this is something fun and chill."

"I love it. Do you sell them?"

"I do. I have an online shop. I'll give you one of my cards."

She dug one out of her purse and handed it to Mia.

"I love handmade jewelry. What else do you have?" Mia noticed her bracelets. "Did you make those bracelets, too?"

Wendy nodded. "Bracelets and earrings, too. I have several pieces with me." She pulled one of the bracelets off. "Here, you keep this one."

Mia slid the bracelet on her wrist. It was a super thin hammered silver with a dark black pearl in the center. "I love it. Are you sure you want to sell it?"

"No, you take this one. And if you really do love it, you can check out the store and buy more."

Mia looked over at Wendy. "Are you serious? This is lovely, Wendy. But I don't want to take your bracelet."

Wendy laughed. "I can make more, and yes, I'd love for you to have it."

"Then you need to give me more of your cards, because I can sell a lot of these for you at my office."

Wendy put her arm around Mia. "Girl, you are my new best friend."

Jamal put his arm around both of them. "I knew the two of you would hit it off."

"Go away, Jamal," Wendy said. "I'm chillin' with my new best friend."

Mia laughed. "I think your boyfriend considered this a romantic weekend."

"Oh, he'll get his romance. For now, though, it's wine time."

Mia was more than ready to get this day started. As Nathan came up beside her, she looped her arm in his and they headed toward the waiting limo.

"Did I mention you look hot?"

She grinned. "You did not. But thanks."

She had a feeling this was going to be a very fun day.

NINE

BY TWO P.M. BOTH MIA AND WENDY WERE ON THEIR WAY to being hammered. Which was pretty funny because the one thing Nathan could always count on with Mia was her control.

She really must have needed to let loose this weekend, because she'd sampled every glass of wine at every winery, and since he wasn't much of a wine guy, she'd finished off his glasses, too. He made sure she ate whatever snacks were offered, because he wanted her to have a good time and not get sick.

Then again, he'd known her a long time. She knew her limits. Right now she was laughing at something Wendy said.

He loved her laugh. She went into it full barrel, tilting her head back, her whole body shaking. When Mia relaxed and let go, she could have fun with wild abandon. That's the way he wanted to see her all the time. Throwing out those inhibitions and allowing herself to have fun. As he sat back and took a sip of the beer he and

Jamal had managed to score at this awesome winery, he was content to just watch her.

"Does she know you have a thing for her?" Jamal asked.

Nathan turned his attention to Jamal. "I don't have a thing for her. We're friends."

"Uh-huh. I have friends who are women, and I don't look at them like that."

"Like what?"

"Like you want to strip her naked and lick every inch of her skin. Which is the way I look at Wendy. Not the way I look at my women friends. My women friends? I look at them as if they're dudes. Do you look at Mia like she's a dude?"

He slanted his gaze over to Mia, who had leaned over to whisper something to Wendy. They were currently sitting in an outside courtyard at the winery. Nathan and Jamal were up at the bar while Mia and Wendy sat at one of the tables. He focused on Mia, on the way her capris hugged her well-toned calves, and the way her delicate fingers moved as she carried on a conversation. He wanted her fingers in his mouth. He wanted to suck on them as he pumped his cock inside of her.

Goddamn.

"No," he answered in response to Jamal's question.

"Does Mia know about it?"

"Know about what? There's nothing to know. We're friends and always have been and that's all we're ever going to be."

Jamal slanted a look at him. "But it doesn't sound like that's what you want."

"It's what she wants."

"Oh, she's friend zoned you."

He shrugged. "I'm not sure that's really what she wants. She's afraid to lose the friendship, though. I keep trying to tell her we won't."

Jamal lifted his beer and took a sip, then studied the women before looking back at Nathan. "Are you sure you wouldn't, though? Mixing sex with friendship can be a dangerous game."

"Maybe. But I value the friendship as much as she does. I just happen to think we can have both."

"You sure she wants you? Maybe she has a guy."

Nathan shook his head. "She doesn't have a guy. I'd know if she did."

"How?"

"Because we're friends and I know everything about her."

"Okay. Then if you want her, go after her. Just know there are risks."

Nathan took a long pull of his beer, then set it on the bar and motioned for the bartender to give them another round. "Yeah, I know. It's what kept me from pushing it with her."

"I guess you have to decide if the sex is worth the risk of the friendship."

He took the beer the bartender offered, wrapping his hand around the bottle. "Yeah."

Looking at Mia, listening to the sound of her laughter, he knew he could maintain the friendship. They had too much to lose to let that go.

He wanted her. Hell, he'd always wanted her. There had been other women after her, but he'd always come back to Mia. He'd respected the sexual wall she'd put up between them, but he'd never stopped wanting more.

He noticed how she looked at him, the way she touched him, and it went beyond friends. With every day they spent with each other, they were growing physically closer. He just had to convince her to break down that wall and add sex to their relationship.

Maybe this weekend would be a good time to test the waters.

"Let's go join the women," Nathan suggested.

"Yeah, let's do that."

They pushed off the bar and went to the table.

"Hey, babe," Wendy said as Jamal leaned over to brush a kiss over her lips.

"Hey yourself. Are you having a good time?"

"I'm having just the best time."

Nathan pulled up a chair next to Mia. "How about you? Having fun?"

"Yes. Are you?"

He lifted up his bottle of beer. "I am now."

She laughed.

"We need to refine your palate. Let's go into the tasting room."

"You do realize I drink wine on occasion."

"Of course I do. But let's go play with some wine." She pushed her chair back and stood. "We'll be back."

"We'll be right here," Wendy said.

Mia took Nathan's hand as they walked into the tasting room. He had no complaints about that so he let her guide him inside. Since they had VIP passes they were allowed to go in and taste the wine as often as they wanted to at the wineries.

Mia went to the counter. "Okay, white or red?"

"Don't care."

"Fine. First, take a sip of water to cleanse your palate from the offending beer."

He tried not to laugh. "Sure." He took a couple of sips of water.

She wrinkled her nose as she studied the menu, then chose a pinot noir. "This winery has an incredible pinot. Smooth and very flavorful. I think you'll like it."

He took a sip. Surprisingly it was pretty decent. "It's good."

Mia's face lit up as if she'd just given him the best gift ever. "So you like it?"

"For wine, I like it."

"Excellent. I've already asked for two bottles of this, so you'll probably end up having some next time you come over."

"Or, I'll have a beer, which you always kindly keep stocked for me."

She grasped his arm. "You know, Nathan, someday I will make you a wine lover."

"Or not."

She shook her head. He picked up a slice of cheese and hand-fed it to her, watching as her lips closed over it. Watching her throat work as she swallowed made his dick twitch.

Yeah, okay, so he had it bad for Mia. She didn't need to know how bad.

He used his thumb to swipe the corner of her mouth, noticing how her focus remained on his face. This wasn't a friends-only exchange. He felt the connection between them, the heat as they stood close.

But he was going to give it time. He gave her his signature grin. "Now you can wash it down with more wine."

"A total win for me." She took another glass of wine and sipped it, then handed it to Nathan. "This one is very good. Try it."

He turned the glass around where her lips had been and took a drink, noticing the way she watched his mouth. When she licked her lips, he knew what she wanted. If they weren't in a public place he'd put the glass down and kiss her.

But she was also more than a little inebriated, and when he made the suggestion, he wanted her sober. So right now it was fun and games and nothing more.

But he still wanted a taste of her, and this was as close as it was going to get for now.

"Good?" she asked, her voice sounding a little raw.

He leaned in closer. "Yeah. Really good."

A tour group had come in, crowding them together. When a

couple pushed up to the counter, Mia laid her hands on Nathan's chest.

"Your heart is beating fast," she said, tilting her head back to look up at him.

"Is it? Must be because your body is against mine."

"Nathan. What are we going to do about this?"

He was about to give her an answer, but Jamal had made his way through the crowd.

"Hey, limo guy said it's time to move on. You two ready to go?"

Mia blinked, then gave Nathan a look of regret. She turned to Jamal and smiled. "Absolutely."

Nathan led her through the group and outside, where Mia met up with Wendy without once looking back at him.

Yeah, not the right time now.

But soon.

TEN

MIA FELT GOOD. LIKE, REALLY GOOD. SHE'D HAD SUCH an amazing time today with Nathan, Wendy and Jamal. Plus, she was pretty inebriated, so that didn't hurt.

They'd hit four wineries and she'd had plenty to drink. She laid her head back on the plump leather of the limo and closed her eyes, and before she knew it she was asleep. She slept the entire ride back to the lodge, only waking when Nathan jostled her.

Ugh. Now her mouth felt like cotton and she had a headache. She went upstairs to her room and downed two full bottles of water and popped some pain reliever. She lay on her bed and closed her eyes for about half an hour. When she woke, she felt immensely better. She texted Nathan, who passed along information about their dinner reservation, which was in an hour.

Plenty of time for her to get ready. Wendy had made a reservation at a Michelin-starred restaurant with an amazing view, so Mia took out the fancy black dress and her heels. Since she was wearing

Wendy's silver bracelet, she chose a long silver chain necklace to go with it. The dress scooped a little low in front so the necklace would bring attention to her cleavage—what little she had. Then again, she wouldn't mind that at all considering the teasing she and Nathan had been doing today.

And what exactly *was* she doing with Nathan? She didn't have an answer to that, nor did she have the time to ponder it because there was a knock on the door. She opened it and tried not to suck in a breath as Nathan stood there wearing black slacks and a white button-down shirt.

"Wow," he said as he looked her up and down. "You know, even dressed casual like you were earlier today, you take my breath away, Mia. But in that dress? Damn."

As compliments went, that one made her warm all over. "Thank you. You look incredible."

"Hey, thanks. So we both look hot." He held out his arm for her. "I'd like you to be my date tonight so all men will be jealous of me."

"You do realize I was already going with you tonight."

"Yeah, but we're the third and fourth to Wendy and Jamal. And we're friends. I want you to be my official date, the woman on my arm. The incredible beauty who only has eyes for me tonight, and I'll only have eyes for you."

She laughed. She couldn't say no to that, especially with the way she felt. "I accept."

Wendy had arranged a limo again, so they rode in style to Auberge du Soleil, a restaurant perched on top of a hill. The views of the valley were spectacular.

"I could stare at this view all day and night," Wendy said as they walked up to the restaurant.

"It's amazing." The hilltop where the restaurant was located offered stunning views of Napa hills and valleys. She wondered how the restaurant got their guests to leave. If it were up to her, she'd stay for hours just to gape at the vistas.

They were fortunately seated at a table right by the floor-to-ceiling windows, which meant the expansive scenery was theirs for the duration of their meal.

"This is stunning," Mia said to Wendy as they sat. "What a wonderful suggestion."

Wendy nodded. "One of my clients mentioned it to me when I told her I was planning a trip up here. She said we had to eat here so I made sure to make a reservation right away."

"Good call."

They were given the wine list first. She and Wendy studied it and decided on a bottle of sauvignon blanc. Even the guys decided to have wine tonight, which made Mia happy, though she knew Nathan was only drinking it to please her.

"You can have beer or something else if you want," Mia told him.

"Wine sounds good. Plus the food's fancy. Wine will go better with it."

He was right about that.

They were presented with the menu, and Mia's mouth watered. The food options looked remarkable.

Wendy leaned over. "What are you having?"

"I think the duck. How about you?"

"The veal, for sure."

Their dinner was a four-course extravaganza. It was a good thing they'd eaten light during the day because this was going to be huge.

"Tell me about your work, Wendy," Mia asked after they'd ordered and the wine had been poured.

"I'm a financial advisor. I do retirement planning and investing as well as insurance. Not nearly as exciting as your work."

"Oh, I don't know about that. You're working with your clients' futures. Plus, money. Money is always exciting."

Wendy laughed. "True."

"But neither of your jobs are as fun as ours," Jamal said.

Wendy shot him a glare. "Oh, please. You run around for a few hours once a week, sweat, roll around in the grass and catch a football. And for that you make millions of dollars."

Jamal grinned. "I know. Isn't it great?"

"You're like an overpaid child."

Jamal leaned over and brushed his lips across Wendy's. "Nuh-uh. A very hot, talented, sexy man."

Wendy rolled her eyes, but she kissed him again. "Okay, I'll give you that."

"Come on, you two," Nathan said. "Don't make us move to another table."

Jamal laughed. "You need a girlfriend."

Nathan leaned back in his chair and put his arm around the back of Mia's chair. "I have a date tonight."

"Oh, so now you two are dating?" Wendy asked. "I thought you were just friends."

"We are," Mia said. "I'm his pretend date for tonight."

Wendy frowned. "I'm confused."

"She looked hot," Nathan said. "So I asked her to be my date tonight so all men would be jealous of me."

"And I said yes."

Wendy shook her head. "I don't understand you two."

Mia smiled. "We're an acquired taste, Wendy. You'll get used to us."

"Mia and I go back a long way." Nathan slid his fingers across the back of Mia's neck. "We're friends, yeah, but there's also some magic chemistry between us."

Wendy took a sip of her wine and leaned forward. "Magic chemistry? Do tell."

"Not much to tell," Mia said, trying to ignore the shivers skidding down her spine in reaction to Nathan's touch. The last thing she wanted was to give Jamal and Wendy the idea that Nathan and she were a couple. "We're friends. Really good friends."

Wendy arched a brow and Mia knew what the unasked question was.

"Unfortunately, not with benefits," Nathan said.

Jamal laughed. "Too bad for you, buddy."

Nathan leaned over and nuzzled Mia's ear. "That could change anytime you want it to."

She picked up her wineglass and took a sip. "Or not."

He swirled his thumb over the back of her neck, giving her goose bumps. "You know I want to change your mind."

She hadn't been this relaxed in months. And she felt really good. Her body tingled with the need to be touched and kissed. She realized there wasn't anyone else she wanted touching her but Nathan.

So she leaned over and whispered in his ear. "Give it your best shot."

She was testing the waters and maybe she was opening up Pandora's Box and she'd regret it. But she'd said the words and she wouldn't take them back this time. She was tired of the back and forth and maybe she just wanted Nathan.

No, there was no maybe about it. She did want him.

So now that it was out there, she'd see what happened.

ELEVEN

THIS HAD BEEN THE LONGEST GODDAMNED DINNER of Nathan's life.

He'd only had one glass of wine so he was pretty much stone-cold sober. And before dinner he was certain Mia had put sex back on the table.

He wanted dinner over with so he could get her alone. Instead, they'd had a fucking four-course meal that had taken eleven hundred hours to eat, so they'd had to endure food and conversation, with Mia occasionally smiling at him and laying her hand on his arm and giving him looks that told him exactly what was on her mind.

Sex. It sure as hell had been on his.

His dick had been semihard for the past two and a half hours. He'd never been more miserable.

And then everyone had to order dessert.

Fucking hell.

He stared down at his crème brûlée as it if were the enemy. He typically *loved* dessert. But right now, dessert was getting in the way of his sex life.

Mia brushed her fingers over his forearm. "Is something wrong?"

Yeah, something was wrong. This fucking meal was taking too long. "No, I'm fine."

She slanted a disbelieving look at him. "Are you sure? You're not eating your crème brûlée."

That was because crème brûlée was a sex-denying dessert. It was evil and had to be destroyed. "I'm full."

She arched a brow. "I cannot believe those words came out of your mouth. You are never full. Usually you eat your dessert and mine."

He shrugged and stabbed his spoon into the dessert.

Die, fucker.

Although maybe if he ate faster they could all get out of there.

He scooped up the offending custard and shoveled it in his mouth in a hurry. He had it polished off in about six bites. He had no idea what it even tasted like. He didn't care. He just wanted it gone.

Their waiter came over and asked if anyone wanted more coffee. He prayed no one said yes.

"I'm fine, thank you," Mia said.

Both Jamal and Wendy declined.

Nathan looked up at the waiter. "We'll just take the check."

While Mia and Wendy went to the restroom, Jamal and Nathan took care of paying the bill. It looked like they were finally going to get out of there.

They stood when Wendy and Mia returned.

"Ready to go?" Nathan asked.

Wendy nodded. "Yes, let's do that." She took Jamal's hand and led the way toward the exit.

Mia leaned in close. "Anxious to leave?"

He brushed his fingers against hers. "You have no idea."

Her lips curved.

The ride back was long and interminable, especially since Mia sat next to Wendy so they could chat. He sat across from them, which meant he had nothing to do but stare at Mia's gorgeous legs.

Dammit. He was not going to ride in this limo with a hard-on while sitting next to Jamal. So he turned his focus on his best friend and talked football instead, deciding ignoring Mia was probably better for his sanity.

He almost audibly sighed in relief when the limo pulled in front of the lodge. He resisted, holding his hand out for Mia to help her.

"I wish there was a place where we could go clubbing," Wendy said.

Jamal nodded. "I think there's a place that has cover bands or jazz musicians. Wanna go check it out?"

"I do." Wendy turned to them. "How about you two? You game?"

Kill me now. Clubbing? If Mia said yes, he might just cry.

He looked over at Mia, who shook her head. "I'm done for. How about you, Nathan?"

Finally. He resisted the urge to shove his fist in the air in triumph.

"Yeah, me, too. I'm heading to my room. You two have a great time."

They waited while Jamal and Wendy left, then Nathan turned to Mia.

"What now?"

She moved into him. "I don't know, Nathan. What do you want to do now?"

He took her hand and led her to the side of the lodge. He couldn't wait another minute, so he backed her up to the wall. "What I've wanted to do all damn night."

He nestled his body against hers and she laid her hands on his chest, tilting her head back to look at him. There was a fire in her eyes that hadn't been there before.

"And what have you wanted to do all night?"

"This."

He put his mouth over hers and kissed her.

TWELVE

MIA KNEW SHE'D BEEN PLAYING WITH FIRE.

Nathan's lips against hers felt like an inferno. Hot and needy and filled with raging desire. She craved more. She clutched his arms to draw that blast of sensual heat closer. He groaned against her lips and her sex quivered in response. She ran her fingers across his chest, moving over the broad expanse of muscle there to seek out his biceps. She gripped his arms and dug her nails into his skin as he sucked her tongue into his mouth.

She wanted to climb all over him, strip him down and do delicious, dirty things with him.

But she realized their surroundings, so she pulled away. "Nathan, we're outside."

He nodded, rested his forehead against hers for a few seconds, then backed away, dragging in a few deep breaths as he did.

"I'm gonna need a minute before we go in."

She noticed his erection straining against his pants, wanted nothing more than to run her hand over his straining flesh, to unzip him and feel his hot, hard cock.

Instead, she took a couple of breaths herself. Maybe some cool night air would rein in her obviously overcharged libido. She decided to look up at the stars. Anything to get her mind off Nathan.

But then Nathan slipped his hand into hers. "Okay. Let's go."

They walked inside and took the elevator up to their floor. Not touching him more took every ounce of restraint she possessed, but she managed it.

She took her key card out of her wallet and slipped it in the door to her room. When she opened the door, she turned to Nathan.

"You're coming in, aren't you?"

"If you're inviting me."

"I'm inviting you." She backed in and he stepped into the room and shut the door.

"If I'm in, I'm in for the night, Mia. So you need to decide if this is what you really want. If you don't, I'll leave."

He was giving her the choice to change her mind again.

"I want you to stay."

His lips curved and he reached behind him to flip the lock, then moved toward her.

She backed against the wall, not bothering to turn on the light in the room. She dropped her purse on the carpet, letting the key card follow.

He nestled his body against hers. "Did you wear that dress tonight for me?"

She tilted her head back. "Yes and no."

"Fair answer." He swept his fingers over the skin of her collarbone. "I like this dress, Mia. But I have to tell you, it drove me crazy."

She felt her heart pounding, heard her own staccato breaths as she struggled with each inhalation. "It did?"

"Yeah. It's low here," he said as he traced his finger over the scoop neck, making her heartbeat skitter. Then he smoothed his hand across her breast and down her rib cage, and grasped a handful of the material of her dress at her hip. "And high here."

She shuddered as he slipped his hand under her dress. She expected him to go right for the goods, but he didn't. Instead, he smoothed his hand over her hip.

"You have the softest skin, Mia. It's what I remember most about our one night together in college. It's like sliding my hand over satin."

His gaze was locked on hers as he rubbed his thumb over her hip and all she could do was hold on to him like he was a lifeline. She had no idea her hip was an erogenous zone, but she was quaking. And when he slipped his fingers under her panties and skimmed her skin there, she let out a low moan.

Then he took her mouth in a blistering kiss that set her on fire. She wanted so much more than this make-out session against the wall. She wanted them naked. She wanted to feel him moving inside of her.

She wanted an orgasm so badly her entire body throbbed with the need of it.

Nathan pulled back. "You're shaking. Are you okay?"

"No. I need . . ." She couldn't put it into words.

He swept his hands down her arms. "Tell me what you need."

"Everything. You and me naked would be a good start."

His lips curved into a wickedly sexy smile. "I can make that happen."

He led her into the room and over toward the bed. "Turn around."

She turned to face the bed. She'd left the drapes open and stared out at the full moon that bathed the room in a silvery glow. Nathan undid the zipper of her dress and she shivered at the contact of his knuckles against her bare skin. He kissed her shoulders when he pulled the dress away. She turned around to face him, his face outlined in the moon's light.

She let the dress drop to the floor.

She was so glad she wore the black underwear to match the dress. Maybe subconsciously she'd known where this night was going.

Nathan's gaze was hot as he looked at her, from her face to her body and back again.

"It's been three years since that night, Mia, and you know what? I've never forgotten a minute of it."

"We were drunk that night."

He undid the buttons of his shirt, then shrugged out of it. "Yeah, we were. I still remember all of it. How beautiful you were. You're even more beautiful now."

So was he. He'd always been lean and muscular, but he'd added some weight and more muscle. He was taller, more imposing. But she'd never felt threatened or powerless when she was with Nathan. He always made her feel safe and cared for.

She reached out and spanned her hands over his wide chest. "You're beautiful, too."

One corner of his mouth lifted. "You're supposed to say I'm strong and muscular."

"Yes, that, too. But there's a beauty in the way you're sculpted. You work so hard to achieve this strength. I admire it."

"So do you." He ran his fingertip over her shoulder, and down over her bicep. "You're strong, Mia. Not in the same way I am, but I know how hard you work on your body, and on your inner strength, too. Your spirit is the strongest thing about you."

He couldn't have complimented her more. "Thank you."

He reached around and undid the clasp on her bra, then pulled the straps from her shoulders. He cupped one of her breasts and teased her nipple with his thumb. "You're like a goddamn work of art. Everything about you fits perfectly."

She didn't have large breasts. They were actually kind of small. But she was petite, so for Nathan to say she was perfect made her feel that way. And when he bent over and fit his mouth over her nipple to suck it between his lips, she let out a moan of pleasure.

This was exactly what she needed, what she craved from him. He popped the nipple out of his mouth and sucked the other one, giving equal pleasure. It was glorious and breathtaking. She wound her fingers into his hair, losing herself in sensation.

He rose and kissed her again and she couldn't resist cupping his erection. He groaned against her lips. Her body flared with a quake of its own.

He pushed her gently onto the bed. She looked up and watched as he undid the zipper on his pants and let them drop, along with his boxer briefs. Then he was beautifully naked.

Talk about a work of art.

"You should always be without clothes."

He smirked. "Around you? Hell, yeah."

He leaned over the bed and grasped her panties, pulling them down over her hips and legs and adding them to the pile of their discarded clothes. Then he crawled onto the bed and lay next to her.

"Did you bring condoms?" he asked.

She rolled on her side and propped her head on her elbow. "What if I said no?"

"Then I'd use my mouth and my hands to make you come about five times tonight. And we'd wait until we got back home to fuck."

She loved that answer. And of course he'd see to her needs without once mentioning his own because that was the kind of guy Nathan was. "Yes, I brought condoms. Did you?"

"I have one in the pocket of my pants."

She shoved at his shoulder.

"You're an asshole."

He pushed her onto her back. "Nah. You like me. And you brought condoms, which meant you were thinking about having sex with me."

"Who says I brought the condoms to have sex with you?"

"I don't see any other random dude in here."

She walked her fingers across his chest. "No, just this random dude. So I guess you'll do."

He rolled over on top of her, captured her hands and raised her arms over her head. "Oh, lumping me in with the randoms, huh? Gonna make you pay for that one, Mia."

His threat made her shiver in anticipation. "Really. In what way?"

He palmed her breast, then ran his thumb ever so lightly over her nipple. "How does this feel?"

"It tickles."

He rolled his fingertip back and forth over the bud until it stood hard and upright. The sensation shot straight to her sex.

"That?"

"Mmm, good."

Then he put his mouth on her, sucking her nipple. He sucked gently at first, then harder, making her squirm, all the while holding her wrists over her head and pinning her lower body with his legs so she couldn't move. He attended to both of her nipples by touching and sucking them repeatedly until waves of torturous need washed through her.

"Nathan."

He lifted his head. "Yeah."

"I need more."

He smoothed his palm along her rib cage and over her lower belly. "More down here?"

She swallowed. "Yes."

When he cupped her sex, he gave her that lopsided grin that never failed to make her heart kick up a fast beat. "You're wet and ready for me, Mia. Want me to fuck you?"

"Yes."

Instead, he teased her with his fingers and his hand until she lifted her hips to meet him. And when he slid a finger inside of her, she gasped.

"I love watching you move," he said. "I love hearing you breathe. Now I want to watch you come. Let me hear you, Mia."

He teased her clit with expertly smooth movements of his hand while dipping his finger in and out of her until she was mindless, seeking only the rush of orgasm. And oh, she was so close. So. Close.

"That's it," he murmured. "You're right there, Mia. Let go." He alternately sweet-talked her with his smooth, sexy voice, then licked her nipples and used his amazing fingers to pleasure her relentlessly until she shuddered and moaned through an amazing orgasm. He stayed right there with her, murmuring his approval as she rocketed through her climax with wave after wave of unbelievable pleasure.

When her hips finally relaxed on the mattress, she expected Nathan to release her arms. He didn't. Instead, he coaxed her right back into another frenzy with his fingers. She was helpless to do anything but ride the wave of his beautiful, relentless torment. This time, she cried out when she came, bucking against his hand with her release.

He let go of her hands and framed her face with his palm. She sifted her fingers through his hair and kissed him, drawing him closer by throwing her leg over his hip. She felt the hard evidence of his erection rub against her as they wound themselves together.

"The condoms are in my bag."

"Yeah, we'll get to that. I need to taste you first."

"That's not necessary."

Again, that half smile that told her he was going to get what he wanted. And what he wanted was her. "You getting off as many times as possible is necessary, Mia."

She shuddered in a breath. "Nathan. The things you make me feel."

"Babe, we haven't even started yet."

He pushed her onto her back, then slid down between her legs and put his mouth on her sex.

She died a little bit again as he expertly slipped his tongue inside of her, then bathed her in the warmth of sensual pleasure with his mouth. She surprised even herself when she came again almost immediately, her whole body trembling with the force of her orgasm.

When Nathan kissed his way up her body, lingering at her hips, her stomach and her breasts, she somehow found her breath again.

He loomed over her and grinned. "Yeah, I'd say you needed those few orgasms."

She reached out to smooth his hair off his forehead. "I guess so."

"Now I'm gonna explode if I don't get inside of you."

She'd wanted that for so long she felt the same way. Her lips curved. "Again, condoms are in my bag. I'll go get them."

"Nah, I'll get mine. You stay right there."

"Great idea, since I'm fairly sure my bones have turned to liquid."

He reached down to their discarded pile of clothes and came up with a condom packet in his fingers. "Let's get this party started."

She was sure the party was already in full swing. But she was more than game to let this particular party go on all night long.

He kneeled above her. She reached out to grasp his cock, closing her hand over the shaft so she could touch him, watching as he closed his eyes.

"That's it. Stroke it."

He was velvety hard in her hands, and as a pearl-sized drop of liquid slid from the tip, she swept it onto her thumb and used it to coat the head, swirling it around with her thumb.

Nathan groaned. "I've thought about you touching me, imagined it when I jerk off."

Hearing him say that made her sex quiver. "Do you think about me?"

"Hell yes. You, naked, spread-eagled on a bed like you are now. Mostly my fantasies revolve around you getting yourself off and me watching you. Or you sucking my cock while you touch yourself and get yourself off."

Her sex thrummed listening to Nathan describe his fantasies in such graphic detail.

"We'll have to make that happen."

He tore the condom open and slid it onto his cock. "Yeah, we will. But now I need to be inside of you."

She needed that, too, nearly quaked with the need for it. "Yes."

He dropped down on top of her, careful to keep his weight off her as he entered her.

It was sweet bliss to feel him ease into her, especially seeing the look on his face, his expression so intense as he seated himself fully inside of her. She could feel her body acclimate and tighten around him.

Other than blissful memories of awesome sex, that one drunken night they'd had together previously was a bit of a blur. She remembered heavy breathing, soft murmurs, some laughing and a lot of orgasms. Now she was fully cognizant of Nathan's crisp, clean scent, the feel of his skin as she smoothed her hand across his shoulder and down his arm, the way it felt to be held against him. Mia thought it would be awkward to be intimate with someone she knew so well as a friend.

It wasn't awkward at all. If anything, she felt as if this was where she was always supposed to be.

"Damn, you feel good," he whispered, then bent to kiss her, a hot tangle of lips and tongues that made her body light up with hot waves of sensation, as if she'd been hit by a lightning bolt of pleasure through her nerve endings.

And then he began to move, and it got better, if that were even possible. She dug her heels into the mattress and lifted her hips to move with him, meeting him with each thrust, her body and mind melding into the powerful sensual forces that flowed through her.

Yes, it had been a while for her, but this was really good. Maybe it was because of the close connection she already shared with Nathan. This wasn't first-time sex with someone she barely knew, where she was always a little hesitant, always held herself back.

She already had a bond with Nathan. He had no expectations and neither did she. Nathan knew her better than any guy ever had, and for that, she felt freer than ever before to give of herself.

What she received in return was way more than she had ever anticipated. So when she felt the tremors of orgasm approaching once more, she let go, knowing she was safe, that he'd take her there with no hesitations.

He cupped her butt and raised her pelvis, then ground against her until she flew. She gripped his arms and wound her legs around his hips.

"Oh, fuck yeah," he said, shuddering as he came with her. She held on to him, feeling every inch of him as he let go.

It was a wild, uncontrollable and very long, satisfying finish. And the best sex she'd had in a long time.

Nathan licked her neck and breathed heavily against her throat. Mia wasn't certain she was even breathing. All she knew was that had been so, so amazing. Even her fingers tingled. That had to be a sign of great sex, right?

Nathan moved to the side of her, then off the bed to disappear into her bathroom for a few seconds. When he came out, he leaned against the doorway.

"I don't know about you, but I'm thirsty as hell."

She rolled over to face him. "I could drink about a gallon of water. There's some in the mini fridge."

He went to the fridge and pulled out two of the large bottled waters, unscrewed the caps and handed one to her. She sat up and leaned against the headboard, watching Nathan as he stood next to the bed and guzzled down at least half of his bottle. She took a few deep swallows herself before setting hers on the nightstand.

Nathan put his down on the other nightstand, then crawled into bed and pulled Mia down next to him.

"That was pretty good for round one."

She laughed. "Round one, huh? It's a good thing I have that box of condoms."

He arched a brow. "Oh, you brought a whole box, huh? Planning an orgy?"

Her lips curved. "Not an orgy, but it's been a dry spell for me."

He cupped her sex and began to rub her with gentle strokes. "Dry spell's over, babe. And I've got lots of stamina."

Despite having had multiple orgasms, her body awakened with renewed desire again. There was something about Nathan touching her that made her hot and feverish with just a touch. And since she figured this was just tonight and then they'd go back to being friends, she intended to use him and use him well.

She gave him a wicked grin. "Good. Because you're going to need stamina tonight."

THIRTEEN

IT HAD BEEN SEVERAL DAYS SINCE HIS WEEKEND WITH Mia at Napa. They'd both been busier than hell and they hadn't seen each other. Mia had told him she'd be swamped with meetings, and Nathan's mind-set was all about training camp coming up. He wanted as much time at the gym with his trainer as he could get so he'd be in top shape.

When he'd dropped Mia off after the weekend, he'd expected awkwardness between them. He should have known better. Mia hugged him and told him she'd had a great time, then smiled and said she'd talk to him sometime next week. Then she'd said goodbye, just as if nothing had happened. As if the sex hadn't happened.

Which was fine with him. Mostly. Except he knew at some point they'd have to talk about where they'd left things and about the status of their relationship.

But for now, he had to get his head wrapped around football.

He already knew he was in prime physical condition. He went

to the gym every day. His trainer was working him hard, and the results were showing. He felt good. He watched what he ate. He was ready for this.

What he wasn't ready for was a visit from his mom and dad. He knew his dad was concerned about him. After Mick had retired, he'd told Nathan he felt like he was dumping him and leaving him to fend for himself. Nathan had assured him he could manage the team just fine, that the year he'd spent learning from his dad and the other backup QB had taught him everything he needed to know. It was important that his dad not feel responsible for him.

If Nathan had been drafted by any team other than the Sabers, and he'd been called up to be a starter, there'd be no one there—including his dad—to rely on. The fact he was taking over as starting quarterback for his own father shouldn't make a difference at all. Not to Nathan and not to his dad.

But this wasn't just a run-of-the-mill kind of thing. It was a huge deal for Nathan. It was a big deal to the team. And to the sports correspondents, too, because it was all they'd talked about the entire off-season, which had dumped an enormous amount of pressure on top of an already pressure-filled situation.

Dad had told him the most important thing he could do was to ignore the media. Nathan knew his father was right, but that was easier said than done, especially with training camp and the pre-season right around the corner. All that hype about whether young quarterback Nathan Riley was going to perform even half as well as Mick Riley was going to amp up in a major way.

Nathan shrugged his shoulders, trying to ease the tension that constantly seemed to be there lately. He pulled into the driveway of his parents' house and got out of his SUV.

Despite his anxiety, he was happy his parents were in town. He went to the door and rang the bell.

His mom answered, his little brother, Sam, whipping around her.

"Nathan!" Sammy barreled into him, throwing his arms around Nathan.

"Sammy!" Nathan was always happy to see his brother. And at the age of six, Sam was like the Tasmanian devil, filled with energy. He picked him up and tossed him around by his arms. Sam laughed uncontrollably.

Then he put Sam down and hugged his mom. "Hey, Mom. How was the flight in?"

"Good," his mom said. "We got in late last night. We would have called but, honestly, we were all tired."

"Not a problem."

"Come on inside. Your dad is in his office on the phone. He'll be out in a few minutes."

Sam grabbed his hand. "Guess what?"

"What?"

"I got new Legos. Wanna play with me?"

"I will in a little bit. What kind of Legos?"

"Some Star Wars ones. They're cool."

"Those are my favorites, you know. Can I take them home with me?"

Sam cocked his head to the side. "Nooo. They're mine, Nathan. But I'll share with you."

Nathan's lips curved. "Okay. We'll hang out and play together. But first I have to talk to Dad, okay?"

"Okay." Sam lifted his head to look at their mother. "Mommy, can I go play out in the backyard?"

Tara nodded. "Yes."

Sam ran off and Nathan followed his mom into the kitchen. He took a seat at the island.

"Iced tea or a beer?" she asked.

"Iced tea sounds great."

She poured two glasses, then sat down across from him at the island. It hadn't always been so informal and easy between them when he'd lived at home. He'd been a little more difficult as a young teen. Attitude and all. He'd given his mom a rough time.

And then Mick had come into their lives and everything had changed. Nathan's whole attitude had shifted and he'd developed a renewed sense of purpose. His mom was happy and in love, and it changed Nathan's perspective on life. After that, he'd been driven to succeed, to be as good as the man who'd adopted him and had never made him feel less than his actual son.

"How's the business?" he asked his mom.

She smiled. "It's good. I'll meet with Maggie and the rest of the team while I'm here. We're looking at expanding the shop."

That was news. "Space-wise or personnel-wise?"

"Both, actually. We've added more people to the business, and we have everyone squeezed into the small space we started with all those years ago. Now we need to add at least two more event planners, and there's no place to put them. So Maggie and I are going to interview event planners, then shop new space."

He loved hearing the excitement in his mother's voice. "I know how much you like to shop. And office space? You'll be in heaven."

She grinned. "I know. We have a real estate agent lined up to spend two days with us showing spaces to lease. We're going to have so much fun."

Nathan laughed. "Are you sure Dad's going to be able to get you on a plane back home?"

"Ha. Maybe not."

"Who's going to watch Sam while you're off having these adventures?"

"Your father, of course. Now that he's retired, he gets to spend more time with Sam. Which they're both enjoying very much."

Nathan was glad that at least one amazing thing was happening because of his dad's retirement.

"Thought I heard you come in."

Nathan slid off the bar stool and hugged his dad, who still looked as young and robust as he had when Nathan was a gawky fifteen-year-old. Nathan couldn't even spot a limp, though his dad had had that knee surgery right after the end of last season.

"How's it going, Dad?"

"Great."

"How's the knee?"

His father looked down at his knee, then back up at Nathan. "Great. Physical therapy is a pain in my—knee actually—but the rehab is going well."

"Don't let him fool you," Mom said. "He complains about it all the time."

Dad lifted his chin. "I never complain."

Mom laughed. "I don't know who's the bigger whiner in the house now, you or Sam."

"I've watched some of the guys on the team go through rehab," Nathan said. "It's tough."

"Yeah. But it'll be fine. I have to be fine. I have to chase after your brother, and you know what a hellion he is."

"He'll love having you around all the time, Dad. Especially now that Mom is going mogul on us."

His dad put his arm around Mom. "She is. This is her turn to shine now that she's supported my career all these years."

Mom nudged Dad in the ribs. "You make it sound like I've done nothing but sit in the stands and act like a cheerleader during your games. You've supported my career plenty. I'll just have a little more time to concentrate on the business now that you're free."

"Yeah," Dad said. "I'm pretty happy about that."

They all sat down in the living room.

"Any thoughts about what your next steps will be?" Nathan asked his dad.

"What next steps?"

"A lot of former players move into broadcasting or coaching."

"Oh." His dad shrugged. "Not right now. I want some time off to finish rehab, play a little golf and play a lot with Sam. He's really looking forward to having me take him to school and pick him up. Being a stay-at-home dad for a while suits me just fine."

"I give it a year or two at most before he's itching to get back into football in some capacity," Mom said.

Dad looked at her. "And you'd be okay with that."

"We've already discussed this and you know I would. You love football. Just because you're not playing anymore doesn't mean you can't be involved in it. And no one knows more about the sport than you. You either need to be coaching or analyzing the games in some way." She grabbed his chin. "Plus, look how pretty you are. I can see you as a sportscaster."

His dad laughed. "Maybe. We'll see."

Nathan felt a little better listening to the two of them talk about the future. His dad didn't seem to be bothered about not playing anymore. At least on the surface. Nathan had worked so hard to get where he was. He couldn't imagine not playing anymore. But he was just at the beginning of his career. He was itching to be at the helm of the Sabers offense, to feel the ball in his hands and know that he was in control.

"Ready for training camp to start, Nathan?" his dad asked.

"Like you wouldn't believe. It's all I've thought about for weeks."

His dad nodded. "The offense will look to you for leadership, that you're ready to grab the reins and run with them. You watched me run that offense all last year. You can handle this team."

He couldn't explain how much his father's confidence in him meant. His dad had always been honest with him, sometimes brutally. If he wasn't ready to take the team, his dad would have told him, even if it hurt.

"Thanks, Dad. I'm anxious to get rolling."

Since thinking about leading the team made his gut tighten, he went to play with Sam for a while. With his little brother, everything was simple and easy. There was never any stress, just building spaceships and rolling around on the floor together. Eventually, they went outside and kicked a soccer ball around.

"I'm gonna play soccer," Sam said.

"Oh, yeah? How about football?"

"That, too. Like Daddy. And you, Nathan. Mommy and Daddy said we're gonna come watch you play this year."

"Great. I'll look for you in the stands. And maybe I'll get to come watch you play, too."

Sam's big blue eyes widened. "You will? Cool."

He could already picture Sam wearing football gear. He couldn't wait for pics.

His mom opened the back door. "Sam, time to come inside and wash your hands."

Sam wrinkled his nose. "Aw, come on. Just a little longer?"

Nathan recognized that look on his mother's face.

"Now."

Sam kicked his toe in the grass and looked down at the ground. "Okay."

Nathan ruffled his brother's dark hair. "We'll play again later." That lit his face up. "Great."

Sam dashed inside and Nathan followed.

"We thought we'd find somewhere to eat dinner," his mom said. "Sounds good."

His phone buzzed, so he grabbed it to take a look. It was Mia. Up for dinner tonight?

He smiled, then texted her back. I'm with my parents and Sam.

She replied with, Want to see them! Let's all have dinner. Invite them to Ninety-Two.

He looked up. "It's Mia. She says she wants to see everyone and invited us to her brother's restaurant for dinner."

"Oh, I'd love to see Mia and Flynn," his mom said, then looked over at his dad. "Mick?"

His dad nodded. "Sounds good to me."

"I'll text her," Nathan said.

They made arrangements to meet Mia at Ninety-Two. He wished he could be alone with her, but he knew how much Mia liked his parents and his brother, so it would be good for all of them to get together.

At least he'd get to see her, and he really needed that.

They needed to talk.

FOURTEEN

MIA WALKED INTO NINETY-TWO AND SAID HELLO TO Carol, the hostess. She spotted Grace, one of the waitresses she'd gotten to know fairly well since she'd officially moved to San Francisco. She waved.

"I have your reservation," Carol said. "And Flynn wanted me to tell you he'd be here in a bit."

"Okay, thanks, Carol."

"Would you like me to seat you now, or do you want to wait for the rest of your party?"

She looked at her phone. She was about fifteen minutes early.

"I think I'll go sit at the bar and wait."

There was an available chair at the corner, so she sat there and ordered a glass of cabernet.

"I can't believe you didn't come back to say hello."

She turned and slid out of her chair to hug Amelia, head chef and her brother Flynn's girlfriend. She was wearing her white chef jacket, her blond hair pulled back in a ponytail.

"I didn't want to bother you while you were cooking. And who told you I was here?"

Amelia stepped back and smiled at her. "Carol did. And other people bother me. You? Never. You're always welcome in my kitchen."

"Do you have a few minutes to sit and have a glass of wine with me?"

"Actually, not at the moment. We're full up and slammed in the kitchen. But you're having dinner here?"

"Yes. My friend Nathan is coming in with his parents."

"Nathan Riley? With Mick and Tara, right?"

"Yes."

"I'll come out later and say hello to everyone. Plus Flynn will be here so he'd make me leave the kitchen anyway."

Mia laughed. "True. Go back to work. I'll talk to you later."

"Okay."

Mia sipped her wine and took out her planner, jotting down some notes that popped into her head relevant to tomorrow's meeting. They were talking with an up-and-coming hockey player who'd had an outstanding season. His team had come close to making the championships and he was touted as a rising star. With a good management company behind him, he could go far.

"Hello, Mia."

She looked up from her planner to see Ken, the restaurant's manager. She smiled. "Hi, Ken. How's it going?"

"It's great. Haven't seen you in here for a few weeks. How's the new company?"

"Busy. But it's going wonderfully. Which is why I haven't been here in a while."

"I'm glad to hear that."

"And how's little George doing?"

Ken grinned. "He's incredible. Growing so fast that Adam and I can barely keep up with him."

"That's how it is with the little ones, I suppose. I want to see your newest photos."

"You mean the ones I took this morning?"

Mia laughed. "Yes. Those."

Ken took out his phone and handed it to Mia. She scrolled through and saw an adorable, chubby-faced little boy who looked a lot like both his dads. She handed the phone back to Ken. "He's beautiful, Ken."

Ken sighed. "Thank you. You'll have to come by the house and see him soon."

"I'd love to. Thanks for the invite."

Ken gave her a kiss on the cheek. "I need to get back to work. I'll talk to you soon."

"See you later."

She was about to go back to her planner when she spotted Nathan walking in with his parents. She tamped down the race of her pulse.

After last weekend and the sex, she was determined she wasn't going to get emotional or involved.

It had just been sex. Plus, he was here with his parents, so she had to keep it friendly. She waved to them and they came over.

"It's been too long, Mia," Tara said as she hugged her.

"I agree. I was so excited when Nathan told me you were in town."

She hugged Mick, too.

"It's good to see you, Mia," Mick said. "Where's your brother?"

"Which one?"

He cracked a smile. "The ugly brother."

"Again, which one?"

He laughed, and so did Mia, who said, "Flynn should be here soon. He said he was looking forward to seeing you."

"Yeah, I'll miss playing with him this season. But the team has Nathan, and I know he's going to kick ass this year."

Mia looked over at Nathan, surprised to see a brief flash of concern on his face before he masked it with a wide smile. "You know it."

She made a mental note to ask him about that later.

"Our table should be ready. Let me go talk to Carol."

She went to Carol, who grabbed menus and seated them in a quiet corner of the restaurant. Mick was as big a celebrity in San Francisco as her brother, so he got looks and waves as they walked through the restaurant. Mick was just as nice as her brother, too, so he stopped to sign some autographs and take selfies with a few people before he joined them at their table.

"That will probably happen forever, won't it?" Mia asked.

"I sure hope so," Mick said with a wry smile.

Their waitress came over and handed them the drink menu. Mia stayed with the cabernet she'd already started. Mick ordered a soda, and Nathan ordered a beer. Tara went with the same cabernet Mia was having.

"Where's Sam?" Mia asked.

"He has a friend who lives next door to us that he doesn't get to see all that often," Tara said. "So he's hanging out with him and having dinner at his house tonight."

"How fun for him."

"Yes. He hates to lose any time with Nathan, but he does enjoy playing with Dexter."

"I'm a novelty," Nathan said. "An hour or so with me and then he'd much rather hang out with kids his own age."

"I'm sure most of us would prefer to hang out with kids our own age," Tara said. "Though I do enjoy seeing both of you."

"Ditto," Mia said. "How's the business, Tara?"

"Great. I was telling Nathan earlier we've outgrown our space, so we're going to shop for a bigger location and hire a couple of new consultants."

"That's incredible. Congratulations."

The waitress brought their drinks, so they paused in conversation. "Thank you," Tara said. "I'm very excited. More importantly, how's your new business?"

"It's wonderful. I was so nervous—still am, actually. But we've picked up several clients already, have a few more that we're presenting to. Everything is running smoothly so far."

Tara nodded. "I know what that's like. My business took off right away, too. We almost had too much business at first. Which wasn't a bad thing, just a little overwhelming."

"Yes. Overwhelmed. That's exactly how I feel. But in a good way."

"It's because you know what you're doing," Nathan said. "You have a solid team, and people know that. They trust you."

She sighed, then smiled at Nathan. "Thanks for your faith in me."

"Why aren't you with Mia's company?" Mick asked.

Nathan paused mid drink. "I don't know. We've talked about it. It almost feels like a conflict of interest because Mia and I are—"

Mia waited, hoping like hell Nathan said the right thing.

"Friends."

She exhaled. That was the right thing to say. They were more than that, maybe. Maybe not. After last weekend she felt more confused than ever. They hadn't laid down the ground rules since last weekend, because she'd been slammed with work and they hadn't had a minute to talk to each other. Hopefully soon they could have some clarification.

"Of course you're friends," Tara said. "But friendship is one thing and business is another."

Mick took a sip of his soda, then leaned back in his chair. "Yeah, I can see how you wouldn't want to muddy those waters, though. Something goes wrong with the business side of things—" He paused to look at Mia. "And I'm not saying they would, but if it did, it could end your friendship."

"Exactly," Nathan said. "And I wouldn't want that to happen."

"Neither would I." Mia gave Nathan a pointed look. "Though I do think MHC is the best management company for Nathan. So I'm a bit torn, as you can tell." She ended on a laugh.

"I might let MHC give me a presentation, hear them out and see if what they're saying is worth the risk." Nathan looked at his parents. "You're both welcome to sit in on that if you'd like."

Mick shook his head. "This is your career to manage as you see fit, Nathan. You don't need your mother and I to hold your hand and walk you through it."

"I agree," Tara said. "Whatever you think is best for your long-term future is what you should do. Your dad and I will always be here if you want to bounce ideas off of us, but you're an adult now. You make the decisions."

"Thanks. I'll think about it."

Mia loved the confidence Nathan's parents had in him. They reminded her so much of her own parents.

There was nothing like having people on your side who fully believed in you.

They started looking at the menu and discussed what they were going to order. Of course, the menu was fluid, one of the things she liked most about Ninety-Two.

"This pasta with shrimp and spinach looks amazing," Tara said. "I think that's what I want. What about you, Mia?"

"I'm looking at the salmon. Or maybe the broiled chicken breasts."

"I think tuna for me," Nathan said.

"I'm having the filet."

Tara smiled at Mick. "I'm not surprised since I've never known you to pass up a good steak. And the steaks here are very good."

Mick grinned. "I know. Amelia makes one hell of a good steak."

"I'll be sure to tell her you said that."

Mia looked up to see her brother standing over her. He put his hands on her shoulders. "Hey, brat."

"What's up, dumbass?"

Mick grinned. "Seeing you two together is just like me with my family. Now I miss them."

"Oh, please," Tara said. "We just had dinner at Gavin and Liz's house last week."

Mick slanted a look at Tara. "I was going for dramatic effect, Tara."

Mia laughed. "I sometimes miss my siblings. But not all that often."

Flynn looked down at her. "I'm deeply offended."

"No you're not."

"Okay, I'm not."

"Can you have dinner with us, Flynn?" Tara asked.

"I don't want to intrude."

"You're not," Nathan said. "We'd like you to join us."

"Well, I am hungry . . ."

Mia rolled her eyes. "You're always hungry."

"Now that you've insulted me, of course I'd be happy to have dinner with you. Thanks."

Flynn grabbed an extra chair and brought it to the table. Mia noticed Nathan scooted closer to her to make room for Flynn. She wasn't sure if it was because he wanted to sit beside Flynn, or because he wanted to sit closer to her.

Either way, she was fine with it, especially when he smiled at her and gave her thigh a light squeeze before turning his attention to Flynn. It wasn't much, but it was enough considering they were dining with his parents.

God, just his touch set her off.

Things really had changed. They had to talk and soon.

"So what have you decided?"

She flipped her attention to Tara, who'd asked the question.

"Excuse me?"

"About dinner."

"Oh. The salmon, definitely. Amelia makes an amazing béarnaise sauce to go with it. Plus I know Nathan will want a bite of it."

Tara laughed. "He used to do that with my food, too. He'd order whatever I didn't so he could taste my food."

"Some things never change, do they?"

"No."

When the waitress showed up to take their order, Nathan turned to face her. "What are you ordering?"

"The salmon."

"Oh, good. I'll have the tuna, then."

Mia laughed, and Tara shook her head.

Nathan looked at both of them. "What?"

"Nothing," Tara said. "Other than you're predictable."

Nathan frowned. "Don't know what that means, but I don't like it." He paused, staring at both of them for a few seconds. "Are you two talking about me?"

"Yes," Mia said.

His frown stayed planted on his face. "Mom, what are you saying to her?"

Tara shook her head. "I didn't say anything. Honest. We're only talking about food."

He gave them both a look of disbelief, then grudgingly turned his attention back to Flynn and Mick.

Mia leaned toward Tara. "I don't think he believed you."

Tara's lips curved into a smile. "He'll get over it."

Mia chatted with Tara about her work. She was fascinated by

the event planning business, and they talked about the expansion. Since Tara had built her business from the ground up, Mia picked her brain about how she started it and what problems she'd encountered along the way. They'd been so engrossed in conversation, before she knew it, their dinner had arrived.

Mia dug in to her salmon. She'd had it here before, so she knew it was exceptionally good. It didn't take Nathan long before he scooped a bite with his fork, so she snuck a taste of his tuna, which was amazing.

"That's really good," she said.

"Yeah. So's the salmon. Mick's steak looks great. We'll have to come back so I can have it next time."

She smiled. "We can do that."

She looked up and saw Amelia coming over. She'd shed her chef's coat and looked absolutely beautiful in a pale blue blouse over navy slacks. She'd pulled her hair out of the ponytail she was wearing earlier and now it lay over her shoulders. She laid her hands on Flynn's shoulders, and he stood to brush a kiss across her lips.

"How was your steak?" she asked.

"Perfect, as always. Are you finished in the kitchen?"

She nodded. "Stefanie is taking over. I thought I'd pop out here for a visit."

"We're so glad you're taking time out to sit with us," Tara said. "Have you eaten yet?"

Amelia sat in the chair Flynn pulled over for her. "I eat constantly in the kitchen while I'm cooking. I have to taste everything, so I'm not hungry. I would love a glass of wine, though."

"I'll get that for you," Flynn said. "White or red?"

"White, please."

Flynn went to the bar.

"The food was amazing, Amelia," Mia said.

"Thank you. I saw you had the salmon. I'm so glad you liked it."

"The pasta was incredible, too," Tara said.

"Thank you, Tara. Where is Sam?"

"Spending the night with friends."

"Here," Nathan said, getting up as Flynn returned with her wine. "I'll trade seats with you so you can sit by Tara and Mia."

Amelia smiled at Nathan. "Thanks, Nathan. It's been too long since I've had an opportunity to catch up and I want to know what's going on. I feel like I'm always buried in the kitchen."

"You say that like it's a bad thing," Tara said.

Amelia laughed. "No, it's definitely my favorite place. But I hear you're expanding your business, Tara. And I want to hear all about Mia's new company."

Amelia looked over at the guys, who were huddled together like they were in the midst of a football game and about to make a call on the next play. She picked up her glass of wine. "Come on. Let's get away from the guys and go outside. I could use some air."

Mia grabbed her glass. "That sounds like a great idea."

Nathan looked up. "Where are you going?"

"Outside."

"Oh. Okay. Have fun."

As Tara and Amelia passed by, Nathan's fingers brushed against hers. She looked down at him. "What?"

He gave her a smile. "Nothing. Just . . . you know."

She didn't know. Or, maybe she did. It was the touch. His touch. And it was everything. "Yes."

Her insides churned with just that simple brush of his fingers to hers.

Dammit. She'd wanted that one night with him, that orgasmic release so she could relax and never let it happen again. But with one touch, she realized she wasn't ready to move on from him. In fact, she wanted a lot more from Nathan.

Which was perplexing as hell.

With a troubled sigh, she stepped outside. She needed to talk to someone about her feelings for Nathan. And the last person she could discuss them with was his mother. So she'd just have to dwell on them tonight.

There was an outside bar and eating area. Tara and Amelia were seated at the bar, the two of them huddled together like the best of friends. Shaking off thoughts of Nathan, Mia joined them.

"So he asked me to move in with him," Amelia said.

"Ohhh," Tara said in response. "So are you going to?"

Mia took a seat. "Wait. Flynn wants you to move into his place?"

Amelia nodded. "Yes. We've been taking things slow, you know. I mean, we love each other. That's a given. But I didn't want to jump into anything. I'm still leasing my house."

Mia nodded. "Right. You said you wanted to keep your own space. But it's been a while since you two committed to each other. And obviously something has changed if he's asked you to move in."

"Yes. A lot of things have changed. We've grown even closer. We've talked about getting a dog."

"Aww," Tara said. "That would be wonderful."

"It would be. But it wouldn't make sense for us to have a dog unless we're living in one place. Especially with Flynn traveling so much during the season. And my place doesn't allow pets. So . . ."

"But a dog wouldn't be the only reason you two would move in together, would it?"

"No." Amelia lifted her glass of wine and took a sip. "He also asked me to marry him."

Mia's eyes widened. "He proposed? When?"

"Last week."

Tara grabbed Amelia's wrist. "And? What did you say?"

Amelia gave them both a serious look.

Oh, God. She turned him down. Flynn had seemed his normal, happy self. But then again, he didn't tell her everything.

But then Amelia grinned. "I said yes, of course. I love that man."

"Oh, my God, Amelia," Mia said. "You scared the shit out of me."

"Me, too," Tara said. She got up and hugged Amelia.

Mia did, too, then whispered, "Brat," in her ear.

Amelia laughed as they sat down. "Sorry. I couldn't help myself. He gave me an amazing ring. It's perfect for me."

Mia searched Amelia's finger. "Where is it?"

"In my purse. I don't wear it when I'm cooking."

"Go get it," Tara said. "You're not cooking now."

"I do need to check on the kitchen. I'll be right back."

Amelia left and Mia turned to Tara. "Secrets. I can't believe they kept it a secret for this long."

Tara nodded. "They probably wanted to be alone with it for a short period of time. You know, to celebrate it by themselves. Engagements can be overwhelming, and then suddenly everyone's bombarding you with wedding questions that you're totally unprepared to answer."

"I suppose that's true. But I'm still going to kill my brother for not telling me."

Tara laughed. "As is your right."

Mia sighed. "I'm so excited for both of them. I've never known two people more in love. It took them a while to get there, too."

Tara nodded. "I know. I even tried to fix them up with different people."

"You did?"

"Yes. Before they got together, Flynn was having all those difficulties finding the right person. I had a dinner party, so I invited him, and he invited Amelia to join him in his misery, or something to that effect."

Mia laughed. "Of course he did. Even back then I knew he liked her."

"Yes, he did."

"So what happened at the dinner party?"

"The two people I fixed them up with ended up with each other."

Mia laughed. "Seriously? That's awesome."

"It is. They're still together, as a matter of fact. A lovely couple. As are Flynn and Amelia. Sometimes people are just right for each other, even if they don't see it at first."

"True."

Mia looked up when Amelia came back outside.

"How are things in the kitchen?" Mia asked.

"Running smoothly, just as I expected. I have a great staff."

"Okay, let's see it," Tara said.

Amelia held out her hand.

Mia gasped. "Oh, my God, Amelia. It's gorgeous."

It was a large emerald cut center diamond, surrounded by diamonds on the setting, with more diamonds on the band.

"I agree," Tara said, taking Amelia's hand. "It's stunning."

"Thank you. I was so shocked. He brought me flowers, cooked me dinner, poured wine and even made dessert. He wrote me a terrible poem—it's kind of become his trademark. And then he got down on one knee and asked me to marry him. It was sweetly romantic and the best night ever. I swooned. Okay, I don't really know what swooning is, but I felt a little weak in the knees. Is that swooning?"

Tara laughed. "Sounds like swooning to me."

"I agree. Who knew my brother was that romantic?"

Amelia grinned. "I did. He's always making gestures like bringing me a single rose to work, or texting me to tell me he misses me. They're not huge, but there's nothing like having someone in your corner, you know?"

"Yes," Tara said. "It means everything. Even after all these years, Mick will still call me every day to see how my day is going. It means so much to me. And he always wrote me a note when he left town."

"Love notes, right?" Amelia asked.

Tara looked down, then back up again. It was so cute to see the stain of blush on her cheeks. "Actually, yes."

"Flynn does that, too. It makes my heart melt."

Mia had no idea what that was like. The few relationships she'd had hadn't worked out. Not that she was all broken up about it since she hadn't put her whole heart into those guys anyway. She'd never had that all-consuming kind of love that Amelia and Tara were talking about. Which was fine. She had her career to consume her. That was her love. It was all she needed.

Maybe someday she'd settle in with a nice, hot guy like Nathan. When she was ready to fall in love. Because if she was ready, she'd want someone like him. Hot, smart, funny, considerate . . .

Which reminded her . . .

"So next week is Nathan's birthday," Mia said.

Tara nodded. "Yes, it is."

"Are you going to be in town still? I'd love to throw him a birthday party."

"That's a wonderful idea. And we could arrange to stay a little longer. What did you have in mind?"

"Nothing yet. But training camp starts not long after so I want to have a big blowout party for him. Invite all his friends and any family that would be available to come. Since you're in town, we could always do it earlier."

"His birthday is just a couple of days after I planned to leave. I could adjust my schedule. And maybe invite a few other family members. I know they'd love to come."

"I could do the food," Amelia said.

Mia looked at her. "I couldn't ask you to do that."

"Why not? Flynn loves a good party and I know he'd pitch in and help me. Just let me know what day and I'll arrange to take the day off."

"That would be wonderful," Mia said. "Thank you, Amelia. Okay, so we'll need a venue. I could probably arrange the clubhouse at my condo."

"Hey, I am an event planner," Tara said. "Let Maggie and I work on that."

Now Mia was excited. "This is awesome. Should we make it a surprise?"

Tara grinned. "Isn't it better that way?"

"I think so," Amelia said. "How often do you get to surprise a guy?"

"Not nearly often enough," Tara said. "We'll leave that part up to you, Mia."

"I can handle that."

They finalized what plans they could. Then Amelia had to head back inside to check on things in the kitchen.

Mia and Tara went back inside. Nathan, Flynn and Mick were still huddled around the table.

Nathan had watched Mia come in. They might have been talking football, but a part of his brain had been reserved for Mia. And when she'd left, he missed her. Watching her come back in made everything within him tighten.

Yeah, that was a big change in their dynamic. Sure, he'd always been happy to see her whenever they were together. But something was different now.

Now he wanted to put his hands on her, to pull her down onto his lap and kiss her and touch her.

"Okay," Tara said. "Breaking up the shoptalk."

Mick slipped his arm around Tara's waist. "Hey, I'm retired."

Tara slid into the chair next to Mick. "Babe, you might be physically retired, but you're always going to be in the game."

"He's going to be missed," Flynn said. "And he's still got keen insights about the Sabers as well as our competition. We were just picking his brain."

Mick leaned back. "You don't need me anymore. Nathan's got this all under control, don't you, kid?"

All that warmth thinking about Mia suddenly dissipated. Nathan sucked in a breath, trying to calm his rapidly beating pulse. "You know I do."

"Yeah, we all know it, too," Flynn said. "This is gonna be one hell of a season."

Nathan had spent the majority of the time listening to his dad and Flynn talk. For the most part, they were reliving the past season. The past season where Nathan had warmed the bench. Sure, he'd watched, he'd listened and he'd learned. But he hadn't taken a single snap in a game situation. They'd had another backup quarterback, and as a rookie, Nathan's job was to absorb, to learn the playbook, to watch his father in action.

Now the backup had been released, a new backup had been signed, and Nathan was suddenly the starting quarterback.

Physically he was more than ready. He knew this game, had known it almost all his life. Hell, he'd been ready from the day the Sabers drafted him.

Getting the team to believe in him? That was something else. You didn't just walk out onto the field as the starting quarterback and gain the trust of the team. You had to prove yourself. He had a lot to prove.

His dad leaned over. "You know you got this."

Nathan nodded and gave his dad a confident grin. "Yeah, I got this."

Okay, so maybe it was more than getting the team to believe in him.

He had to believe it, too. And until he held the ball in his hand and started calling plays, it still didn't feel real to him.

FIFTEEN

MIA SAT DOWN NEXT TO NATHAN AND RAN HER HAND over his back. "Everything okay?"

Funny how she could always pick up on his moods. "Yeah, it's fine. How about you?"

She smiled at him. "I've had a fantastic dinner, and got to visit with your mom and Amelia. So far it's been great."

Nathan took a quick glance over the table. His mom and dad were busy talking with Flynn and paying no attention to them, so he smoothed his hand over her back. "Want to come home with me tonight?"

Mia gave him a questioning look, then shot her own glance across the table before answering. "That's a loaded question."

"Not really. Unless your answer is a flat-out no."

"We have things to talk about."

He arched a brow. "Things?"

"Yes. You know, about last weekend."

He wasn't sure he liked the direction of this conversation. "Okay. Let's talk about them."

"Not here, obviously. We'll go to your place after we leave here."

"Sounds good."

What didn't sound good was the direction of her thoughts.

Fortunately, they wrapped things up and his mom and dad said their good-byes.

"We'll talk again, Mia," his mom said as they hugged.

"Soon. I had a great time tonight."

"Me, too."

Amelia came out from the kitchen to say good night to everyone. Nathan hugged his parents.

"You want to come back to our house?" his dad asked.

"Uh, I have plans tonight."

"Oh. Sure. Call me tomorrow."

"Will do."

After his parents left, Mia stood.

"Well, I'm going to head out," she said, sliding a short glance at Nathan.

"Okay, see you later," Nathan said. It was obvious Mia didn't want to give his parents or Flynn any idea that they'd be meeting up later.

He was okay with that, but they were friends. It wasn't a big deal for the two of them to hang out and he didn't think anyone would blink twice if they'd left together. But he wasn't Mia and he had no idea what was going on in her head.

So about five minutes later he said good-bye to Flynn and Amelia and headed out to his car. Mia was still there in the parking lot, leaning against her car waiting for him.

"Thought you'd already left," he said as he came up next to her.

"That would be pointless since I don't have a key to your house."

"We can go to your place, ya know. Since you hate my décor."

She snorted out a laugh. "Good point." She pushed the button on her key fob and unlocked her door. "Let's go to my place. Your fridge is probably empty anyway."

"It is not. But I don't have wine."

She slid into the car seat and looked up at him. "Another reason we're going to my place."

Several clicks caught her attention and she looked over to see that same photographer she'd spotted in Napa.

"Nathan, that's the same guy who was taking pictures of us last weekend."

Nathan whirled around. "Yeah? Where?"

When she peeked around Nathan's form, the man was gone. "He was right there, two cars away."

Nathan wandered off to search the parking lot but the guy wasn't lurking around. He came back to Mia and he could tell she was upset. Her arms were crossed tightly over her middle and her gaze kept darting left and right. "I didn't see anyone, Mia. Are you sure it was the same photographer?"

"Yes. Mid-forties, short, light curly hair and glasses."

"Wow, you're good."

She frowned. "At what?"

"At memorizing what people look like."

"I just remembered him because I thought it was strange he was taking our picture. And then here he was again. I know I saw him, Nathan."

"I believe you. But the pics he took of us in Napa never showed up anywhere. You said you searched online, right?"

"I did."

"Then don't worry about it. I'm not news." Nathan grinned. "Not yet, anyway. Wait 'til the season starts."

She rolled her eyes. "Nathan, this concerns me."

"Okay. I'll keep an eye out for him. And I'll follow you home."

"All right."

He got into his car and drove behind her all the way to her place. When he pulled into Mia's complex, he parked on the street, lingering to make sure no one had followed. There were no cars on the street at all. Satisfied the guy hadn't followed them, he walked with Mia up to her door.

Once inside, Mia made a beeline for the kitchen and began uncorking a bottle of wine. He followed her and watched her work, enjoying the sight of her gorgeous legs as she reached up into the cabinet for a glass.

She'd worn a dress tonight, a navy blue one that skimmed along the edges of her knees and hugged tight to her body. He'd wanted to put his hands on her and smooth his palms over the soft fabric, but since his parents had been there, he'd resisted. Plus he wasn't sure what the boundaries were between Mia and him yet. They'd had that fun weekend in Napa and hadn't talked about it since. He knew what he wanted, but he had to be sure she wanted the same thing.

She had amazing legs. He could imagine them wrapped around him as he thrust into her. The thought of the two of them tangled together made his dick twitch.

She glanced over at him. "You want a beer?"

He wanted her. But for now, he'd settle for a beer. "Sure."

He went into the kitchen and Mia handed it to him.

"Let's go sit down in the living room."

He cocked his head to the side. "I hope the next thing you say isn't 'We need to talk.' Because that's the kiss of death."

She laughed. "It isn't, doofus. Though I would like to talk about that photographer. That worries me."

She kicked off her shoes and tucked her legs underneath her, then took a sip of her wine. She looked relaxed, which made him feel better. He didn't want her upset about some dumbass photographer who didn't have a picture of anything other than Mia and him talking at her car.

He took a long pull of his beer. "Tell me what's bothering you."

She inhaled and let it out. "You. Me. What that photographer has in mind with those photos."

"Babe, there's nothing in those photos other than you and me having a chat in the parking lot. It's not like there's anything scandalous. We weren't making out, I didn't have my hand up your dress and you weren't sucking my dick."

She spit out a laugh. "Nathan."

"Okay, so maybe that was the direction my mind was going over dinner tonight."

"While your parents were there? Nathan. I'm shocked."

"No, you're not. Tell me you didn't think about the two of us together."

She took a sip of her wine, and he saw the desire in her eyes. "Maybe. But I'm also conflicted."

"In what way?"

"Our friendship. You know what that means to me. And now I'm also wary of stalking photographers and what that could mean."

"The photographer means nothing, and we'll always be friends. I think you're just trying to avoid having sex with me again."

She lifted her chin. "Utter bullshit. And I think you have a penis ego problem."

He gave her a confused look. "Huh?"

"Your penis has an ego. You and I had sex last weekend and because I didn't immediately jump right on board for another go at it, your penis is offended."

He laughed. "Oh, is that it?"

"Yes."

"Uh-huh. You wanna know what I think?"

"Of course."

"I think you're trying your damndest to keep from diving into the zipper of my jeans to get to my awesome dick."

She rolled her eyes. "I went three years without your dick, Nathan. I'm sure I can live without it for three more years."

"So the sex sucked."

She laughed. "It did not and you know it."

"If the sex blew your mind you wouldn't be telling me you want to be just friends."

"I never said I wanted to be just friends."

He leaned back. "So what do you want?"

"I . . . don't know exactly. This all happened so fast and we haven't had time to talk about it."

"Do we have to analyze it? Can't we just go with it and see what happens?"

She looked at him like he'd suddenly started talking a language she couldn't fathom. "Of course we have to talk about it. We need ground rules and . . . things."

He raised a brow. "You mean you'll need to add a section in your planner for 'Mia and Nathan's Relationship'? Will there be bullet points?"

She shoved at him. "You know, sometimes having someone know you so well can be a detriment. No, moron. What I mean is I need to think about this. We need to talk about it. Are we in a relationship? Are we still friends? Are we going to get emotional about this or are we just having fun? And yes, dammit, I will be making notes in my planner about it."

His lips curved and he laid his beer down, took her wineglass from her hand and set it on the table, then pulled her onto his lap. "You know, I love that you're so analytical about everything, Mia. It's who you are. But sometimes, you just have to let things happen."

She wound her arm around his neck. "Sacrilege."

He grinned, then kissed her. And when she turned and pressed against him, and he felt her body surrender to him, it was all he'd wanted, all he needed. He swept his hand down her back, soaking in the softness of her, breathing in the sweetness of her scent.

When he pulled away, she gave him a confused look. "You stopped."

"Yeah. I don't want you to think I'm in this just for the sex. Because we do have a friendship, Mia, and that's important to me, too. I want to fuck you. But I want to date you, too."

She sighed. "That's such a lovely thing to say."

He laughed. "Is it?"

"It is." She laid her palm on his chest. "I want to fuck you, too. And date you. And be your friend. And have wine and beer with you and do everything with you."

"Everything, huh?" He smoothed his hand over her dress. "Did I mention you look hot as fuck in this?"

"You didn't mention that. But thank you."

"Look. I get that you're angsty over this change in our relationship. You're worried for nothing, Mia. I can't imagine not being friends with you. And the sex is good. Really good. Right?" As he spoke, he ran his hand along her thigh, then slid it up her back. She responded by leaning into him, so he knew damn well she was affected by his touch. He needed her to at least acknowledge that.

She inhaled a deep breath, and let it out. "Right."

It had taken everything he had to stop kissing her, but he wanted her to understand there was a lot more to them than just being fuck buddies. He knew the friendship part was important, and he could take things slowly. Even if slowly meant he'd go home with his dick hard tonight.

He slid her gently off his lap.

"You're really okay with this?" she asked.

"No sex. Just hanging out with you tonight? I'm always okay with it."

He picked up her remote and turned on the television, then watched TV with her for an hour or so before leaving. He never wanted her to think he was with her only for the sex, though after all these years she should already know that. When she started yawning, he got up, said good night and left her with a kiss on her forehead.

"See you later," he said.

"I'll see you, Nathan." He saw the regret on her face, and for some reason that made him feel better.

SIXTEEN

MIA HAD MISSED NATHAN OVER THE LAST WEEK, BUT
she'd had work to keep her busy, along with planning Nathan's
surprise birthday party, so she hadn't had much time to dwell on
it, which was a good thing.

And okay, maybe she was dodging him because she didn't want
to do or say anything that would spoil his surprise party. Running
her business was always a great excuse for her limited time, and
Nathan was awesome about understanding when she had to put
her job first.

Nathan was pretty awesome in general.

She'd met with Tara and Amelia earlier in the week. Tara had
secured a venue for the party. Amelia had planned the menu and
taken care of hiring cooks to assist her. It was up to Mia to wrangle
the guest list and to get Nathan there without him becoming sus-
picious.

For that part she'd brought in Nathan's friend Jamal. If

everything went according to plan, Nathan wouldn't have a clue what was going on until he stepped through the doors.

They'd arranged to have dinner with Jamal and Wendy. He wouldn't suspect a thing.

She was grateful the event was on a Saturday so she didn't have to go into the office. She'd wanted the entire day to help Tara, though when she arrived at the venue, Tara and her event crew had everything well in hand. The tables and chairs had been organized to create a dance floor and plenty of areas for people to stand or sit and chat. Tara had secured a deejay for the evening and his area had already been set up. Mia helped with the decorations and then she called Amelia, who was preparing the food for the evening. Amelia was happily on schedule and confident the menu would be perfect. When Mia hung up, she pulled out her planner, so she and Tara could review Mia's checklist one last time to make sure they'd covered everything.

"Are you nervous?" Tara asked.

Mia shook her head. "No. It's all under control. I'm more excited than anything. I want this to be a great party for Nathan."

Tara laid her hand over Mia's. "It will be. Don't worry."

She fielded several calls from people who were attending to confirm the time or give directions to the venue. The number of Sabers team members who had said they were attending, including coaches and staff, surprised her. She just hoped they could pull off the surprise aspect. The more people who knew about the party, the bigger chance someone would spill to Nathan. Though he hadn't said anything to her yet and they'd had several phone conversations, so it was likely he didn't know.

Perfect.

On her way back home, Nathan called her.

"Hey, what's up?" she asked.

"Nothing. I was just wondering what you were doing?"

"Oh. Uh. Heading to the gym for a workout. How about you?"

"Did that this morning. Just chillin' now. Thought I'd come over and hang out with you. Maybe when you get back from the gym."

She had a million things to do before the party tonight. "Sorry. I need to stop by work and handle some paperwork, and then I have some errands to run. So I can't."

"No problem. I'll see you for dinner, okay?"

"Sure. Oh, and, Nathan?"

"Yeah?"

"Happy birthday."

He laughed. "Thanks. See you later."

She hung up, realizing her pulse was racing. She'd tried to act nonchalant. Hopefully she'd pulled it off. She supposed she'd find out when she saw Nathan later. In the meantime, she was going to hit the gym and work off some of this nervous energy so she wasn't a total stress ball tonight.

She wanted this to be Nathan's best birthday party ever.

SEVENTEEN

NATHAN KNOCKED ON MIA'S DOOR, HEARD HER MUM-
ble or holler something that sounded something like the door was
open, so he tried the knob. It turned, so he walked in.

"Mia?"

"I'm upstairs finishing up. I'll be down in a sec. Shit. Stupid dress."

His lips curved. "Need some help?"

"No. Yes. Come up here."

He went upstairs and into her bedroom, where Mia stood in
front of her full-length mirror making a face at herself.

"What's wrong?"

She whirled around to glare at him.

"I got this dress and I don't know how they expect single
women to dress themselves when the damn zipper goes from Af-
rica to Canada. Would you mind?"

He made a twirl motion with his finger, so she pivoted. He

couldn't help but notice her bare skin or the damn sexy flimsy-as-fuck underwear she had on.

"You did that on purpose," he said as he drew the zipper up.

She gave him a look over her shoulder. "Did what on purpose?"

"Wore that underwear."

She sat on the bed and slid into her shoes. "No idea what you're talking about. It's not like I planned on having a pain-in-the-ass zipper, Nathan. What I planned on was to be ready when you got here. You look amazing, by the way."

He looked down at himself. Mia had told him to dress nice, no casual clothes. "Nice" to him was black slacks and a matching black button-down shirt. "Thanks."

Mia stood, and holy shit, that dress formed to her body like a second skin. It was a dark silver that shimmered in the light. And she wore damn-high-as-heaven shoes that made her legs look a mile long.

"You're really trying to kill me, aren't you?"

She frowned. "What?"

He walked over to her and pressed a kiss to her cheek, then whispered in her ear, "What I mean is, you look hot as hell in that dress and those shoes."

She leaned back and smiled at him. "Oh. Thank you. I'm finally ready, and thank you for the assist."

"Anytime. You'll of course let me know if you need help getting *out* of the dress."

She laughed, then pressed her palms to his chest and brushed a soft and oh-too-short kiss across his lips. "You, of course, would be the first to know. And happy birthday again."

He sucked in a breath, really wishing they were staying in tonight. They could order in, and when they were finished eating he could take that dress off of her.

Mia started out of the bedroom and toward the stairs, though, so he supposed that wasn't going to happen.

Dammit. He'd thought about her all week long. She'd been busy. He understood work was her first priority, so he hadn't pushed to see her. And he'd had his own shit to do with workouts and agent and PR meetings.

But now he was more than ready to spend his birthday with Mia.

They headed down the stairs. "So where is this place we're going to dinner?"

Mia grabbed her clutch and a sweater. "It's a trendy new bistro. I thought we'd give it a try. Jamal and Wendy are meeting us there, right?"

Nathan nodded and pulled the door open for her. "Yeah. I texted him that I was picking you up, and he said they were heading out the door so they should already be at the place when we get there."

"Perfect."

The drive took about twenty minutes. Nathan noticed Mia's face was buried in her phone. "Got a hot guy you're texting with?"

Her head shot up and she shoved her phone in her purse. "What? No, of course not. It was . . . uh . . . Monique, about some work stuff. Sorry."

He frowned and studied the road ahead of him. Mia was always forthcoming about who she was texting with. He knew all her friends, and he didn't believe for one damn second that she'd been texting with Monique. Or that it was work shit.

Which meant it was some guy. And he didn't like the tightening in his gut in reaction.

They hadn't laid down ground rules about their relationship. They weren't exclusive, and now she was texting with some asshole, no doubt about meeting up with him later as soon as her obligation to have dinner with Nathan on his birthday was over.

"You know, you don't have to have dinner with me tonight just because it's my birthday."

She looked over at him. "What? I want to have dinner with you."

"Do you? Because it's obvious you'd rather be somewhere else."

"Nathan, what are you talking about?"

He motioned with his head toward her purse. "You. Texting. With some guy."

She laughed. "I was not texting with some guy. I told you it was Monique."

"Uh-huh."

She reached over and smoothed her hand over his thigh, which did not help his disposition in the least.

"Trust me when I tell you there is no place I'd rather be right now than with you."

"Okay."

He still felt unsettled, and more than a little pissed off. Which he had no right to be. Mia was free to see whomever the hell she wanted to see and there wasn't a damn thing he could do about it.

Which only unsettled him more.

Her phone buzzed and she gave him a quick worried glance, pulled the phone out of her bag and looked at it.

"Sorry. It's work stuff."

Yeah. Work stuff. Sure it was.

She typed a quick answer and with a guilty look at him, slid the phone back in her bag.

Shit.

Maybe he needed to start dating around again, and he wouldn't feel like this. The only problem with that was the only woman he wanted to see was Mia.

"It's this exit," Mia said.

He nodded and took the exit, then followed her instructions to the location.

"This looks like a warehouse," Nathan said, but there were a ton of cars parked there.

"I think the restaurant is in the back," Mia said.

He shrugged, his mind on Mia, her phone and her legs. So, whatever. They'd eat and then she could go out on her date.

They parked and walked to the restaurant. He held the door for her and she slipped inside.

Damn it was dark in here. How were they supposed to even read the damn menu?

The lights flipped on and Nathan blinked as a bunch of voices shouted "Surprise!" in unison.

It took him a few seconds to register what was going on, but then he saw his mom and dad, and Jamal and Wendy, and . . . holy shit, was that Uncle Gavin and Liz? And his grandparents?

He looked over at Mia, who leaned against him and laid her hand on his chest.

"Smile, Nathan. It's your birthday."

She grinned at him, then stepped away. After that, he was surrounded by his friends. Teammates. His family.

His mom cupped his face. "Happy birthday, Nathan. Are you surprised?"

He hugged his mom. "Stunned is more like it. I thought you had left two days ago."

She laughed. "That's what we wanted you to think."

His dad gave him a clap on the back, and then Gavin and Liz greeted him.

"Look at you, all grown-up," Liz said. "It makes me feel old. And I am not old."

"No, you aren't," Gavin said, squeezing Nathan's arm and putting the other around Liz.

"I'm really happy to see you both. Did you bring Genevieve?" Nathan asked.

Liz nodded. "Yes. She's with Sam and the nanny at your parents' house. And very anxious for a visit from you."

"I'll definitely make time to come to the house to play with her."

He looked over to see his grandparents were there, which made him tear up.

"I can't believe you're here," he said to his grandmother.

"We wouldn't miss it," she said. "And Jimmy loves San Francisco, so we're making a trip out of it."

"Happy birthday, kid," his grandfather said, and folded him into a big hug.

Nathan could barely breathe. And when he spotted his Aunt Jenna and her husband, Tyler, he realized what a hell of a party someone—he looked for Mia but didn't see her—had put together.

He hugged Jenna. "How are you?"

"I'm fine." Jenna rubbed her belly. "Baby's fine. We're so happy to see you."

"Yeah, we figured we'd better get out here to this party before you become famous," Tyler said.

Nathan laughed. "Here I thought you were the superstar. Or so you keep telling me."

Tyler shot him a grin. "Well, you know, hockey off-season, so I'll let you take the ball and run with it for now."

There were so many people to talk to, to thank for coming. He chatted up his Sabers teammates, some of his college friends who'd made the trip—Christ, he couldn't believe some of the people who'd come.

It was at least an hour before he found Mia, sitting at a table talking to Monique, Jamal and Wendy. He pulled her from her chair and hugged her.

"You did this."

She shrugged. "Your mom and me and Amelia, who made the

food we're about to eat. And I was texting your mom in the car, not some guy. Though I appreciate the slice of jealousy I saw."

He'd downed a couple of beers while he was chatting with everyone, so he was a lot more relaxed now. "Me? Jealous? Don't know what you're talking about."

She gave him a knowing smile. "Sure. Anyway, isn't it great? So many people showed up. I guess for some reason people like you, though I have no idea why."

He wanted to kiss her so badly he could already taste her on his lips. But considering there were about a hundred and fifty people watching them at the moment, he had to rein it in. So instead, he kissed her on the cheek. "Thank you. Seriously, thank you. This is a really amazing birthday."

She splayed her hands on his chest and gave him a look that told him she wished that kiss had been on her lips, too. "You're welcome, Nathan. I hope it's everything you could imagine, and more."

He leaned in and whispered to her, "You have no idea what I'm imagining right now."

She turned her face to his. "Oh, I think I do."

His mother came over. "Nathan, your grandfather wants to talk to you."

Mia smiled at him. "We'll chat later."

He walked away with his mom, but gave Mia a lingering look.

Yeah, they'd definitely chat later.

EIGHTEEN

THE PARTY WAS IN FULL SWING AND GOING GREAT. MIA had had a few moments of panic in the car on the way over. She'd known Nathan was pissed at her about the texting, but she just had to sit back and let that play out until they got to the venue.

The look on his face when he walked in the door had made it all worth it. He'd been truly shocked, and she couldn't have been happier.

She'd made it a point to meet his family. Fortunately, Tara had taken her around and introduced her to his grandparents. Jimmy and Kathleen Riley were lovely people and she could see where Mick got his sense of humor as well as his loving warmth from. She'd met Jenna and Tyler and was excited to talk to them about their upcoming baby, who was due in December. They also talked hockey.

Mia really loved hockey. It was too bad none of her brothers had been born with the hockey gene. So she'd spent some time talking with Tyler about his successful season with the St. Louis Ice, and some of the other players on the team.

When he discovered she had started up a sports management company, he insisted she give him her card. Then Liz Riley came over. She knew Liz because a couple of her new clients were represented by her. She was a formidable and very savvy sports agent and Mia really liked working with her.

"Are you interested in Mia's company managing you?" Liz asked.

"Thinking about it."

"We should totally talk about it," Liz said. "As much growth as you're having both as a player and a brand, it's something you should consider."

Mia vibrated with excitement, but she knew this wasn't the time or place.

"I don't want to talk shop at a party when you should be enjoying yourself," Mia said. "You have my card, and Liz knows my number. Please give me a call or send me an e-mail whenever it's convenient for you and we'll set up a meeting."

Tyler nodded. "I'll do that."

She made her way through the crowd, checking to ensure everyone had a drink and was having a good time. Tara's staff was handling everything perfectly, and there were plenty of bar stations set up to serve the guests.

She went into the kitchen to see Amelia supervising the crew she'd hired.

"It smells amazing in here."

Amelia nodded and smiled. "I hope everyone loves what we've cooked up tonight."

"I'm certain they will."

Soon, dinner was served—buffet style to make it easy on everyone.

There were salads, along with crab cakes and beef tenderloin, and various amazing side dishes. Mia's stomach rumbled as she breathed in all the delicious smells. She helped Tara and her crew wrangle everyone to the various stations so they could fill up their plates and start eating.

Once everyone had been through the line, Tara made Mia grab a plate.

"Come on," Tara said. "Now it's our turn."

They got food and Tara led them to an unoccupied table in the corner. She signaled to one of her staff, who arrived with two glasses of wine.

"Now, this is perfect," Tara said after she took a sip of her cabernet.

"Thank you, Tara. I could have gotten my own drink, but I really appreciate you handling it."

"You've been on your feet the entire time talking to people, getting them drinks and chatting up Nathan's team members and the Riley clan. You know you're not working this party. I hired staff to take care of that. You're supposed to be having fun."

Mia smiled. "I am having fun. I got to meet members of Nathan's family that I hadn't met before. He's spent so much time talking about them that I felt I already knew them."

"I'm glad you've had a chance to meet them. They're all wonderful and sometimes a pain in the ass."

Mia laughed. She dug into the food, which was amazing, of course. Everything Amelia created was outstanding.

She looked around, hoping Amelia had stopped to take a break. She smiled when she spotted her at a table with Flynn. She was sipping on a glass of wine and listening to Flynn and some of the guys from the team chatting.

Good.

Her gaze drifted to some of the nearby tables, settling on

Nathan, who was deep in conversation with his dad, along with his grandparents and his family. It made her heart squeeze to see him so relaxed. Clearly his family centered him.

"So tell me, Mia, how do you really feel about Nathan?"

Her gaze zipped back to Tara. "I'm sorry. What?"

Tara graced her with an all-knowing smile. "You can be honest with me, and it won't hurt my feelings if you say you don't care about him."

"I adore him, Tara. He's one of my best friends."

Tara laid her fork on top of her plate. "But there's more to it than that, right?"

Oh, God. Was it written all over her face? Had she betrayed herself with some kind of emotion even she wasn't aware of? "Honestly? I don't know. We've been friends so long, and here and there it's been more than that. But I've tried so hard to keep it strictly platonic, because my friendship with Nathan means so much to me, and I'm scared to death of losing it."

Tara nodded. "I can understand that. I also see the way he looks at you. I get the idea he wants more."

"He does."

"The question is, do you?"

"I . . . don't know. Yes and no, which is a terrible answer, I know."

"I know you're conflicted. But you have to either tell him friendship is all you're ever going to offer, or you need to fall headlong into some kind of relationship with him. Dancing around it isn't good for either of you, especially with what's going on in both your professional lives. You don't need the additional emotional conflict in your personal lives."

Tara was right, and Mia realized she'd been teasing the edge of friends, friends with benefits or a full-on relationship for a while now. And that wasn't fair to Nathan. It was time to make a decision.

"Of course you're right. I need to decide."

Tara reached across the table and laid her hand over Mia's. "I love my son, of course, but I also care about you, Mia. And I don't want to lose your friendship, either. So I understand your dilemma. I don't want either of you to get hurt."

"Thank you, Tara. Neither do I."

She took a deep breath and let it out, then reached for her glass of wine to take a long swallow, hoping it might give her some clarity. Though she doubted it. She needed more than alcohol to give her the answers she needed.

What she needed was to talk to Nathan, to be with him, to figure out the right answers.

She didn't have to look far because after Tara left the table to check on her staff, Nathan slid into the chair next to her.

"Where the hell have you been all night?"

She'd had just enough wine to feel relaxed. "I've been here the whole time. Are you having fun?"

His lips curved. "I am." He put his beer on the table and reached under the table to lay his hand on her thigh. "I really want to pull you onto my lap and kiss you for putting this all together. And okay, I want to kiss you because you're smart and beautiful and because I always want to kiss you."

She tingled all over as she took in his words. "Thank you. And you're welcome. Your mom and Amelia did a lot of the work."

"I'll bet you did a lot, too. My mom told me this was all your idea."

"I just suggested it. Everyone else ran with it."

He looked around. "Dammit. Too crowded in here."

"Too crowded for what?"

"For me to kiss you."

"Nathan." She said his name with a laugh. "Are you drunk?"

"Maybe a little. But you look really nice, and you smell sweet."

He moved closer to her. "And I want to spread your legs and eat your pussy and make you come."

Mia's clit quivered and she went instantly damp. She took a swallow of wine. "Is that right?"

"Yeah."

It was at that moment she knew exactly what she wanted. She stood. "You need to come with me."

She had seen the room earlier in the week when they'd done the walk-through of the venue. It was a huge coat closet, used in the winter.

But it wasn't winter and there weren't any coats in there. So no one would be using the space. She looked around to make sure no one followed them. But just to be sure, she wandered a bit aimlessly for a few seconds along the hallway.

Nathan looked at her. "Where are we going?"

Finally, she took his hand. "In here."

She opened the door to the coat closet, flipped on the light, then closed and locked the door behind her.

"Oh. A coat closet. Haven't hidden in one of these since elementary school."

She pushed him up against the wall. "I'll want to hear that story sometime. But right now, I have something else in mind."

"Yeah? What's that?"

She pressed into him and splayed her hands over his spectacularly fine chest. Then she scraped her nails up the crisp cotton of his shirt and over his shoulders, and swept her hand around his neck to draw his head closer to hers.

"We'll start here."

When their lips touched, she felt as if she'd melted on the spot. His mouth was delicious, his tongue sending pinpricks of sensation all over her body.

Nathan wrapped his arm around her waist and tugged her closer. She responded with a moan of absolute delight.

She hadn't realized how much she'd wanted his mouth on hers until right now. And now that she had it, she wanted to stay like this for hours, exploring and tasting. But she knew she couldn't risk it, so she pulled away.

Nathan arched a brow. "I'm hoping you had something more in mind than just a short make-out session."

"I do. It's your birthday present."

She caught the sparkle in his eye.

"Oh, good. I hope my present involves you getting naked."

"We might get there at some point tonight. But for now?" She grabbed a thick coat out of the box marked "Lost and Found" and propped it on the wood floor.

Nathan looked down at Mia. "Are you serious?"

Mia didn't answer, just gave him the hottest smile with her gorgeous, red-painted full lips. Nathan's cock rose to attention, and when she unzipped his pants, he couldn't think of anything he wanted more than Mia's sexy mouth wrapped around his dick.

She reached into his pants and rubbed his shaft. He was pretty sure he forgot how to breathe.

And when she pulled his pants down and then his boxer briefs, her warm hand circling his cock, he let out a groan. Fortunately, the venue was loud and there was music, and hell, he tuned it all out anyway. All he cared about right now was Mia, the way she looked up at him, that fiery blue light in her eyes as she leaned in and put her lips over him.

"Christ."

Her mouth was wet heat, her lips suctioning around him as she brought him into her mouth.

"Oh, fuck yeah. Suck it, Mia."

He didn't know what he'd done to deserve this, but all rational thought fled as she bobbed her head forward and engulfed him. He'd never felt anything so good, so torturously, mind-alteringly hot in his life. His balls tightened and he could blow his load right now into her sweet, hot mouth. But he wanted these amazing sensations to linger, wanted to watch the way his cock kept disappearing and reappearing in and out of Mia's mouth. He could hold back. He could wait.

But then she cupped his balls and gave them a light massage as she pressed the roof of her mouth down over his cock and flicked her tongue over his shaft.

He wrapped his hand around her head, needing to control her movements.

"Just like that. Oh, fuck, suck it like that."

And for all that was holy he thought he was a master at control but Mia was the mistress of blow jobs and he could only take so much.

"I'm gonna lose it here, babe," he said, so into the rhythm he found himself shoving his hips forward, feeding his cock into her mouth deeper and deeper until the first spurts of come jettisoned from his cock. And then it was like an explosion. He might have yelled as he came. He didn't know, because his brain exploded with his orgasm and he felt light-headed, palming the wall for support as Mia took what he gave her. He watched her throat work and it was so damn hot it made his knees weak.

He wasn't even sure he was breathing when it was over. In fact, he was pretty sure his heart had stopped a long time ago.

Maybe he was dead. If he was, that had been one hell of a way to go.

Mia finally let go of him and he pulled her up and took her mouth in a hot kiss that made her moan and got him fired up all over again.

He rubbed her bottom lip with his thumb. "I'm not sure, because I think you blew my brains out my ears with that blow job, but I am almost certain I mentioned something about wanting to lick your pussy. And then we came in here and it was all about me, not all about you."

She gave him a wry smile. "It's not my birthday today."

"So, can it be my birthday every week?"

She laughed. "No. But I sure enjoyed that."

"I know I did." He looked around and found a sturdy-looking table at the back of the closet. "And there's something else I'll enjoy."

He led Mia to the back of the closet, then picked her up and sat her on the table. He spread her legs and lifted her dress over her hips.

She shuddered, then looked up at him. "I don't know, Nathan. We've already been gone awhile. We should get back to the party."

He knelt on the floor between her legs. "I promise I'll make you come fast."

The scent of her as he pulled her underwear to the side was enough to make him hard again. And the look on her face when he smoothed his hand over her thighs spurred him on to make this good for her. He could tell she was pent up and needy.

Yeah, he knew what that was like.

He flicked his tongue over her clit, heard her deep breath and wanted to give her more. So he put his mouth over her and laid his tongue flat.

She moaned, a long, low sound that told him he'd hit the right spot.

She tasted like salty honey as he smoothed his tongue over her and inside of her. She leaned back on her elbows and spread her legs wider, giving him full access. And when he slid a finger inside of her, she released a sound that made his balls quiver.

"Oh, yes. Just like that, Nathan. Fuck me with your finger and suck my clit."

He loved how verbal she was, that she gave him direction and told him what she liked. And damn if he didn't love giving it to her. And when she began to writhe against him, he knew she was close, so he pressed his tongue harder against her clit, rolling it over and over to give her the rhythm she needed to fall right over that cliff into orgasm.

"Oh, yes. I'm coming. I'm coming."

He bathed her pussy as she rocketed through her climax, using his lips and tongue to ratchet up her pleasure. She reached out for him and he grabbed her hand, giving her something to hold on to as she rolled through the spasms.

Then he kissed her thigh and stood up to smile at her.

She finally lifted her head. "Holy shit, Nathan."

His lips curved. He righted her underwear, smoothed her dress back in place and lifted her off the table, making sure to hold her in place while she got her bearings.

She lifted up and kissed him. "Thank you."

"Yeah, that was fun."

"And now you really need to get back to your friends and family." She brushed her fingertip over his lips. "But first, stop in the restroom and wash your face."

He laughed. "Yeah, I'll do that."

He started to leave, but then turned to her and pulled her into his arms. "We're going to continue this later. Naked. I want to be inside of you."

She looked up at him, her beautiful blue eyes clear as she met his gaze and nodded. "Yes."

He'd expected argument or waffling. There'd been none. He

was happy about that. He brushed his lips across hers. "See you later."

She nodded and he stepped away, unlocked the door and ducked out.

He smiled as he made his way to the men's room.

Best damn birthday ever.

NINETEEN

THE PARTY WRAPPED UP AROUND MIDNIGHT. MIA WAS
surprised that so many people had stayed that long, but then again
they had the deejay and a dance floor and the bars, so of course
everyone wanted to party. Nathan's grandparents had stayed 'til the
end, and had even been out on the floor dancing with everybody.

She was so happy about the turnout, and it seemed everyone
had a great time.

The best part was, Tara had brought in a cleanup crew, so they
didn't have to stay to clean up this mess.

"You're the best, Tara." Mia hugged her.

Tara gave her a squeeze back. "You're the one who took care of
the invites. I was blown away by how many of Nathan's friends and
teammates showed up."

"And you brought in the family in droves. He was so happy
about that."

Tara grinned. "Well, we're just awesome, aren't we?"

Mia laughed. "I guess we are."

"Hey, anytime you want to leave sports management and come to work for me, you'd make an incredible event planner."

"It's good to have a backup plan. Thanks, Tara. Especially since my start-up is new. You just never know."

"You know I'm joking, right?"

"I wasn't. This party planning thing was fun. I could see myself doing it."

Tara laughed. "Okay, mogul. Time for you to go."

They walked to the door together. Nathan was chatting with Jamal, Wendy and Mick.

"Okay, we'll see you later."

"I'll see you at the gym on Monday," Jamal said.

"Nah. Probably at the gym *tomorrow* morning."

Jamal grinned. "You got it. We'll see which one of us shows up first."

"It'll be me."

"I dunno, Nathan. You look pretty out of it. You've had too many beers. My guess is you sleep in."

"Hey, I'm not the one who was downing shots of whiskey with the offensive linemen. So I'm pretty sure you'll be the one sleeping in, asshole, while I'll have already run three miles and put in a hard iron press for thirty minutes before you even drag your ass out of bed."

Mia rolled her eyes and grabbed Nathan's arm. "Yeah, and then you can both compare dick sizes. Tomorrow. Good night, everyone."

"Hey, I wasn't done insulting Jamal," Nathan said as Mia took the keys from him and clicked the doors to unlock his SUV.

"Uh-huh. You can continue it in the morning."

"Hey," he said as he climbed in. "You driving?"

She got in the driver's seat. "I am."

He buckled his seat belt, then turned to her. "Are you okay to drive?"

"I'm fine. I only had a couple of glasses of wine the entire night."

"Okay, then. Drive it like you stole it."

She laughed. "I don't think I'll be doing that. But since we're in your vehicle and mine's at my town house, how do you feel about coming back to my place?"

He leaned his head back against the seat and closed his eyes. "I feel pretty great about it."

Yes, Nathan was seriously inebriated. She was glad he'd had such a good time.

She drove to her town house and pulled Nathan's SUV in front. By then he was lightly snoring, so she turned off the car.

"Nathan."

No response.

"Nathan."

Still nothing. She shoved at his shoulder. "Hey, beerhead, we're here."

He woke up and looked at her. "Great. Where's here?"

"My place."

"Okay. Let's get this party started."

She rolled her eyes. "Yes, let's do that."

Nathan slid out of the car. Mia got her keys and went to the front door. Nathan followed behind her. They went inside and she locked the door behind her, knowing Nathan wasn't going anywhere tonight.

She laid her bag down and went into the kitchen. "How about some water?"

"A beer would be good."

She laughed. "No more beer for you."

He came up behind her and wrapped his arms around her, nuzzling her neck. "Did I ever tell you how good you smell?"

She leaned into him, enjoying the feel of his hard body against her. "You might have mentioned it."

"Let's go upstairs. I want to get you naked."

"Sure. I'm going to grab a glass of water first. How about unzipping my dress?"

He drew the zipper down. "Don't be too long."

"I won't."

Nathan disappeared up the stairs and she filled her glass with water, deciding to get a glass of water for Nathan, too. She checked a couple of text messages on her phone, mainly thank-you messages from party attendees. She smiled at that, then made her way up the stairs.

When she got to her bedroom, she leaned against the doorway and sipped her water, then shook her head.

She knew Nathan well. He could handle his liquor up to a point, but she'd watched him do several shots of whiskey with his friends and teammates, and she knew for a fact he was shitfaced. He might seem normal, but she'd been through this with him on countless nights out. And as soon as he sat still or lay down, he was out.

Like now. He'd taken off his shoes and had propped himself into a sitting position on her bed, no doubt to wait for her to come up.

And he was sound asleep.

She smiled, slid out of her dress and went into the bathroom to wash her face and brush her teeth. When she was done, she nudged him.

"Hey, let's get you out of those clothes."

He cooperated, so she got him undressed and under the covers. And when she turned out the light and climbed into bed, he turned and nestled against her.

She closed her eyes.

TWENTY

MIA ROLLED OVER AND BLINKED, THEN REACHED HER arm out for Nathan.

His side of the bed was empty. And cold.

She frowned, then reached for her phone.

Okay, it was seven a.m. and way too early to get up. She looked over at the bathroom door, but it was open and the bathroom was dark, so he wasn't in there. Did he get up and leave already?

No. Nathan wouldn't do that without waking her up to say good-bye. At least she didn't think he would. It wasn't like they'd spent the night together a lot.

She got out of bed and saw his clothes from last night laid over the chair.

Okay, he was still here. Somewhere.

She slid into a tank top and a pair of shorts, then started downstairs. The smell of coffee hit her halfway down. She kept coffee around for guests, but normally she brewed tea. When she turned the corner at the landing, Nathan was there, leaning against her kitchen island while he drank a cup of coffee.

Wearing just his boxer briefs.

She had to gape for a moment at the picture he presented. Wide shoulders, broad back, muscled thighs. She was fully awake now, for sure. If only a nearly naked beefcake like this could present himself in her kitchen every morning, it would be the best wake-up call ever.

She made her way into the kitchen. Nathan turned his head and leveled his thousand-watt smile on her.

"Morning."

"Good morning. You're up early."

"I got plenty of sleep. You're the one who's up early. I thought you might want to sleep in."

"I'm good, but thanks." She filled her teapot with water, then set it on the stove and went to grab a cup and the tea diffuser.

"Thanks for taking me in last night."

"You're welcome. I'm glad you had fun at your party."

He laid his cup on the counter and tugged her against him. "I was surprised as hell. And I had a great time. Thank you."

He was rubbing her back, and she had to admit it felt good to be pressed against his warm body. And when he grasped the nape of her neck and pulled her forward for a kiss, she didn't resist.

This was what she'd wanted last night—a continuation of what they'd started in the coat closet. She raised up on her toes to get closer, to run her hands over all the glorious, exposed muscle of his arms and shoulders. He responded by cupping her butt and drawing her against his now-hard cock.

Her sex was now sharply awake and ready for him.

Until the teapot whistled. She pulled back. "Sorry."

He gave her a look that was all raw hunger and need. "Turn it off."

She flipped the burner knob to off, then went back to Nathan, who drew her against him.

"I'm hard and I need to be inside of you," he said. "You sleeping naked in the bed next to me when I got up this morning? That was torture. I wanted to wake you up and fuck you."

She lifted her gaze to his. "Why didn't you?"

He bent and took her bottom lip between his teeth, teasing her before kissing her again, more deeply this time. She moaned against his mouth, flicking her tongue against his.

He pulled his mouth from hers. "Because you needed to sleep. But now you're awake and we started something last night that we didn't get to finish."

She smoothed her hands over his chest, using the pads of her thumb to roll over his nipples, and was rewarded with his sharp intake of breath.

"I agree. I'm ready for you."

He flipped her around so she was facing the island, then slid his hand inside her shorts. She quivered at his touch, a hot fire of need sparking inside of her.

She tilted her head back and rested it against his collarbone, arching her hips forward to meet his questing fingers.

"You're wet," he whispered against her ear.

"I need to come. You make me so hot, Nathan."

He slid a finger inside of her, using his hand to massage her clit. With his other hand he reached under her tank top to massage her breasts and nipples. She could already feel herself falling, her body quivering in response to the magic his hand and fingers aroused within her. She felt as if she was floating on a cloud of delicious sensations, and before she knew what was happening, she was climaxing with a loud cry.

Nathan pressed his fingers in and out of her while she rode out her orgasm, leaving her spent and taking in deep breaths. He kissed the back of her neck.

"Stay like this. I'll be right back."

He disappeared up the stairs and was back in a hurry with a condom in his hand. He drew her shorts down, then his boxer briefs, and put the condom on. He spread her legs and put his arm around her, shielding her body from the kitchen island.

"You ready for me?" he asked, teasing her pussy with the head of his cock.

She gripped the edge of the counter. "Yes."

He slid inside of her with one thrust, then stilled. Her skin broke out in chill bumps, every nerve ending feeling the intense pleasure of his cock swelling inside of her. It was the sweetest sensation, and she reached down to rub her clit, making her sex quiver with powerful quakes.

"Oh, fuck yeah," he said. "I feel that."

He withdrew, then drove into her again, this time with more force, grasping her hips as he powered into her over and over while she strummed her clit with frenzied strokes.

Her body tightened around him as she spiraled toward orgasm again.

"Yeah," he said, reaching up to cup her breast, to tease and pluck her nipples. "Take me with you. Come on my cock, Mia."

His words were a dark whisper of promise, his voice deep and husky and telling of his own need. She pushed her hips toward him and lost herself in the sensations that wrapped around her, in the musky scent of Nathan and her own sex mingling together, in the way his warm breath caressed her, the way he kissed and nibbled on her neck.

When she came, it was with an unintelligible cry and mix of words. Nathan bucked against her and dug his fingers into her hips, only adding to the wild pleasure that sent her toppling into a deeper, more penetrating orgasm. And when Nathan wrapped both arms around her and shuddered against her, she felt that connection to him while they both rocketed into oblivion.

Sometime a few minutes later she came out of the fog. She was still bent over the island and Nathan was draped over her back.

"We're sweaty," she said.

"Yeah." He disengaged from her and she turned to face him.

"I need tea. But I need a shower first. Want to join me?"

"Definitely. Let me grab a pair of shorts and a T-shirt from my car first."

She arched a brow and looked at him. "You're naked."

He laughed. "I'm going to grab my pants from upstairs."

"Good call. I'm not posting bail for your indecent exposure."

She went upstairs and started the shower, and got in once the water was hot. Nathan joined her a couple of minutes later. They both washed and rinsed, then got out and dried off.

Mia dressed in shorts and a T-shirt and Nathan put on the clothes he'd grabbed from his car. She headed downstairs to start the tea brewing process all over again and Nathan poured himself another cup of coffee.

"That was one hell of a great start to the day," he said as he took a swallow of coffee.

Her tea finally ready, she grabbed a seat at the island. "Yes, I'm fully awake now. And you told Jamal last night you were going to show up at the gym bright and early and mentioned something about kicking his butt."

He pulled up a bar stool and sat next to her. "I did? Huh. Guess I'll be late."

She thought for sure he'd want to run right out of there considering how competitive he was. "I guess so."

"What are your plans for today?" he asked.

"Catching up on work stuff."

"I could make you breakfast. Are you hungry?"

"Actually I am. I'll help you cook."

"Sounds good."

They worked side by side and made spinach, artichoke and to-mato omelets. She poured juice and they sat at the island and ate. Mia picked up her phone and scanned social media.

She frowned when she saw the pictures.

"A photographer snuck into the birthday party last night."

Nathan swallowed. "Yeah?"

"Yes. Look."

She slid her phone across to him. "There are pictures from the party. And we did not invite photographers."

He looked at the photos, then passed her phone back to her. "They got some good shots. You should grab those."

"Nathan. This is serious."

"Why?"

"How did a paparazzo even know about the party?"

He downed the last of his coffee, then got up to make another cup. "Come on, Mia. That many people there? Plus my parents, Ty-ler, Gavin, other teammates. It was bound to attract some attention."

She rubbed her temple and read the article on the sports news site about the party. It was fairly innocuous, but still, it irked her that someone had been at the party sneaking pictures and she hadn't even noticed. "I . . . guess."

She did a search using Nathan's name and "birthday party." More articles and photos came up. She found one of the two of them together, his arm slung around her. She chewed on her lower lip as she read the article, this one on a sports gossip site. "Here's one questioning whether or not I'm gunning to be your new girl-friend. Ugh."

"You're going to have to tune all that out, Mia."

She couldn't believe he'd even suggest that. "It's hard to tune that out. I'm trying to build a business, and part of my business is not 'gunning to be Nathan Riley's new girlfriend.'"

He brought his cup to the island and sat next to her, then reached over to grasp her hand. "You're right. I'm sorry. To me it's all fluff and no one pays attention to it. I'll try to keep a closer eye out in the future."

"Thank you. I will, too."

They sat in silence for a while and Mia searched more sites but didn't find anything on the party, which she supposed was a good thing. She decided to set her worry aside, at least for now.

"So now your birthday is over and the next thing up is training camp. Are you excited?"

He scooped up a forkful of omelet and slid it between his lips. He nodded, swallowed and said, "Yeah."

That didn't seem enthusiastic.

"Nervous about leading the team?"

"Sort of. I mean, it's a big fucking deal, ya know? I know they're looking to me to walk onto the field and be Mick Riley. Only I'm not."

She laid her hand on his forearm. "I don't think anyone is expecting you to be anything like your dad, Nathan. And if the team didn't feel you had the skills at quarterback to lead the team, then they wouldn't have made you the starter."

He let out a sigh. "I guess. It'll be fine, I'm sure. I'm just anxious to get started."

"I'm sure you are. And I'll bet all this anxiety you're having is fear of the unknown. You had so much confidence in Texas, right?"

"Well, yeah."

"That's because you knew what you were doing. This is no different. As soon as you take the reins on the offense, you'll get back in your groove."

He leaned back on the bar stool. "This is different. It's the pros. A lot more eyes on me."

She understood his anxiety more than he knew. "When I had the idea to start up this company, in theory and as long as it was in my head, it was fine. The reality of it is so much different, because you're right. Everyone's watching to see if you fail."

He rubbed her back. "I've never known anyone more determined to succeed than you. You have the skills and the knowledge and the background, Mia. You'll make a go of your business, and you'll be the best at it."

She hadn't been fishing for compliments, but his certainty about her abilities sure felt good. "Thanks for your confidence in me. I feel the same way about you, Nathan. You've got this."

He swept his hand up her back and into her hair. "Then I guess we're both going to kick some ass, aren't we?"

She gave him a smile. "Hell yes we are."

He brushed his lips across hers, lingering for a few seconds and making her breath catch before he pulled back to take a swallow of coffee.

"So . . . about last night."

She tilted her head. "What about last night?"

"In the car on the way to the party. I thought you were texting a guy."

"Oh." Her lips curved. "I wasn't. I was texting your mom."

"Yeah. Well, when I thought you had a date, I didn't like it."

She tried to fight the smile. "Okay."

"So I'd like you to be with me, Mia. Just me. Try me out for a while. I know you'll like me."

She laughed. "I'm not seeing anyone else, Nathan, and have no intention of doing so. And I already like you."

"Good. And ditto. I'm not seeing anyone else, either. And this is different from what we were before. Now we're dating. In a relationship. Ya know?"

His broad grin made her melt. "Yes. I know. We'll try it out for size and see how it goes."

So now they were officially in a relationship. Which was weird since they'd been friends for years. She mentally crossed her fingers, hoping this worked out between them without ruining what they had.

TWENTY-ONE

MIA HAD PACED AND PONDERED AND THOUGHT AND agonized about this, tossing the idea around in her head and throwing it away multiple times. But she was running out of time and she needed to make a decision. Or at least ask the damn question. Which she wished she had asked a couple of weeks ago. But their status had changed only a few days ago, and oh, why was she worrying about this?

She finally grabbed her phone and called Nathan Tuesday afternoon. He picked up.

"Hey, what's up?"

"Are you busy?" she asked.

"Nah. Just doing some things around the house."

"I need to ask you a question, and you can feel free to say no."

He paused. "Okay."

"My brother Barrett is getting married this weekend in Texas. I need a date for the wedding."

He paused again. "I don't know anyone in Texas, but if you give me a few hours I'm sure I could rustle someone up for you."

"Funny."

"So you're asking me to be your date for the wedding?"

She liked that he made this easy for her. "Yes, I would really like it, if you're not busy this weekend, if you'd come with me and be my date for my brother's wedding. It's super last minute and all and you can feel free to say no."

"I'd love to come with you, Mia."

She exhaled. "Thanks. I hate going to these things solo and I would have asked you sooner, but our relationship just changed recently and before that I was going by myself. But now you and I—you know—God, I'm not making any sense."

He laughed. "I said I'd be happy to go, babe. Just text me the details."

"Great. I'll make the travel arrangements. We'll go up Thursday night and come home Sunday night if that doesn't interfere with anything you're doing."

"Right now I'm only doing gym time and a few meetings. So my schedule is clear."

"Perfect. I really appreciate this, Nathan."

"Not a problem. I'm sure it'll be fun. I like at least one of your brothers, and your parents."

She laughed. "You'll love my entire family. I promise."

They hung up and she felt as if a giant weight had been lifted off of her. She went to her office window and looked out over the bay. It was foggy today, and she wanted nothing more than to be outside to feel the salty spray on her face.

She didn't feel it was necessary to have a date for the wedding. She didn't. She was an adult and a businesswoman. She didn't need a man to feel complete. It was just that a lot of her friends would be there. A lot of her married friends who would then ask her endless questions about her dating life. That was what she didn't need.

But now she was dating Nathan. Which would likely bring about a whole new set of questions. Then again, no one would have to know if they didn't tell anyone.

She rubbed her forehead with her finger.

Relationships were fraught with baggage, both external and internal. She was going to have to have a discussion with Nathan about whether or not to discuss their relationship while they were with her family. Did she really want to get into it with her parents? Her brothers? God, her brothers. The inquisition could be mind-boggling, both for her and for Nathan. And right now things between Nathan and her were so new, so tenuous, the last thing she wanted or needed was for her family to insert themselves into the middle of it all.

No. Absolutely not. She'd let everyone believe they were still just friends and leave it at that.

Now that that was out of the way, she made Nathan's flight arrangements to coincide with hers, and called her mother.

"Mia, it's so great to hear from you."

"How goes the wedding planning, Mom?"

"It's all under control over here. Harmony's mother, Diane, and I have been on the phone daily going over the checklist, and we have everything covered. Harmony and Barrett will be in town soon and we'll do final dress fittings, and pick up the tuxes, and oh, by the way, I'll have your dress here."

"Thanks, Mom." It was so sweet of Harmony to ask her to be a bridesmaid in her wedding. And even sweeter that she had chosen the most beautiful dresses to wear. Not all bridesmaids were that lucky.

"So what's up?" her mom asked.

"I'm bringing someone with me to the ranch."

"Oh? And who's that?"

"Nathan Riley. You remember him from college?"

"Of course."

"He's a friend, so separate bedrooms for us."

"Okay. I'll jot his name down on the guest list."

She loved that her mother didn't ask probing questions.

At least not yet. She imagined her mother would want to get a feel for her relationship with Nathan. Then she'd ask the probing questions.

Which was fine. Her mom could ask all the questions she wanted.

Mia intended to divulge nothing.

TWENTY-TWO

NATHAN PULLED INTO THE DRIVE OF THE DOUBLE C ranch.

"One hell of an impressive place," he said to Mia.

She sighed. "To me, it's always been home."

"It must have been great to grow up here."

She unbuckled her seat belt and turned to him with a smile. "It didn't suck."

They were surrounded by barking dogs of all shapes and sizes when Nathan exited the rental car. He bent and petted all of them, until a whistle sent them scurrying. He recognized the man on the porch right away. It was Easton Cassidy, football legend and Mia's father.

"Hey, Dad," Mia said, making her way to the front porch to give her father a hug.

"Hey, baby girl." Easton surrounded his daughter with a tight hug. "It's been forever since I've seen you."

She laughed. "Only a few months. You look good."

"So do you."

Nathan stood on the ground, waiting.

"Nice to see you again, Nathan," Easton said.

"You, too, Mr. Cassidy." Nathan made his way up the porch steps to shake Easton's hand.

"I've told you before. Call me Easton. How's your dad doing with his retirement?"

"He seems fine with it. He's happy to be able to spend time with my little brother."

"I'll bet he is. I'll have to give him a call and tell him all the fun things he can do now that he's retired."

"Like buy a ranch?" Mia asked with a teasing smile.

"He should definitely buy a ranch."

"Yeah, I can't see my mom being ready for that just yet," Nathan said. "But maybe several years down the road."

Easton laughed. "Come on inside. Your mom just made some fresh lemonade, Mia, and some of your brothers are here."

Easton held the door for them and they walked inside. It was hot as blazes out, so Nathan was happy the air conditioner was cranked to arctic levels in the house.

The Cassidys' house was huge. Nathan could tell it had been designed with four boys in mind. Lots of room to run around, no precious trinkets sitting about on the tables. Everything had a rustic but modern feel to it with dark hardwood floors, exposed beams on the tall ceilings and one hell of a dining room table that looked handmade. The house was pretty enough that a woman would love it, but also comfortable and somewhere a guy would like to live. Kind of a best of both worlds thing.

They made their way into the kitchen, which boasted an oversized island. Mia's mom, Lydia, leaned against the island talking to Grant, Mia's oldest brother, and Tucker, one of the twins, along with their wives. It was always easy to recognize Tucker since he wore glasses.

"Oh, you're here," Lydia said, coming around the island to fold Mia into a hug.

Mia hugged her back. Then she had to hug Grant and his wife, Katrina, and Tucker and his wife, Aubry.

"You all remember Nathan Riley? And if you don't, this is my friend Nathan Riley."

"Hey, Nathan," Grant said. "Good to see you again." Grant introduced his wife, Katrina.

"We haven't met yet," Tucker said. "Great to meet you. This is my wife, Aubry."

"It's nice to meet all of you."

"And it's wonderful to see you again, Nathan," Lydia said. "It feels like forever, though I know we saw you at the game last year when we came out to see Flynn play."

"It's good to see you again, Lydia. Thanks for letting me tag along to the wedding."

"We're happy to have you."

"How does it feel taking over as Sabers quarterback?" Grant asked.

"Daunting."

Grant laughed. "Yeah, I know that feeling. But you're gonna do great. Unless you play our team. Then we'll kick your ass."

Nathan smiled. "Somehow I think Flynn would disagree."

"Disagree about what?"

Flynn and Amelia walked in, hand in hand.

"That Grant's team will kick the Sabers' ass," Mia said.

Flynn walked over and patted Grant on the back. "Keep being a dreamer, buddy."

Easton beamed a smile. "I love when the family comes to-gether. Such warmth."

Lydia laughed. "Go check the ribs, Easton." She turned to Mia and Nathan. "There's lemonade and iced tea in the fridge, along with beer. And, Mia, you know where the wine is."

"Okay." Mia turned to Nathan. "What would you like?"

"I'll take a beer."

"Grab one for me, too," Flynn said. "Amelia?"

"I'd love a glass of wine."

"White or red?" Mia asked.

"Whatever you're pouring for yourself."

"That makes it easy."

Nathan pulled two beers—then three, when Tucker asked for one. He ended up following the guys outside, where they hung out with Easton while he finished smoking the ribs, which smelled amazing.

"How'd you manage the time off, Tucker?" Nathan asked.

"I just pitched yesterday afternoon's game so I won't be in the rotation again for several days. Coach wasn't all that happy for me to leave, but they let me off anyway. And it helped that I gave them plenty of notice."

"Plus, he sucks and they don't like to use him that often," Flynn said.

"Yeah, that's why my earned run average is so low."

"I don't know why you let him bait you," Grant said. "You should just tell him to go fuck himself."

Tucker took a swallow of his beer. "Oh, right. Go fuck yourself, Flynn."

Flynn smiled over his beer.

Nathan didn't have brothers close in age, but his dad, uncles and their cousins sparred like this all the time. He knew it came from a place of affection. It was amusing as hell to listen to—and to be a part of. Once he'd become an adult, the Riley clan had used insults to show him how much they loved him.

"How are you feeling about this season, Nathan?" Easton asked him.

"Honestly? Equal parts raring to go and nervous as hell."

"I think you'd be in trouble if you weren't split down the middle like that," Grant said. "If you're overconfident you'll fuck it all up. If you're too scared to even move from under center, you'll fuck it all up, too. I'd say you're right where you need to be."

"I agree," Flynn said. "It's natural to be nervous. Hell, we all were when we first started out. But as long as you know you've got the skills, you'll do great."

Tucker nodded. "My first time on the mound starting a game I thought for sure I was going to either throw up or pass out."

"You pitched seven solid innings and won," Easton said.

Tucker's lips lifted. "Yeah. Only gave up one run. It was a decent outing for my first trip to the mound."

"My first time at defensive back, some five-foot-seven running back skirted past me as if I was frozen," Flynn said. "Hell, I might have been."

"I remember that," Tucker said. "We were all at the game that day yelling from the stands because we were wondering when the hell you were going to move your ass."

Flynn frowned. "I moved my ass plenty after that. And after the coach pulled me and screamed at me for like five solid minutes. The very next play I got past the offensive tackle and nearly sacked the QB."

Nathan laughed. "A real come-to-Jesus moment for you, was it?"

"Like you would not believe."

"I did get sacked in my first game as a starter," Grant said. "Some big burly defensive end flattened me so hard I couldn't breathe."

"Yeah, we all thought you were dead," Easton said with a grin.

Nathan shook his head. "But you got up and then you threw a forty-yard touchdown pass."

Grant looked over at Nathan. "You remember that."

"I watched a lot of football before I ever got to play."

"Studying the game is the best way to learn the right way—and the wrong way—to play," Flynn said.

"You're right about that," Easton said. "Okay, these ribs are done. Go grab the pan from your mom, Tucker, along with the barbecue sauce so I can get these babies on the grill."

"You got it."

They spent the next half hour jawing about sports while Easton finished with the ribs. Nathan went inside to get everyone more beer. Mia was at the kitchen island surrounded by her mother and all the women and was so engaged in conversation and cooking she didn't even notice him. He was fine with that. He knew how much being with her family meant to her.

He'd also been introduced to Katrina's younger sister, Anya, and her brother, Leo. Leo ended up outside with them—minus the beer, since Leo was underage.

But since Leo also played football, he fit right in and he and Nathan had a discussion about how Leo hadn't started playing football until his sophomore year in high school. Now he was going to play wide receiver in college.

"So you decided on the University of Texas, huh?" Nathan asked.

"Yeah. I got lucky and received several offers, but I really liked Texas."

Nathan nodded. "It's a good school. Grant went there, as you know. So did Mia. So did I. Great football program."

"Great academically, too. I like the coach and the team and what they have to offer. I can't wait to start."

Nathan remembered what it was like being a freshman in college, just waiting for football season. "Already getting started on your practices?"

He nodded.

"Hey, if you have any questions, text or call me."

They traded numbers.

"Thanks, Nathan. Oh, and I'm excited to watch you lead the Sabers as quarterback this season."

"Thanks. I'm pretty pumped about it."

Easton said the ribs were ready. Grant went inside and came out with several serving trays. They piled the ribs on those and went inside.

"Those can go on the dining room table," Lydia said. "We're all set up."

He had no idea what else they'd been fixing in here, but whatever it was smelled damn good. When he made his way to the dining room, Mia waved him over, so he sat next to her.

There were also a lot more people who'd showed up, including a few older guys who looked a lot like Easton. Mia introduced Nathan to Easton's brothers—her uncles—along with their wives, though his brother Elijah was single.

The food spread was spectacular. Besides the ribs, there were baked beans, green beans and salad and corn on the cob, along with corn bread and fruit salad. There were pitchers of iced tea and lemonade, along with pitchers of lemon-infused water. Nathan poured a glass of water.

"Dig in, everyone," Lydia said.

Nathan and Mia waited while the elder members of the family took their portions. Then they served themselves. Nathan dove into the ribs and devoured several of those before he even began to tackle the side dishes.

"Hungry?" Mia asked.

He used one of the napkins to wipe his mouth and chin. "I've been smelling these ribs for a couple of hours now. I couldn't wait to taste them."

"My dad makes pretty exceptional ribs."

"Yeah, he does." He made sure to tell Easton how good they were.

Easton beamed a smile.

"Thanks, kid."

Nathan was pretty sure he could have devoured every rib Easton had pulled off the grill. But the competition was fierce with all these guys and he kept eyeing the plate, sure they were going to run out.

They didn't. Obviously the Cassidys were used to feeding hordes of hungry mouths, because by the time everyone was finished, there was still food left over.

Nathan was so full he could barely stand.

But then everyone got up and started carrying dishes into the kitchen. It was a lot like hanging out at his grandparents' when all the family came over. When Flynn and Grant and Tucker and the rest of the guys began to put food away, Nathan dug in to help. There were so many of them it didn't take much time at all to get everything cleaned up and put away.

Teamwork, man. Worked every time.

Flynn handed him a beer from the fridge, and he followed the guys outside onto the back porch. Plenty of places to sit, so he pulled up a white Adirondack chair and settled in.

"When do Barrett and Harmony and her family get in?" Flynn asked.

"Tomorrow morning," Easton said. "Harmony had some last-minute business things to finish up this afternoon, and they didn't want to rush into a flight tonight, so they're flying in early tomorrow morning. They should be here by noon."

Mia had told him that Barrett and Harmony had decided to get married here on the ranch. They had already decorated a couple of barns for the ceremony and the reception, and there were plenty of guest cottages for those who'd be staying over at the wedding. Plus they had a block of rooms reserved at one of the hotels in Austin for the rest of the guests.

He'd heard a lot about Cassidy weddings lately. Two of her brothers—Grant and Tucker—had gotten married last year, so Mia had shared details about the weddings and showed him pictures.

She'd looked pretty in the wedding photos. Then again, Mia always looked pretty. In or out of clothes. He probably shouldn't be thinking about her not wearing clothes while he was sitting around with her brothers, but it was hard not to think about her. He heard her laughing inside and damn if he didn't want to go in there, wrap his arms around her and kiss her. He craved the taste of her lips on his.

His dick quivered just thinking about it, which meant he needed to stop thinking about it. At least until he could get her alone.

He wasn't sure how he was going to accomplish that. On the flight here, Mia had explained to him that she wanted to keep their relationship private, not tell her family they were dating yet. She didn't want probing questions from her family.

He totally understood that and he was more than willing to respect her terms. This was her ground, so she could play it however she wanted to.

Which didn't mean he wouldn't try to grab some alone time with her. And enjoy being her date at the wedding.

Time to direct his thoughts elsewhere. He thought about all these Cassidys. All these weddings in such a short time must have been a whirlwind of crazy for the Cassidys. Mia had loved it, had spent hours talking to him about the weddings.

This was the first one Mia had invited him to, though. He wasn't a wedding kind of guy, but he'd gone to plenty of them over the years with the Riley clan. And this was important to Mia. He was happy to be here with her.

Between hanging out with the guys and with Mia, he was going to have fun.

The group broke up about an hour later. He was bunking with Leo, which suited him just fine. He liked the kid and they had plenty in common. He tossed his bag on the double bed upstairs in the main house, then went downstairs to grab a glass of water.

Mia was in the kitchen.

"Did you find your room okay?" she asked.

"Yeah. I'm with Leo."

She grinned. "Leo is awesome."

"He is. Where are you bunking?"

"Not too far from you. In my old room. By myself."

That gave him ideas. "Oh, yeah? You'll have to give me a tour."

She arched a brow. "Thinking of invading my inner sanctum?"

He looked around but didn't see anyone. The TV was on in the living room, but that was far enough away that no one could see them. Still, he didn't want to risk someone walking in on them, so he kept his distance. "Maybe. If you invite me."

She reached out and skimmed her fingertips across his chest. "Well, we could—"

Flynn walked into the kitchen and Mia snatched her hand back.

"I hope you didn't drink all the beer."

Nathan maintained a casual pose, as if he and Mia had just been chatting. "No guarantees."

Flynn grabbed three beers from the fridge. "Luckily for you there are still beers here. So I don't have to kick your ass."

Nathan laughed.

"And why aren't you guys in here watching the game with us?"

Flynn asked. "It's the bottom of the seventh and L.A. and Texas are tied."

Nathan looked over at Mia, who shrugged. "I wouldn't miss it."

So much for having some alone time with Mia.

"Me, either," Mia said.

Nathan nodded. "Yeah, let's go watch some baseball."

TWENTY-THREE

MIA ADORED WEDDINGS. SHE WAS NOWHERE NEAR ready for her own, but there had been so many Cassidy weddings in the past year they had filled her heart with love and absolute joy.

Having watched her brothers Grant and Tucker marry the women they love had been wonderful. She already felt like Katrina and Aubry were her sisters. She loved them both so much. And now her brother Barrett was going to marry Harmony, and she'd gain yet another sister.

After growing up with four annoying brothers, having all these women become a part of her life was nothing short of a miracle.

Hopefully sometime soon Flynn and Amelia would be planning their wedding and then she'd have four sisters to counteract the effects of all that Cassidy testosterone.

They'd celebrated Flynn and Amelia's engagement last night with a round of champagne for everyone. Amelia said she didn't want to make a big deal out of it because this was Harmony and

Barrett's celebration, but Mom had insisted that it was still a big deal and they should at least do a toast.

She was so happy for her brother, who had showed some smarts by asking Amelia to marry him.

As soon as Barrett and Harmony arrived on the ranch this afternoon, it had been chaos. But it was wonderful chaos. Barrett was his usual laid-back self, and Harmony was excited. They all dragged her upstairs to ogle her wedding dress and talk about the plans for today.

"Are you nervous?" Katrina asked her.

"A little. Nervousness mixed with excitement and a touch of 'Oh my God I can't believe the day is finally here.'"

Aubry laughed. "I felt the same way on my wedding day. Like it took forever to get here, then once the day came there was so much to do. And it was over so fast. I wanted it to go on forever."

"You looked like a freakin' fairy princess in your wedding dress," Mia said, remembering the blush-tone dress Aubry wore on her wedding day that complemented her peachy complexion and blond hair. She'd looked stunning.

Aubry grinned. "I kind of did, didn't I?"

"And of course Katrina looked like she'd just stepped off one of her photo shoots," Harmony said, "with that sleek silk wedding gown and her body that made us all jealous."

Katrina smiled. "Thank you. I loved that dress. After doing so many wedding shoots in so many designer dresses, I just wanted simple."

"You made simple look elegant," Anya said. "Which I told you was the best choice."

Katrina looked over at her younger sister. "Well, you know me best, don't you?"

"And now we can't wait for Harmony to get all dressed up and walk down the aisle," Mia said. "Or down the barn aisle."

Harmony laughed. "I know. It's crazy to think we're getting married here. But it's so perfect. Even my mom loves it here."

"That's because your mom has the hots for my uncle Elijah," Mia said.

"Oh, she so does. Any opportunity she has to get next to that man she takes it. Did I tell you he asked her if she was bringing a date to the wedding?"

Mia sat on the bed in Harmony's bedroom and leaned against Katrina's knee. "You did not. What did she say?"

"She said she absolutely did not bring a date, she wasn't seeing anyone and she was leaving all her dances open for him."

Aubry laughed. "I don't know why those two aren't seeing each other more frequently."

"Well . . ." Harmony let the word trail off.

"What do you know that we don't know?" Amelia asked.

"He might have made a trip down to Tampa a time or two."

Mia laid her hand on her heart. "He did not. Did he, really?"

"Yes. I'd say there's definitely something going on with my mama and Elijah."

"That is awesome," Aubry said. "I'm really pulling for those two."

Mia made a mental note to keep her eye on her Uncle Elijah and on Diane, Harmony's mother, who was conspicuously absent from this get-together.

"Hey, Harmony, where is your mom, by the way?"

Harmony shrugged. "No idea. She conveniently disappeared as soon as we got here."

Katrina laughed. "I'll bet Elijah is nowhere to be found, either."

"Either that or she's with my mom going over last-minute planning," Mia said.

"I like the idea of her hiding out in some corner of the ranch making out with Elijah," Aubry said.

Harmony laughed. "You're all a bunch of sloppy romantics."

"Let's find out," Mia said, sliding off the bed. "I'm hungry anyway."

They went downstairs and found Mia's mother in the kitchen going over a list. Diane wasn't with her. They made sandwiches and sat at the island.

"Lydia, have you seen my mother?" Harmony asked.

Mia's mom looked up. "She was in here with me a while ago, but then she said she had a call to make and she disappeared. Did you look in her room?"

"Checked her room before we came down here," Harmony said. "She's not in there."

Amelia made a "hmm" sound, then said, "Interesting."

Lydia frowned. "What's interesting about that?"

"We think she's off with Elijah somewhere," Mia said.

"Oh. She probably is. They've been seeing each other."

"So you knew about that?" Mia asked.

"Of course."

"How come I didn't know about that?" Mia asked. "How come none of us knew about it?"

"Maybe because it's none of your business."

Mia rolled her eyes. "Oh, come on, Mom. There's romance brewing."

Her mother gave her a direct stare. "And would you want the entire family knowing *your* romance business?"

Mia didn't answer. She definitely would not like the entire family knowing what was going on between Nathan and her. Instead, she took a bite of her sandwich and a long swallow of iced tea.

"That's what I thought," her mom said.

"So much for us skulking around the ranch to find Elijah and Diane," Aubry whispered to Mia.

Mia turned to her. "I know. Moms ruin all the fun."

"I heard that, Mia," Lydia said. "And since none of you have anything to do other than gossip, I have a list of items that need taking care of. Mia, go get the tractor and mow the front property."

Mia wrinkled her nose. "What? Me? Why can't one of the guys do that?"

"Because I have the guys doing other things."

She sighed. "Fine."

After they finished eating and cleaned up, Mia went upstairs and grabbed her tennis shoes and a ball cap, then shoved her hair into a ponytail. On her way through the kitchen toward the back door, she noticed everyone else had left.

"Where is everyone?" she asked her mom.

"I gave them things to do. Everyone except Harmony. She's the bride and she gets a pass. She has enough to deal with."

"Huh. Fine. I guess I'll go mow."

"I guess you will."

She headed out back where the tractors were located. On her way, she saw her dad painting the outside tables, Flynn and Tucker were taking folding chairs from the storage barn over to the wedding barn, and Barrett and Nathan were pulling weeds.

She laughed at that. The bride-to-be got a day off, but the groom-to-be had to pull weeds.

Awesome.

She started the tractor and pulled it out of the barn, then dropped the deck and began mowing the side yard along the fence line before moving to the front of the property.

It was already hot as blazes outside and she was going to be a dripping, sweaty mess by the time she was through. She decided to consider this her workout for the day.

NATHAN DIDN'T MIND PULLING WEEDS. HE WAS USED to sweating outside, and any kind of physical activity worked for him. He'd gotten his run in with the guys before dawn this morning, taking in the sprawling acreage as he did his three miles listening to the sounds of nature and cattle. It had been amazing.

Now, sweat slid down his back and into his face as he took the last of the weeds he'd pulled and tossed them in the trash can.

"Water?" Barrett asked.

"I'd like to surround myself in a pool of it right now."

Barrett laughed. "I'll be right back."

Nathan took up a spot in the shade alongside the house, pulled off his ball cap and swiped his forearm across his brow. He heard the sound of an engine, so he glanced over and spotted Mia running the tractor.

Damn if she didn't look hot as fuck operating that thing. It was three times her size and she was flying across the lawn like she was master of that monster.

What the hell was it about watching Mia mow the damn lawn that made his dick hard? Or maybe it was watching her do anything that made his dick hard?

"Hot?"

He jerked his head around to see Barrett standing there with a tall glass of ice water for him.

"Oh. Hell, yeah. Thanks."

Shit. He really needed to shift his focus away from lusting after Barrett's little sister. He guzzled half the glass of ice water, hoping it would cool him down in more ways than one.

"I think we're done out here," Barrett said. "Too bad we didn't get the easy job like Mia over there."

He looked over to see Mia turning the corner and head out to mow the front of the property. "Does she do that a lot?"

Barrett shrugged. "Mom probably told her to do it."

"Pretty hot out here today."

"She's tough. She can handle it. Besides, she loves mowing,

even though she grumbles about it. If you ask her if she'd rather do dishes or mow the lawn, she'll take mow the lawn anytime."

Nathan cracked a smile. "Is that right?"

"Yeah. I think that has to do with growing up with four older brothers. We were always fighting over running the tractor and Mia often got the short end of the stick. As soon as she was tall enough to sit on the tractor, Dad let her start mowing and driving the trucks around the property. Then we got stuck doing dishes."

Nathan laughed. "Sucks for you."

"For sure."

The door opened and Harmony stuck her head out. "Babe, I need you."

Barrett looked over at him. "Saved by groom duties."

"Later, Barrett."

Barrett disappeared inside, and Nathan finished his glass of water and set it on the table by the back door. He thought about finding the guys to see what they were up to, but for some reason he found himself wandering toward the front yard.

Mia had mowed most of the front area and looked to be about ready to finish up. He circled around back, grabbed his glass and took it inside.

Lydia was in the kitchen, along with Diane. They were heads together creating some centerpiece decoration thing and barely noticed him, so he refilled his glass with ice water, along with a second one. He slid out the door without anyone asking him questions. Once he was out the door, he realized he was acting all stealthy for no reason at all.

Everyone was busy and no one was paying attention to him, so he walked out front in time to see Mia pulling the tractor toward the barn. He followed her in there.

She shut off the tractor and turned to him.

"You following me?" she asked.

He handed her the glass of water. "Thought you might be thirsty."

"I am, thanks." She downed half the glass in a couple of swallows, kind of like he had with his first glass. She took off her ball cap and her hair was stuck to her head. Sweat glistened all over her arms and neck, and her T-shirt clung to her breasts in a way that was more attractive than it should be, all things considered.

"You're all wet."

"No shit. It's hot out here. I need a cool shower. This is one of those days I want to go whine at my dad about never putting in that swimming pool I always begged him for."

He laughed. "I grumbled at Barrett about wanting to surround myself with water."

She leaned against the tractor. "How was weed pulling?"

"It's my dream job. I'm thinking of giving up football just so I can pull weeds every day for the rest of my life."

She laughed. "I want to be at the press conference when you announce your retirement before the season starts."

"No one will miss me. My dad will come out of retirement and lead the Sabers to the championship game again."

She took another long swallow of water. "Thought about all this while you were weed pulling, huh?"

"It's good to have a long-range plan in mind."

"You're an idiot, Riley."

He gave her a half smile. "That's why you like me."

"No, I only tolerate you."

He looked around the barn. It was filled with farm equipment, from mowers and tractors to accessories for those. Then there were hoes and rakes and hoses. He also noticed there was storage up above accessible with a ladder.

"What's up there?" he asked.

"An old-style hayloft."

"Oh, like the kinds you see in old movies?"

She frowned. "What?"

He shifted to lean against a wood column in the barn. "Come on, Mia. Haven't you ever watched old movies, where the couple climb into the barn hayloft and make out?"

She looked up at the loft, then back at Nathan. "Apparently not. And there's no hay up there. Though we have storage and horse blankets."

"Sexy. Let's go up there and make out on the horse blankets."

She laughed. "I don't think so. Horse blankets aren't comfortable. Besides, I'm sweaty."

"So am I. Let's get even more sweaty."

"It won't be romantic."

"Wanna bet? I can make anything romantic."

"Are you throwing down the romance gauntlet?"

"Yup."

She stood. "Fine. But if I end up with hives or fleas from the horse blankets, it'll be your fault."

He cocked a grin and grabbed her hand. "Aren't you just full of adventure today?"

"No. I'm hot and sweaty and I need a shower."

He followed her up the ladder. "You're very sexy when you're grumpy."

"Shut up, Nathan."

This might not be ideal, and Mia might be cranky as fuck, but he'd change her mind about being up here. And it might be his only chance to get her alone. So even though it was hot and they were sweaty, they were together.

He'd make this work.

MIA WANTED NOTHING MORE THAN A NICE, COOL shower right now to rinse off the grass and sweat. Instead, she was climbing into this airless, hellish loft with sweat pooling between her breasts and every bit of clothing she wore sticking to her skin. Her hair was plastered to her head and neck and she felt disgusting.

So. Not. Sexy.

She got to the top of the loft and turned to wait for Nathan. He made it up there and looked around.

"Hot as fuck up here," he said.

"See? It's not like the movies. There's no springtime breeze flowing through the opening. No birds singing. It's like hell up here. Can we go now?"

"I see your point." He came over and wrapped his arms around her and it suddenly got twenty degrees warmer. "But we're alone. Doesn't that count for something?"

"I can think of better places to be alone. Like my nice cool shower in my bathroom."

"You're ruining my fantasy here, Mia."

"And I'm about to pass out from the heat."

He gave her a look of concern. "We can't have that. Let's go."

She tilted her head back to meet his gaze. "Seriously?"

"Yeah. Your face is bright red. Come on."

He held her hand as they made their way back down the narrow staircase. She actually felt a little dizzy, which she would not admit to Nathan. But when they hit the barn floor she was happy as hell to be out of that hot loft.

He didn't hesitate once they got there, just took her by the hand and led her toward the house. They went in the front door and he marched her up the stairs and right to her room. Fortunately, they didn't run into anyone along the way. He went inside with her and shut and locked the door.

She was so happy to have her own bathroom, because what she needed right now was privacy. And a shower. She really wanted a shower.

She turned to Nathan. "I'm stripping and getting in the shower. You coming with me?"

"You sure about that?"

She pulled her top over her head and dropped it on the floor. "I wouldn't have asked if I wasn't sure. Can you unhook my bra?"

"Yeah." He undid the clasp and she pulled it away from her sticky body and let that drop, too. "Yuck."

She went into the bathroom and turned on the water, shimmied out of her shorts and underwear, then stepped in the shower.

Oh. Heaven. She tilted her face back and let the lukewarm water rain down over her.

She heard the shower door open but she didn't move. Nathan could just wait his turn.

"I'm hoarding all the water for a minute," she said. "At least until I rinse all this sweat off of me."

"I can handle standing in my sweat while you cool down. Take all the time you need."

She sighed in happiness and let the refreshing shower continue. When she felt like most of the sweat was off of her, she stepped out of the way and let Nathan move in. He rinsed off and took her body wash and did a quick once-over on his body. Then he grabbed her shampoo and poured some in his hand.

"Tilt your head back."

She did and he washed her hair while she leaned back against his chest. He massaged her head in gentle, circular motions. Other than an orgasm, having Nathan wash her hair was the best sensation ever.

"Rinse."

She rinsed her hair, conditioned it, then stepped out of the water. Nathan was there with soap in his hand.

She felt revived now that she'd gotten out of the heat—and that damned loft. She stepped forward and turned so Nathan could apply soap to her back. His hands on her body felt so good. After she rinsed, he soaped up his hands again and spread them over her shoulders and down her breasts, circling his thumbs over her nipples.

She sucked in a breath as pleasure spiraled. He continued to wash her breasts, teasing her nipples until they were taut, tight buds. He moved his hand over her stomach and cupped her pussy, rubbing back and forth in light, easy motions.

"Nathan." She gripped his arms.

"I know what you need to relax you. You need a good orgasm. The kind that makes you scream."

Her sex quivered and pulsed with tingling sensation. And when he released her and took the handle of the shower head off to rinse her, then got down on his knees and put his mouth over her, she had to palm the wall for support.

Water rained down over her head and shoulders, warm and inviting, while Nathan's mouth and tongue performed a magical dance over her quivering pussy, taking her right to the edge. She was pent up, hovering right near the precipice of orgasm. She wanted to stay right there, to feel those tingling sensations until the end of time.

But she couldn't hold back and she came with a strangled cry, her limbs shaking as the waves of orgasm pounded over her. She was gasping for air when Nathan stood and kissed her, taking the remaining breath she had with a passionate kiss that left her legs trembling.

He reached around and turned off the shower, then dragged her out with him. He reached for a towel and dried both of them off.

"I need to be inside of you. I need to fuck you."

She nodded, feeling satiated and drugged with pleasure, yet needing exactly what Nathan wanted, too.

"Condoms are in the drawer on the bedside table," she said.

He took her by the hand and led her to her bedroom. He opened the drawer and put a condom on his beautiful, hard cock, then lay on the bed and pulled her on top of him.

"Ride me," he said.

With a shuddering sigh, she climbed on top of him and slid onto his shaft, her body still experiencing the aftereffects of that mind-blowing orgasm. So when she was fully seated on top of him, she tightened around him.

"Fuck. Do you feel that?"

"Yes." She moved forward, sliding against him. The sensations were so good they almost made her weep with joy. She held on to his arms and soaked in the heated passion in his gaze.

"My dick got hard watching you mow the lawn," he said. "Do you have any idea how fucking sexy you looked doing that?"

That made her lips curve. She had felt sweaty and awful. To hear Nathan say she looked hot was everything she needed to hear. She dug her nails into his arms and rocked against him, dragging her clit along his pelvis, bringing herself even closer to coming again.

And when the pulses sparked within her, he grasped her hips.

"Yeah, I feel it. Now come on my cock and take me with you."

His gritty voice was all it took to make her take off. She dropped down on top of him and ground against him, splintering with her orgasm.

Nathan groaned and grasped her butt, drawing her closer as he shuddered. She put her lips against his and kissed him, lost in the pleasure of his cock, of her own climax and of how it felt to be connected to him.

After, she lay on top of him listening to the beat of his heart against her chest. She was exhausted. Nathan stroked her back and she closed her eyes and let herself drift off.

When she woke up, they were curled together, her leg flung over his. She had no idea how long they'd been asleep, but someone was knocking on her door. She tried to blink back the cobwebs.

"Hey, Mia. Are you in there?"

It was Aubry. Mia pulled herself out of the bed and grabbed her robe that was draped over the nearby chair. She slipped it on and cracked open the door.

"I'm so sorry," Aubry said. "Were you napping?"

"Just a short nap. The heat from mowing zapped me."

"Okay. Your mom sent me to look for you. It's time to get ready for the rehearsal."

"Got it. I'll be right down."

"Sure." Aubry's lips lifted. "You might tell Nathan the guys were looking for him, too."

Mia looked over her shoulder to see Nathan sitting up in her bed. And obviously Aubry had spotted him, too.

Well, shit.

"Will do. And, Aubry? Try not to spread that around."

"Hey, I've been where you are. Trust me, I saw nothing."

"Thanks. I'll see you shortly."

She shut the door and leaned against it, then looked over at Nathan. His hair was tousled from sleep, the sheet barely covering his best parts. She wanted to climb back in bed and sex him up again. And again.

He dragged his fingers through his hair and smiled at her. "Who was that?"

"Aubry. It's time to get ready for the wedding rehearsal."

"Oh. Yeah. I'd better get out of your way and let you handle that."

He slid out of bed and grabbed his clothes, coming toward the door.

"You're going to get dressed, right?"

"Why? My room is right across from yours. And my clothes are dirty."

She shook her head. "Hang on."

She popped the door open a crack and took a peek outside. No one was in the hall. "Okay, go."

He leaned over and kissed her. "See you later."

"Okay."

He dashed across the hall and opened the door, then quickly shut it. She wondered what was going to happen if Leo was in there.

That was his problem to explain, she supposed.

She went into the bathroom and looked at her hair. Since she'd fallen asleep with it damp, it was a hot mess. At least she didn't have super-long hair anymore, so she rinsed it in the sink, dried it and flat ironed it into submission.

Much better now. Then she did her makeup, grabbed her dress and heels and put those on, along with her jewelry. All in all, she'd done it in record time.

She went downstairs and into the living room, searching for Harmony or her family. No one was in there. They weren't in the kitchen, either, so she went outside toward the wedding barn, which was just outside the front door and across the newly paved walkway. When Mom had heard Harmony and Barrett wanted the wedding here, she'd insisted the walkway be paved.

Personally, Mia was grateful for that because she would not have wanted to make this trek on gravel while wearing heels.

She made her way through the barn doors. She remembered this barn being filled with hay. Now it was bright and shiny and painted like new. The floors had also been cemented, and it was filled with chairs for tomorrow's ceremony. There was a beautiful white arbor at the front of the barn and by tomorrow the place would be filled with flowers.

"Aubry said you took a nap."

Mia turned to see her mother had come to stand beside her. "Yes."

Her mom laid her hand across her forehead. "Are you feeling all right?"

"I'm fine, Mom. I was just hot and tired after mowing, so I took a shower and laid down on the bed for a minute to close my eyes, and I guess I fell asleep."

Her mother nodded. "I'm glad you're okay."

"I'm sorry I overslept."

"It's all right. You didn't miss anything. The minister was running late so we're just about to get started."

"Oh, good."

Suzanne, the wedding planner, came up to Mia's mom.

"I think we're ready now, Lydia. I'm trying to get everyone in position, so if you can take your place, we'll get started."

Mom nodded. "All right."

All the women settled in at the back of the barn, along with Harmony's brother, Drake, who'd be walking her down the aisle since her father was deceased.

"You glow, honey," Mia said to Harmony. "Are you excited?"

Harmony laid her hand across her stomach. "Equal parts excited, can't believe this is finally happening and I might throw up."

Mia laughed. "Well, you look gorgeous. And happiness thrives on your face."

Harmony grabbed her hand and squeezed. "That's the best thing you could have said to me. I might not pass out now."

Mia laughed. There was nothing more beautiful than a bride-to-be. And Harmony was definitely beautiful. She wore a copper-colored sundress that brought out the beauty of her rich, umber skin. She might be nervous, but her genuine smile didn't show it.

So they followed Suzanne's instructions and lined up in order. Mia was first, so she started down the aisle, listening to Suzanne tell her how to walk, at what pace and where to stand once she got to the altar. She noticed Nathan sitting in one of the chairs watching it all. He gave her a wink as she took her position. Suddenly the barn got a lot warmer even though it was nicely air conditioned in there, another addition for the wedding.

The rest of the bridesmaids walked down the aisle, then Harmony with Drake, who handed her off to Barrett. Mia's eyes teared up watching her brother with Harmony. She was going to have to hold it together or she'd be a weepy mess tomorrow.

They did a run-through of walking down the aisle and the ceremony one more time. The pastor and the wedding planner seemed satisfied after that, so they were finished.

They all went to the house, where dinner was being catered. Mom always liked to cook, and Diane did, too, but Barrett and Harmony insisted the wedding preparations were stressful enough, so dinner tonight and tomorrow night were going to be catered events.

Mia had had countless conversations with her mother about this, and Mom wasn't keen on the idea, but she'd finally given in. And since Mom had already been involved in both Tucker and Aubry's, and Grant and Katrina's weddings, Mia didn't want her overwhelmed any more than she already had been with Barrett and Harmony's wedding. The last thing she needed was to be stuck in the kitchen cooking up a meal for a large group of people. She should be wandering around enjoying the company.

The caterers did a great job and the food was already spread out in the kitchen by the time they came in. Plus, there was a bar set up, which, of course, was where everyone headed first.

Mia decided on a sparkling water, since she still felt dehydrated from her time in the sun this afternoon. She noticed Nathan went for a glass of ice water instead of a beer. She made her way over to him.

"Still thirsty?"

He looked around and then leaned in. "For you? Yes."

Why was it that every time he said something sexual to her, her body went up in flames? She would have thought that since they'd already had sex a few times, she'd be immune, that the newness of it would have worn off by now.

Apparently she was not immune to Nathan Riley. She was going to have to shore up her defenses. The last thing she needed was to become emotionally attached to him. Fun and dating was one thing. Love? That was something entirely different. She wasn't ready for that.

Fortunately, Barrett came over, putting an end to that unruly thought process.

"I don't know about you two, but I'm hungry."

"That's nothing new for you," Mia said. "Aren't you nervous at all about tomorrow?"

"Nah. Marrying the woman I love? I can't wait."

Barrett's love for Harmony made Mia's heart squeeze. She leaned her head against his shoulder. "That's incredibly sweet and I love you."

He smiled down at her. "Love you, too, brat. Now we should go nudge Mom about starting the food line."

Nathan laughed. "I wouldn't object to that."

"Fine," Mia said. "I'll go tell Mom you're all starving to death and if food isn't served right now there's going to be growling and whining."

"Mostly growling," Barrett said. "Men never whine."

"Ha," she said as she walked away. She found her mother talking to Diane.

"The men are whining about eating."

"Don't they always?" Diane asked. "I swear, every time Drake is over for dinner, he's the first in line. And it's not like the boy is starving."

Mia's mom laughed. "Mine are the same way. It's all the calories they burn. It was like that when they were growing up, too."

"Tell me about it," Mia said. "It's a miracle there was ever any food left by the time a plate was passed my way."

Diane put her arm around Mia. "Harmony said the same thing.

She also accused Drake of dumping all the meat onto his plate and all that was left for her were bits and pieces that had fallen off the bone."

Mia nodded. "Sounds about right."

"Yeah, you're not starving, either," her mom said. "Come on, let's go round up Barrett and Harmony so they can be at the front of the line."

"And I'll be right behind them before the guys eat all the food."

Her mother gave her a teasing smile, but Mia hadn't been joking and she did get in line behind Harmony and Barrett. Not that she was all that hungry, but she had seen the pineapple rice on the menu and she wanted to be sure she got some, along with the chicken kabobs.

She grabbed a seat at the dining room table next to Harmony and Alyssa, Harmony's best friend and maid of honor. Lachelle, Harmony's friend from college and another bridesmaid, sat on Mia's other side. Lachelle had three-year-old twins and also worked as a coordinator for at-risk youth, so Mia spent a lot of time at dinner talking to Lachelle about her work and her family life.

"Twins and such an important job that I'm sure takes up a lot of your time," Mia said. "How do you juggle it all?"

Lachelle took a sip of iced tea, then laid her glass on the table. "Honestly? I have an amazing and supportive husband. He spends just as much time with Marcus and Mateo as I do. We share kid duties, so when he's busy, I take on more with the kids. When I have something come up, he's right there to pick up the slack. I sure couldn't do this alone."

"Sure you could," Harmony said. "You're Wonder Woman."

Lachelle laughed. "You'd like to think that, but no woman is Wonder Woman. Not a woman with twin boys, anyway. But I love my work as much as I love my husband and kids. I'm profoundly fortunate to have all these loves in my life. Someday Miss Harmony over there will find herself doing the same since she loves her work as much as she loves Barrett."

Harmony laid her fork down. "Hopefully without the twins. Not that I don't love your boys, because I do, but, honey, I'd like to have my kids one at a time."

Mia laughed. "I'm sure that would be easier."

"What about you, Mia?" Alyssa asked. "Any hot guys you're hiding from us? All the Cassidys seem to be settling down. Are you next?"

Mia shook her head. "The only love of my life right now is my business. It's all I can handle at the moment. Men will have to take a backseat to that."

She realized as she said the words that Nathan was sitting at the far end of the table. He'd been in conversation with her dad and Flynn. But as she glanced over, she saw he'd been looking at her. She wasn't sure if he heard what she said, but he wasn't smiling. He resumed his conversation with her father.

Surely he hadn't heard. And what if he had? It wouldn't have hurt his feelings in the least, right? Sure, they were in a relationship. But it was a fun, uncomplicated, having-sex kind of relationship.

And nothing more.

But after dinner, she found a minute to get him alone.

"Were you listening in on my dinner conversation with Harmony and her friends?"

He frowned. "What? No. Why?"

She shrugged. "Never mind. No reason."

She started to walk away, but he grasped her arm. "What was it you didn't want me to hear?"

"It's stupid, really."

"Mia, nothing you say is stupid. Tell me."

"Alyssa asked me if I was steady with any guy. I told her the only love of my life right now was my work. And at that point you and I connected visually and I could swear you were shooting daggers at me, like you heard what I was saying and you were mad."

He laughed. "Why would I be mad at you about that? We aren't in love, Mia. We're just having some fun. Right?"

"Right." She laughed, too.

He swept his hands down her arms. "Relax. This is supposed to be light and easy between us. So don't stress about it."

"I won't."

But later, she played their conversation over in her head.

We aren't in love, Mia. We're just having some fun.

It was exactly what she'd wanted to hear. What she'd needed from him. She should have been relieved.

So why, when he'd said the words, did her stomach tighten and her heart feel crushed?

Dammit. She was not falling in love with Nathan. She would not allow that to happen.

TWENTY-FOUR

MIA LOVED WEDDING DAYS. SHE'D GOTTEN UP THIS morning totally refreshed, chalking up the disappointment over her conversation with Nathan last night to exhaustion.

They were exactly where she wanted them to be. Where he wanted them to be, too. Having sex and having fun with it, with no emotional entanglements. She wasn't falling in love with him. He was her best friend and they were slowly building on their relationship by dating. She needed to just have fun and go with it and not stress over every little thing. Nathan certainly wasn't taking it all so seriously, and neither should she.

More certain than ever of where they stood, she dismissed last night's weird emotional state, determined to soak in all the love from Barrett and Harmony's day.

The guys had all taken off for Austin to go play golf, which left the women alone to enjoy the day. The wedding was scheduled for six p.m., so they had massages scheduled, followed by manicures and pedicures. They also had hair and makeup artists coming in. It was going to be a fun spa day.

Mia was looking forward to being pampered.

First they all gathered in the kitchen to make breakfast. It was a free-for-all of women chatting while peeling potatoes, breaking eggs and slicing fruit. Mia sipped on her coffee while talking with Katrina about her last photo shoot.

"It was beautiful. We were off the Amalfi Coast. Not only was the scenery breathtaking, but I could spend a week just wandering through the history of the place. I told Grant we have to vacation there during the off-season."

"I've looked at pictures," Mia said. "It's lush and breathtaking, and I agree with you about the history alone. Maybe I'll hide in your luggage."

Katrina laughed. "As work goes, it didn't suck. But of course I didn't get nearly enough time to play tourist. I want to take the kids with me. I think Leo would love it for the history and Anya would enjoy it for the food."

"I'm down with any place that has amazing food," Anya said from across the kitchen island.

Amelia put her arm around Anya. "I love this girl."

Mia smiled.

Breakfast ended up being quite a feast, from the croissants Anya made to the eggs Benedict Amelia had put together. Then there were fried potatoes and fruit salad and sausages along with freshly squeezed orange juice they used to make mimosas. Mia sat at the table and thought about what an amazing family she had, only enriched by these incredible women who'd fallen in love with her brothers.

She was very lucky.

"Who's minding your interior design business while you're

busy getting married and taking a short honeymoon, Harmony?" Amelia asked.

"I have an incredible assistant who's scary good at what she does," Harmony said. "Rosalie has it all under control."

"So you won't worry something will fall through the cracks while you're gone?" Mia asked.

"You mean like *you* are right now?" Mia's mom asked.

"Maybe." She wouldn't mention how many calls she'd made already, or how many times she'd e-mailed everyone at the office. She had the utmost trust in her staff, but MHC was her baby.

"Oh, I was totally like you when my business first started out," Harmony said. "It was hard for me to even leave for an hour to go to a dental appointment without freaking out that the whole place would go under while I was gone."

Mia nodded.

"After a while, you start to realize that you hired awesome staff for a reason," Harmony said. "Because they *are* awesome, and because they can do the job. And then you start to relax knowing your company is in good hands."

"I know you're right and I have the best people at MHC. But still, it is hard to be away from our babies."

Her mother patted her hand. "You know that right now Monique is cracking the whip on your amazing staff. She has it all under control."

"I know. She's sending me regular updates and all is as it should be. It's still hard to let go."

Harmony smiled. "It'll get easier with every month. I promise."

Mia hoped so. She didn't want to spend the rest of her life worrying about her company every time she had to leave town. But they were in the middle of negotiating some very big deals at the moment, and she felt like she needed to be there. But she also knew there were going to be times like this, and her team could handle it.

"I'm wondering if we could just all live together here on the ranch and do this every morning," Alyssa said. "I mean, I get that some of you have husbands that you might miss and all, but this is pretty awesome."

Mia swirled her mimosa around in the champagne glass. "I could get used to it."

"I don't know," Aubry said. "I'd miss the sex."

Aubry looked over at Mia's mom. "Sorry, Lydia."

Mia's mom laughed. "It's okay, Aubry. I already knew you two were having sex."

Aubry laughed.

"I mean, the men are great and all," Katrina said, "and you can't deny the sex is outstanding. But sisterhood? No one is going to understand you as well as another woman can."

Anya held up her glass. "I'll drink to that."

Katrina frowned. "Who put champagne in her glass?"

Mia grinned. "I did. She's close enough to twenty-one and she's not driving anywhere today. She's entitled to one mimosa."

Anya cracked a smile. "It hardly has any champagne in it, and you let me have wine in Paris, Katrina."

"I did. But that was Paris. And that's all you get today."

Anya rolled her eyes. "Yeah, okay, Sis."

It must be totally fun to have a sister. But Mia realized she had several now, and she couldn't be happier about that.

After breakfast, they cleaned up the dishes. The massage and mani-pedi staff arrived with all their equipment. Mom had them set up in the dining room, living room and several of the bedrooms.

Mia had her manicure and pedicure first. She sat side by side with Aubry. The two of them were alone in her mom's bedroom since it had a lot of space. And now her feet were relaxing in a warm bubbly spa while she was getting her nails done.

"So," Aubry said. "Want to tell me what's going on with you and Nathan?"

She knew Aubry would eventually bring that up. "Nothing's going on. We're just having some fun."

"You two have known each other a long time. Were you friends all through college?"

Mia nodded. "Yes. But nothing was going on back then, either. We're just friends."

Aubry raised a brow. "I had guy friends in college and medical school. I never had sex with any of them."

"Maybe you missed out, then." She gave Aubry a grin.

Aubry laughed. "Ew. No, I did not. Trust me."

"You're only saying that because you're married and totally in love with my brother. Back then, some of your guy friends were probably hot."

"Okay, maybe they were. But I think we were all so stressed about medical school and grades and just trying to keep our sanity that was all we could think about."

"Oh, come on, Aubry. You never had sex while you were in school?"

"I did. And had one relationship that ended badly, so I focused on school instead of guys."

Mia nodded. "I understand that. That's why I'm not having a relationship. I have my business to think about and that's occupying most of my thoughts."

"Your one true love?" Aubry gave her a wry smile.

"Yes. That's it exactly."

"Then it makes sense for you to have sex with your best friend."

Mia looked down at the women doing their manicures. They were good at their jobs, because they were focused on their tasks and, while Mia was sure they were listening in, their facial expressions betrayed nothing of their thoughts.

"It's working for both of us right now. Nathan is just about to start the football season and he has a lot of pressure on him, too. Keeping things simple between us is the best way to go."

Aubry's nails were finished, so she leaned back in her chair. "Sure. As long as neither one of you gets emotionally involved."

"Right. And that's not going to happen. We both know what we're doing."

Aubry let out a soft laugh.

"What?" Mia asked.

"Oh, nothing. I'm sure you totally have it together. Just like Tucker and I did."

Mia frowned. "Hey, that's not funny. You two are married now."

Aubry gave her a knowing smile. "Exactly. And so are Grant and Katrina and now Flynn and Amelia are engaged. Oh, and of course Barrett and Harmony are getting married today. And you know what the common thread was binding all of us together?"

She didn't want to know the answer, but she knew she had to ask. "What?"

"None of us wanted to get involved. None of us were in the market for love or a relationship. And none of us planned on falling in love." Aubry held out her hands. "Look at all of us now, Mia. So you know, best-laid plans and all."

Mia lifted her chin. "That's not going to happen with Nathan and me. We've been friends for a long time. How we feel about each other is different."

"Uh-huh."

She did not like Aubry's tone. "What's that supposed to mean?"

"It means that once you introduce sex into a relationship, it changes everything."

Her manicurist had just finished with her, and the team was

taking a break before pedicures, so Mia shifted in her chair. "That's exactly what I told Nathan. Only my reasoning for keeping sex out of our relationship was because I was afraid to lose our friendship."

"I don't think that should be your biggest concern. But I do understand it. I know how close you and Nathan are. If it were me and I had a guy friend as my BFF, I'd be hesitant to have sex with him, too. Because like I said, sex changes everything."

Mia sighed. "Dammit, Aubry."

Aubry laughed. "Sorry. But it's true. It changes the entire dynamic of your relationship. However, I will say this. If anyone can manage it, it's you, Mia."

"Thanks. I'm going to try my damndest."

She thought about—or more like worried about—what Aubry had said. In fact, she pondered it all through her pedicure. By the time she was on the table for her massage she was a tight bundle of tension and the massage was more painful than enjoyable because she wasn't able to relax.

"Try deep, cleansing breaths," her massage therapist said. "In through the nose, out through the mouth."

She did. She settled into the massage, determined to fall asleep if possible. But then she thought about Nathan, about all the things Aubry said and how things would change in her relationship with him.

She had been wary of introducing sex into their relationship, though she had to admit she was having a great time with him now that they had. The sex was amazing, and being able to see him more often, to touch him and be intimate with him had sparked desires in her that had lain dormant for far too long.

Nathan was an amazing lover, so generous, so passionate.

But at what cost? She was always going to worry about their relationship ending, about something going wrong between them.

Dammit. She could not relax. She even practiced her yoga

breathing, tuned in to the gentle music, even tried to fall asleep. Nothing worked because she couldn't clear her head. She was tense. Tense, tense, tense. She felt bad for her massage therapist, who Mia was sure took it personally.

Mia got up at the end of her session.

"I have a lot on my mind."

Evita, her therapist, sighed. "I can typically work with that. I'm not sure why I couldn't release the tight knots in your muscles."

"It's not your fault. But thank you. It was a lovely massage."

She got dressed and left the room, hoping Evita's next client was someone a lot more relaxed. She passed Harmony on the way out.

"How are you doing, honey?" Mia asked.

Harmony grinned. "I'm having a fantastic day. How was the massage therapist? I'm next with her."

"She's amazing and you're going to love her."

"I can't wait. I'll see you soon."

Evita was going to have a great time giving a massage to the happy bride-to-be.

Mia went to her room and took a shower to wash off the massage oil, then slipped into a sundress. She went downstairs and found a group of women in the kitchen. There were small sandwiches and snacks laid out—her mom and Diane's work, no doubt. Given the stress and activity of the day, her mom wouldn't want anyone to get hungry. Mia grabbed a few carrots to nibble on and made herself some green tea. Maybe that would relax her.

She pulled up a chair next to Amelia.

"Did you get your massage?" she asked.

Amelia nodded. "It was heavenly. How about you?"

"Yes. It was perfect." She wasn't about to tell anyone how bound up with tension she was.

"What time is hair and makeup?" Katrina asked.

"According to the schedule, they should arrive around three."

She picked up her phone. She had an hour to kill, so she took her tea and went upstairs to her room. She grabbed her planner and sat in the chair next to the window. The sun was bright, and the day was hot as blazes, but the air conditioning made the room perfectly comfortable.

She opened her planner and flipped to a blank page, then settled in to make some notes. But it wasn't work that was on her mind, it was Nathan. Nathan and her, and their friendship.

She divided the page into two columns, titling one "Friendship" and the other one "Sex."

On the Friendship side, she listed all the things that mattered to her: trust, length of their friendship, the fact she could count on Nathan for everything, that she could tell him all her secrets and that their friendship had, for the most part, been non-sexual, which had made it uncomplicated.

On the Sex side, she wrote "Fun, Adventurous, A Tension Release, Hot, Steamy," and then smiled as she wrote, "The Best I've Ever Had."

She tapped her pen against the paper. "Isn't that the damn truth?"

On the Sex side she also wrote, "Complicates Things. What If It Ends? Could End Our Friendship." And then there were the scary photographers, who'd been stalking them here and there. She still couldn't make sense of what they wanted, but if word of their relationship got out, it could spell bad tidings for both of them. And then there was the family issue. She didn't need her family nosing around her relationship with Nathan. With the season about to start, the last thing Nathan needed was to be at odds with one of her brothers.

Her brothers had always been protective of her. She had no idea how any of them would react to her seeing Nathan. Plus Flynn played on the same team with Nathan. So she added "Work Complication for Nathan" to the Sex side.

She sighed. So many unknowns. Which was why she put three underlines under "Uncomplicated" in the Friendship column.

She compared lists, searching for clarity but finding none. Of course their friendship would always come first. She could live without the sex. She'd done that plenty of times. The problem was, she was now having a sexual relationship with Nathan.

And that's where *un*complicated had become *complicated*.

She sighed, closed her planner and headed downstairs. It was time to put thoughts of her oh-so-complicated relationship with Nathan away for now. Because it was wedding day for Barrett and Harmony, and that's the only thing she intended to think about for the rest of the day.

TWENTY-FIVE

SO FAR, IT HAD BEEN AN AWESOME DAY. THE BEST
thing about not being involved in a wedding was that you could
kick back and relax.

Nathan had played golf with all the guys this morning, which
was a blast. He'd shot a decent game, so at least no one had been
able to give him shit about that. He mentally thanked his dad for
dragging him around golf courses from the time he was a teenager. At the time, he hadn't appreciated it, but Dad had always told
him golf was a social game as well as a game of skill and patience,
and that someday all those lessons would come in handy.

He'd been right. His dad was always right, dammit.

They'd had lunch in Austin, then driven back to the ranch to
get ready for the wedding.

Since he had no official wedding duties, he asked what he could
do to help. Easton told him he could assist in supervising the
set-up of the reception barn since Lydia was busy getting her hair

done and she'd handed him a clipboard saying it was essential everything be done right.

"So you want me to handle this?" Nathan asked, looking over a
checklist.

Easton slanted a grin in his direction. "Yeah. Because I have to
handle the liquor."

"The drinking of it or the stocking of it?"

Easton laughed. "I wish we could start drinking. But I don't
think Barrett would be very happy with me if I was inebriated before his wedding even started. So I'll settle on supervising the
stocking. With maybe one beer."

Nathan smiled. "Okay, what do you need me to do?"

"Just make sure everything on this list gets checked off. And, I
guess, it's supposed to look good."

Nathan gave Easton a wide-eyed look. "How am I supposed to
know if it looks good?"

Easton slapped him on the back. "Hell if I know. Good luck, kid."

So now he was watching people set up tables and chairs and put
down linen tablecloths and flower centerpieces and whatnot. Definitely things that were out of his wheelhouse, but hey, he had a
checklist, so he supposed he was good to go. He just hoped these
people knew what they were doing, because if something got
screwed up, he was the one with the damn clipboard.

He wished Mia was here. In fact . . .

He pulled his phone out of his back pocket and texted her.

Where R U?

He waited. Five minutes later he got a return text.

Getting makeup done. What's up?

Dammit.

He replied with, Nothing. Have fun.

She replied right away with, Do you need me?

She had no idea how much he needed her right now, but if he

said he did, she'd come running. And it was hot as fuck out here and her makeup would melt.

He could handle this shit.

So he replied with, No, I'm good. C U L8r

He took his clipboard and wandered the barn, counting all the tables. They were all up and in place according to the plan, so he checked that off. Then he did the same with chairs. Tablecloths had all been put on. Next he had to do the place settings.

What the fuck did he know about place settings?

"What did you need?"

He spun around to see Mia standing there. She was gorgeous. Her hair was perfect, like it always was, and her makeup looked— he supposed, like makeup. He didn't know, since she always looked pretty. But the sundress bared her shoulders and her neck and he really wanted to put his mouth on her neck.

"Should you be out here?" he asked.

She frowned at him. "Why shouldn't I be out here?"

"Because you had your makeup done and it's hot."

She rolled her eyes. "I'm not a freaking snowflake, Nathan. Now what's going on?"

He pointed to the clipboard. "Your dad put me in charge of this after your mom put him in charge of it and I'm not sure I know what I'm supposed to do."

She took the clipboard from him. "Let me see it."

She scanned the list, then looked over the barn. She started wandering around to inspect a few of the tables. She handed the clipboard back to him. "It looks great. The team knows what they're doing, so your job is to just stand here in case anyone has questions. And if they do, text me and I'll ask my mom."

He was so relieved. "Thanks. I didn't want to screw it up."

She grasped his arm, lifted up on her toes and pressed a kiss to his lips. "That's sweet. I have to go. See you later."

"Okay. Oh, and, Mia?"

She had started to walk away, but stopped. "Yes?"

"You look really pretty."

Her lips curved. "Thanks, Nathan. You look hot and sweaty."

He grinned. "Thanks. Later, Mia."

She wandered off and he relaxed into his job, figuring all he had to do was monitor things. Now that the stress was off of him, he appreciated how nice the barn looked. Even though the reception was taking place in the barn, the tables were round and sturdy, and they'd been fancied up by the nice linens. Bright lights were strung over the wood beams, and they'd cleared a dance floor at the front, where there was a long table set up for the wedding party.

It should be a fun night. They just had to get Barrett and Harmony married so they could get to the party portion of the evening.

Nathan was more than ready to party.

TWENTY-SIX

MIA STOOD AT THE FRONT OF THE BARN AND WATCHED her brother Barrett declare his love for Harmony. She blinked back tears as he recited his vows to love and honor Harmony for the rest of his life.

She'd cried tears of happiness for each of her brothers at their weddings and for the women she'd grown to love like sisters. She loved Harmony just as much and couldn't wait to welcome her into the Cassidy fold.

Her brothers had all made wonderful choices in women and as Barrett and Harmony sealed their bond with a kiss, she sniffled and smiled.

After the ceremony, they took what Mia thought was about a million photos before they made their way from the wedding barn to the reception barn. She was happy to walk in there first to the cheers of the crowd, then stand in a line with the other bridesmaids and groomsmen as Barrett and Harmony were introduced as husband and wife to wild cheers and applause.

Then they had their first dance, and it was so sweepingly romantic. Harmony looked beautiful. She'd chosen a very simple A-line wedding gown with a sweetheart neckline that clung to her curves and looked stunning on her. She'd worn her hair up, a few tendrils curled around her face. The only jewelry she had on were her mother's pearl necklace and matching earrings. Simple, yet exquisite. She glowed.

Oh, and Barrett looked nice, too, she thought with a grin.

After the bride and groom finished up, the bridal party danced, which was kind of hilarious since Mia was partnered up with one of the defensive linemen from Barrett's team who towered over her by at least a foot and a half. But he was so sweet to her and so cautious as they moved around the floor. He didn't step on her toes once, which was awesome considering he had enormous feet.

"I practiced with my wife," Jacob said while they danced. "She told me if I crushed your toes she'd never speak to me again."

Mia laughed. "You're doing great, so I think you're safe."

After the dance, her obligations as a bridesmaid were mostly over. She had to sit at the head table with the bridal party during the toasts, and then there was dinner, which was spectacular. She was happy that dinner was catered, even though Barrett and Harmony had kept the guest list small. Only family and close friends had been invited and it ended up being intimate and sweet rather than ostentatious and crowded.

It was lovely and her brother looked happier than she'd ever seen him.

She got up from the table to stretch her legs and walk off dinner. She made her way to the bar to grab a cocktail.

She'd had champagne for the toast, but otherwise she'd avoided alcohol so she could stay clearheaded today. Now she was ready to party. She decided on a dirty martini. She took the glass and walked away from the bar, wandering about the crowd.

She spotted her uncle Elijah dancing with Diane. The deejay was playing a slow song, and the two of them were bundled up so tightly together that it was like they were one body.

Oh, there was definitely something romantic going on between the two of them.

"I think my mama might be in love with your uncle."

She turned to see Harmony standing next to her. "I think you might be right. Isn't it great?"

Harmony's lips curved. "It sure is. Your uncle is an amazing man. He's flown out to Tampa a few times and stayed at Mama's house. They get along well and Mama deserves to be happy. She's been focused on work and on me and hasn't taken the time to do anything for herself for as long as I can remember. It's time she has some romance—some love—in her life."

Mia draped an arm around Harmony's shoulders. "I agree. They seem happy together."

"I think so, too. Mama said Elijah would be willing to move to Tampa. Mama really doesn't want to leave there. It's home. And he likes it out there."

"That's awesome, Harmony. So maybe before long we'll have another wedding in the family."

Mia saw tears glisten in Harmony's eyes. "Nothing would make me happier."

She saw Barrett approach and put his arm around Harmony, then glare at Mia.

"Did you make my wife cry?"

Mia rolled her eyes. "I did not."

"These are happy tears," Harmony said. "I've been crying them all day, in case you haven't noticed."

"I understand why you'd cry. It's pretty magical, being married to me."

Mia made a gagging motion. "I might throw up."

Harmony laughed.

"Suzanne said we have to do the flower and garter thing," Barrett said.

"Oh, okay." Harmony squeezed her hand. "You'd better be there to catch the bouquet."

Not a chance. "Definitely."

She watched them head off, Barrett taking Harmony's hand. She pivoted and started back to her table, then spotted Nathan standing alone by the front of the barn.

Changing direction, she went to where he was leaning against the double-wide doors. He looked magnificent in his dark gray suit and his burgundy tie, his crisp white shirt making a nice contrast.

Of course, when didn't he look amazing? Whether he was in jeans or dressed up like he was tonight, Nathan always made her catch her breath.

She shook her head, realizing she had it so bad for that man.

The doors were closed to keep the air conditioning in, but they'd put up clear doors to let in what light was left of the day.

"Pondering great things?" she asked.

He pushed off the wall and turned to face her, offering up a smile. "Nah, just taking a breather. You look beautiful."

She looked down at her coral dress. She'd been a bridesmaid on more than one occasion. Some dresses she loved. Some she'd hated. This one she loved. It was comfortable and pretty and she could move in it. Both the color and the cut were flattering and she'd wanted to kiss Harmony right on the mouth after she'd chosen them. Every one of the bridesmaids looked like a million bucks in their dresses. What bridesmaid could complain about that?

"Thank you. You look pretty hot yourself."

So hot, in fact, she wanted to touch him. But she was also mindful of the fact there were over a hundred people nearby, so she kept her hands to herself.

"How goes the wedding festivities and your duties as bridesmaid?"

"Duties are complete."

Just then, the deejay announced that Barrett and Harmony would be tossing out the bouquet and garter.

"Shouldn't you be up there fighting for the bouquet?" Nathan asked.

Mia twirled her olives on a stick around her martini. "Not on your life. What about you? Anxious to grab that garter?"

"Only if you're wearing one."

Her nipples tightened at the thought of him lifting her dress in search of a garter. "Now I might have to go steal it from the winner."

"Yeah? And what if it's one of your brothers?"

"Well, three of my brothers are now married and therefore ineligible. And if it's Flynn . . . well, dammit."

He laughed, then turned his head to the front of the barn when squeals of laughter and applause were heard.

Mia looked, too, as one of the wedding guests caught the bouquet. It was Harmony's best friend, Alyssa.

Mia smiled. "That should make Harmony happy."

"Here. Hold my beer."

"Changed your mind about the garter?"

"You could say that."

He shrugged out of his suit jacket and slung it over a nearby chair, then headed into the crowd of anxious men waiting for the garter.

Mia made her way to the front of the barn to watch.

Nathan had taken up position toward the back. Not a good sign. The garter didn't weigh much, and wouldn't fly like the heavier bouquet. But she mentally crossed her fingers for him anyway.

If anything, it would be fun to watch. She took a sip of her martini and got in closer.

"My money is on Flynn," Amelia said, coming up to stand next to her. "I told him if he caught the garter I'd set a date for our wedding."

Mia smiled. "Is that a point of contention?"

She shrugged. "He's in a hurry. I'm not."

Mia laughed.

Barrett took the garter off Harmony. She knew that wasn't Harmony's keeper garter, it was a spare for the throwaway.

Barrett stood with his back to the crowd of men, who all jostled each other out of the way. Nathan and Flynn elbowed each other, then a few other guys got into the mix.

"It's a good thing Aubry's a doctor," Mia said. "We might need her after this."

Amelia snickered.

And when Barrett threw it, the damn garter sailed like it had a football attached to it.

That's when Nathan pushed his way into the crowd.

"Oh, my God," Mia said.

Nathan caught the garter. And then he was tackled to the ground like he actually had a football in his hand.

Amelia took a sip of her wine. "This is even more entertaining than a football game."

Mia laughed. "Right?"

Everyone laughed and applauded when Nathan stood, holding the garter up in his right hand.

"Guess I don't have to pick a wedding date yet," Amelia said. "Flynn will be so disappointed."

"You're so mean, Amelia."

"Aren't I? Now I'm going to refill my wineglass."

Amelia wandered off, and Mia watched as Nathan and Alyssa

had their photos taken with the newlyweds. When they were finished, Nathan made his way back to her. She handed his beer to him.

"Nicely done."

"Thanks. I do like to win."

"And you can take that winning attitude into this season with the Sabers."

He took a long swallow of his beer. "Now you sound like my coach."

She laughed.

"Okay, now come with me."

She arched a brow. "Where are we going?"

"Someplace where we can be alone."

She looked around. No one was watching them, so she laid her martini down on the table and followed Nathan outside. He took her to the barn where the wedding ceremony had been held. It was dark in there. The lights had been turned out, but all the chairs were still set up.

Nathan turned on the light switch and the room was bathed in all the beautiful lights from earlier.

He took her hand and led her to the back row of chairs.

"Take a seat."

She did, and he knelt in front of her.

"You aren't going to propose to me, are you?"

He laughed. "No."

Instead, he pulled out the pretty beige-and-white garter. "This belongs on you."

She inhaled a deep breath as he swept her dress up over her knees, then smoothed his hands over her legs.

"You know, as soon as we started talking about it, I had a visual in my head of you wearing this." He slipped it over her right shoe then up along her calf, her knee, and slid it just above her knee, his fingers dancing along her skin.

She shivered, passion bursting within her like a newly formed star. Breathing became difficult as he teased her thighs with light touches of his fingers.

"Turn off the lights and lock the door," she said.

He got up and locked the door, then flipped off the light switch, casting the barn in darkness. She heard his footsteps on the concrete, but she couldn't see him.

Until she felt his warm breath on her cheek, and his lips brush hers. She reached up to caress his face. He wrapped his hand around the nape of her neck and kissed her, this time more deeply, pressing his mouth to hers.

She moaned, flicking her tongue against his. He pulled her from the chair and put his arms around her, their bodies molding together in a heated embrace. Mia wished they were alone somewhere so she could get naked with him. But even in the main house, someone could walk in, someone could hear them. For now, this would have to be good enough.

His mouth was on hers, his hands roaming her body, and nothing was going to stop this runaway train of hot passion. Not if she had anything to say about it.

So when he sat her down on the chair and spread her legs, she was on board. He lifted her dress and smoothed his hands up her legs again, taking his time to map every inch of her, his fingertips making their way along her thighs. She leaned back in the chair as he swept his thumb over her, rubbing back and forth over her sex. He gently removed her underwear and she had no idea what he did with it.

She didn't care. Not at the moment. She wanted an orgasm. She wanted his mouth on her pussy. That was her need and only Nathan could give that to her.

Now all she heard was her own labored breathing. And Nathan's, too. And when his mouth took over for his fingers, she gasped, gripping the back of the chair next to her like an anchor in a storm-tossed sea.

He bathed her sex with hot, wet licks of his tongue, making her writhe in the chair until she twisted upward, gasping as sensation overcame her.

"Nathan. You're going to make me come."

She felt out of control as a blast of orgasm slammed into her so fast and furious she grabbed on to his arm for balance. Nathan stood, pulled a condom out of his pocket and unzipped his pants. He knelt and cupped her butt, then slid inside of her while she was still quivering from her climax.

His cock swelled within her, sending her into a wild spiral as he tunneled in and out of her. She dug her nails into his shirt and held on, her eyes adjusted to the darkness enough to soak in the passion in his eyes.

He kissed her. She tasted herself on his lips, which only made her arch against him, wrapping her legs around him so he could drive deeper and harder within her.

She came again, and this time, he groaned and went with her, both of them shuddering against each other.

He laid his forehead against her, then kissed her, this time a gentling kiss.

Mia trailed her finger along his jaw. "This is getting to be a habit with us."

"What's that?"

"Hiding out in locked rooms having sex."

He laughed. "At least this time the room was bigger than a coat closet."

"True."

They disengaged, and Nathan found some paper towels for them to clean up. It was the best they could do for now since there wasn't a bathroom in the barn.

Nathan went over to the door and flipped on the light switch.

He handed her her underwear and she slipped it back on, then straightened her dress. "How do I look?"

"Like I want to undress you and do this again."

Her lips curved. "Good enough, then. I'm going to head over to the house."

"I'll go with you."

He unlocked the door and inched it open. "No one's out here."

They walked outside and toward the house. Nathan ducked into the downstairs bathroom, and Mia went up to her room. She brushed her hair and fixed her makeup, then went back down. She noticed Nathan was nowhere to be found, so he must have gone back to the reception.

But as she was heading toward the door, she heard her mother's voice in the kitchen.

"You two aren't fooling anyone, you know."

She halted mid-stride, winced, then turned and walked into the kitchen. "Oh, hi, Mom. Were you talking to me?"

Her mother was sitting at the kitchen island sipping on a cup of coffee. "There's no one else in here, Mia, and you know damn well I'm talking to you. I saw you and Nathan sneak in here."

"You did, huh?"

"Yes, I did. So what's going on with you two?"

"Nothing's going on."

Mia got the infamous Lydia Cassidy "Don't Bullshit Me" look that had always been typically reserved for Mia's brothers when they'd tried to get away with something.

"Okay, fine. We're . . . hanging out. Having fun together. It's nothing more than that."

"Uh-huh." Her mom continued to sip her coffee, which irritated Mia, so she came over and pulled up a chair on the island next to her.

"What do you mean, 'Uh-huh'?"

"It means that I've watched you two over the past couple of days. I've been watching you two for years. It's more than just hanging out. It's always been more than that."

"Mom, we're friends. We've always been friends. And, trust me, it's nothing more than that."

Her mother took another sip of coffee, then said, "Uh-huh."

"Dammit, Mom. We're friends." Mia looked around before continuing. "We just happen to be friends who are currently having sex."

Her mother shot that all-knowing look across the bow of her coffee cup. "And that doesn't complicate your friendship at all, does it?"

Mom was the second person who'd brought that up this week. "I don't know. Maybe. We're trying *not* to let it get complicated. Why does it have to be complicated?"

Her mother shrugged. "I don't know. Because sex is a complicated thing, and because it's impossible to mix sex and friendship without it getting emotional?"

Mia frowned, irritated by the cross-examination. "Quit getting all lawyerly with me. It is not impossible. We've been handling it just fine so far."

Her mother smoothed her hand over Mia's arm. "I just don't want you to get hurt."

"I am not going to get hurt."

"Okay. You're a smart, capable woman, Mia. I believe you know what you're doing."

"Thanks, Mom."

"But if you ever need me—for advice, complaints, a shoulder to cry on—anything at all. You know I'm always here for you."

Mia wanted to object, to tell her mother that her life was going just perfectly and she had nothing to complain about. She wasn't going to screw up her friendship with Nathan. She had this totally under control.

Mia laid her head on her mother's shoulder. "I know. You'll always be in my corner, no matter what. I love you, Mom."

"I love you, too, Mia."

TWENTY-SEVEN

TRAINING CAMP HAD BEEN GOING WELL THE PAST TWO weeks, actually better than Nathan expected. Offense was clicking, and he'd felt from the first day as if he belonged. He had to thank his offensive linemen and receivers for that. They never once made him feel like an outsider, or that they had any regrets that his dad was no longer leading the team.

They looked to him for leadership, and he was going to give it to them.

They'd worked a few practice sessions with the L.A. team, and even though it hadn't been a real game situation, it was better than running drills with his own team. It had made him even more charged up for the season to start. With the first preseason game coming up this weekend against Seattle, he was amped and ready to get rolling.

His least favorite part was all the reporters hanging around. The best part? The fans and autograph sessions. After his shower today, he did press first and handled all the typical questions about how the team was doing, how he felt heading into the season. The same questions he'd been getting for the past couple of weeks.

"Have you spoken to your dad recently?" one of the journalists asked.

"Every day."

"Does he give you advice about how to handle the team?"

Nathan was used to this question, too. It irritated him, but his dad had actually given him a lot of good advice on how to handle the sports media. He'd said to be kind, and give short answers. So he smiled at the reporter. "No. He told me when he retired to handle the job like it was mine, not his. That's what I've been doing."

"We've seen photos of you with Mia Cassidy, the daughter of Easton Cassidy and your teammate Flynn's sister. Anything going on there?"

After the photos that had been circulating, he'd been expecting that question.

"Mia and I went to college together. We're friends and of course she's Flynn's sister. Since she also works in San Francisco, she hangs out with us. Nothing more."

Since there was no bait to hook on that question, they moved back to questions about his work ethic, how training had been going and the like.

Kids were the best, and they were excited to spend time with him. He liked hanging out with them, too. The adults were great and supportive for the most part, though he'd occasionally get as much grilling from fans as he did from the media.

"Do you think you'll be as good as your dad?"

"How nervous are you about the first game?"

"How do you think you'll feel if you screw this up?"

Yeah, no pressure.

There were also several women in the mix of fans. Some were

legit fans and their enthusiasm was great. And then there were those who Nathan could tell were hanging out for a chance to hook up with him. The flirting and the way they touched him was a surefire clue that they wanted more than just a photo op or an autograph. He'd learned a long time ago to be polite, but not engage in any flirtation. Because first, photographers were always hanging out at these autograph sessions, and second, there was only one woman he was interested in.

They hadn't seen much of each other the past couple of weeks. Since they got back from Texas, Mia had been slammed with work and he'd been busy with practice. This week he'd been in L.A. for the games, though they'd texted a lot and had a few phone calls. He'd just returned yesterday, and then he'd had practice today. He wanted to see her.

When he finished up the autograph session, he texted Mia.

What are you doing?

She texted right back. Up to my eyeballs in contracts. How did practice go?

He smiled as he made his way to his car and sent her another text. Good. Wanna hang out tonight?

She replied with, Sure. Have some things to wrap up here so I'll be a few more hours. How about pizza night?

He sent her a reply. Sounds great. Text me when you're home.

He tossed his phone on the center console and started the engine, then smiled.

Yeah, he was excited about seeing Mia tonight.

TWENTY-EIGHT

MIA HAD THE WORST HEADACHE. SHE'D GONE OVER A particularly difficult contract with MHC's attorney, still not certain they were going to be able to come to terms with Roland Green. Some of his requirements were outrageous and she wasn't going to agree to them.

But dammit, she wanted to sign this guy. He was an up-and-coming basketball star and she knew they could do great things for his career. But they were a management company, not ass kissers, and she wasn't going to allow her staff to be at his beck and call at all hours of the day and night.

She rubbed her temple and propped her feet on her sofa, wishing she could soak in a hot tub and sip on a glass of wine and totally forget about this day. But she'd texted Nathan when she got home and he was on his way over. Which was probably a better idea anyway. She needed the distraction so she didn't spend the evening alone dwelling over the problem.

Since she was still in her work clothes, she went upstairs and changed into a pair of shorts and a T-shirt. She thought about doing thirty minutes of yoga, then realized it would only make her pounding head worse, so she went back downstairs and headed straight for the chardonnay she'd opened yesterday. She poured herself a nice tall glass, then went into the living room and propped her feet up on the table while she sipped the wine.

Oh, yes. This was good. She rested her head against the back of the sofa, closed her eyes and took several more swallows of wine.

Maybe she should institute a wine hour at work. That could definitely be beneficial, especially on days like today. Of course, if she did that, they'd all be drunk by noon and that might be bad for productivity. Then again, think of the employee loyalty. She'd probably win some kind of national award.

Her lips curved.

The doorbell rang, so she got up to answer it. She hadn't realized how much she missed seeing Nathan until he stood there at her front door wearing dark jeans and a very soft-looking gray T-shirt. He was tanned from practicing outside, his dark hair falling over his forehead.

She did not want to feel the things she felt for him, but it had been two weeks. She knew they were both professionals and busy. Nevertheless there it was, that pang of feeling, of the need to wrap her arms—and legs—around him and make him hers.

So dangerous.

"Hey, come on in."

She shut the door behind him, trying to act nonchalant about this driving need to climb all over him.

But then he pulled her into his arms and kissed her—a long, deep, soul-shattering kiss that left her breathless, and those mental walls she'd tried to construct around her emotions came crumbling down.

"I missed you," he said.

Everything inside of her squeezed tight, and warning bells clanged loud in her head.

Don't get your heart involved, Mia.

Right. That was getting more and more difficult every time they were together.

"I missed you, too. I'm having a glass of wine. Would you like a beer?"

"No, thanks."

"What? Are you sick?"

He laughed. "No. Just trying to leave the beer for maybe once a week now that we're into the season. I'll take a glass of ice water, though."

"Oh, that's right. You don't drink much when you play. I can't believe I forgot that."

She took her wineglass into the kitchen and refilled it, put ice and water into a glass for Nathan, then brought it into the living room and handed it to him

"Thanks. That's a fairly good-sized pour for you. Is that glass number two? Three? Four?"

She laughed and sat next to him on the sofa. "Two. I had a shit day."

He leaned back on the sofa. "Tell me about it."

"A difficult client is being ridiculously demanding with contractual items and I don't know that we'll be able to come to terms. Which is sad because I really want to sign him."

He nodded. "Sometimes athletes can be dicks. What's he asking for?"

"Personal representation at all of his games, both home and away. Personal cell phone numbers of all of our staff, who should be available to meet his needs twenty-four hours a day. Limo service to his games. Specific requirements like photo ops and body-guards and things we don't provide."

Nathan arched a brow. "Did you explain to him that's not what MHC is about?"

"Yes. I told him we were there to manage his career, not his personal life. He said if we want—and I quote—'the privilege of managing him'—unquote—then we'll give him what he wants."

Nathan made a face. "Dump him. He's a diva and he's not worth it, no matter how high profile he is."

"That's what Monique said. Among other things that I won't repeat."

His lips curved. "I can imagine what Monique thought of the guy. She doesn't much care for athletes with big egos. Sounds like this guy's ego is huge."

"Yes. And she thinks his dick is tiny."

Nathan laughed. "It probably is. Seriously, though, Mia, drop him. He's bad news."

She sighed and swirled the wine around in her glass. "You're probably right. He should be some other management company's headache. Right now he's mine. My head is killing me."

"See? Take it as a sign. You don't need this particular headache."

When her two best friends agreed, she needed to listen. And in this case, she knew in her heart she needed to step away from Roland Green. She nodded. "You're right. I'm going to have to pass on this guy. I can't inconvenience my entire staff because some prima donna athlete thinks everyone should kiss his ass."

"Now you're thinking clearly."

She lifted her wineglass. "I don't know about clearly, but I know what I want—and don't want—for my company."

"Good for you. Protect what's yours and don't let anyone step on it. No client is worth it. I don't know who this guy is, but even if he's some huge superstar, he's still not worth the hoops you and your staff would have to jump through to keep him happy."

She half turned to face him. "Thank you for helping me find clarity."

"You know I'll always be here for you."

There was a knock at the door.

"That's the pizza," Nathan said. "I ordered it on my way over."

She wanted to kiss him for taking care of dinner. She was hungry. She was tired. She'd totally forgotten about pizza.

He hadn't, though. He paid the delivery woman and brought the pizza into the kitchen. She followed him and took plates out of the cabinet, then got out silverware and napkins.

"Fancy."

She frowned. "What?"

"I'm fine with just a paper plate. Or even a paper towel. It's just pizza, Mia. And I sure as hell don't need a knife and a fork to eat it."

"I don't have any paper plates. And I just wanted to offer the knife and fork option."

He grabbed a slice and bit into it, talking to her as he chewed. "You've seen me eat pizza before. It's not like you don't know me."

"You can feel free to eat with your hands. As long as you eat in the kitchen. I'm putting mine on a plate and eating in the living room. And turning on the TV. To watch baseball."

He gave her a long stare. "You drive a hard bargain, Ms. Cassidy."

Mia gave him a triumphant look, then made her way into the living room. She chose a spot on the sofa, then grabbed the remote and turned on the TV, scrolling until she found the baseball game. Nathan came in with his plate and sat next to her.

"Your uncle Gavin is playing tonight," she said.

"Yeah. They're playing Washington. It's a good matchup."

They ate their pizza and watched the game. Mia ate two pieces, then set her plate on the table and finished off her glass of wine while she watched Gavin Riley knock a fastball into left field that bounced into the corner.

"Hell yes," Nathan said as Gavin ended up with a double.

"He is so good."

"My dad got me tickets to see one of Gavin's games when Mom first started dating Dad. We flew into St. Louis and went to the game, and I got to go to the locker room and meet Gavin and the rest of the players. It was a great trip."

Her lips curved. She could imagine what that must have been like for Nathan as a young teenager with a case of hero worship for both Mick and Gavin Riley. "Obviously a memorable one for you."

Nathan grinned. "It was very cool."

After they finished eating, she took their plates into the kitchen, then grabbed her planner, flipping to one of the notebooks. She took out her pen and, as the innings progressed, made some notes on the Washington pitcher who had a wicked arm, was incredibly good-looking and was about to become a free agent. He was being coveted by almost every team. He was also shopping new management.

"Don't you ever turn it off?"

She glanced over at him. "Turn what off?"

"Work."

"Of course I do. But I'm making notes about a player."

"Interested client?"

"He might be."

"And you can't tell me which one, of course."

"Right."

A few minutes later, Nathan asked, "It's not my uncle, is it?"

She laughed. "No."

"Someone on his team, then, huh?"

"Nathan, I can't tell you. Some of these athletes currently have management companies and are looking to make a change. After we sign them, they go up on our website as clients of MHC. Until then, it's confidential, for obvious reasons."

"Yeah, right, I knew that. You've only told me a hundred times. Sorry."

She laid her notebook to the side. "It's not that I don't trust you. You know I do. But the first thing I tell prospective clients is that everything we do while we're courting them is strictly in confidence."

"I appreciate that. And it's good that you're not willing to mention it even to me."

"Or my brothers—who have asked, by the way. Or my parents, or anyone outside of MHC. So it's not just you."

He slid his fingers into her hair, and the way he rubbed it made her tingle all over. "That's what makes you so trustworthy. Your clients will appreciate it."

He always made her feel better about her choices, even when she couldn't tell him anything. Even when she had to keep reminding him she couldn't tell him anything.

"Thanks."

They watched another inning. Mia made notes and Nathan was pretty quiet. Once they went to commercial, he looked over at her planner.

"What kind of notes do you make?"

She set her planner aside. "Mostly my thoughts about how to present to that particular athlete. What we can do for him to shape his brand. What his strengths are in his sport, and how we can build on that, in terms of marketing and from a contract perspective. If a player is doing exceptionally well, he can make a lot more money when his contract is up. I also note questions I'll want to ask him during the meeting."

"What kinds of questions?" Nathan asked. "If I can ask that."

Her lips curved. "You can. I'll ask how he feels about the team he's currently playing for. If our attorneys and agents are going to represent him in contract negotiations, we need to know if he wants to stay or if, in his mind, he's already looking toward moving to another team.

"I also watch them play. Are they as good as the reports we've been getting on them? It's my job to build MHC into a well-recognized sports management company. I'm not going to do that by signing failures."

He leaned back against the sofa. "Wow. You're tough."

"I have to be. I want to build a successful company, and not every athlete is going to be good enough to be represented by us. We aren't going to be the right fit for everyone."

"Like the guy we talked about earlier that you're going to walk away from."

She nodded. "Headache guy."

He laughed. "Yeah. How's the headache, anyway?"

"Still present, but down to a dull roar now."

"You need a hot bath to soak away the tension."

"That sounds ideal."

"Come on." He stood. "Let's go take a bath."

She arched a brow. "You're going to take a bath?"

"I'm not, no. But you are."

She looked up at him. "I don't know, Nathan. The whole bath thing would be a lot more fun if you were going to be in the tub with me."

He looked down at her and leveled her with a hot look that promised sex and a lot of it, which was exactly what she needed to erase the last of this tension.

"Done. Now let's go."

She turned off the TV and followed him upstairs. When they got to her room, she turned to face him. "You, strip. I'll start the bath."

She started to go into the bathroom, but he grasped her hand.

"No, you strip, and I'll start the bath. I'm supposed to be catering to you, remember?"

"I don't remember that conversation at all, but I'm not going to object." She stood in front of him and pulled her top off.

He stared.

"Shouldn't you be running my bath?"

"Oh. Right. Yeah. I'll get on that."

He disappeared into the bathroom and she smiled, then shimmied out of her shorts and underwear. She grabbed the elastic she had on her wrist and wound her hair up into a messy bun on top of her head.

The bathroom was already steamy warm when she walked in. And Nathan was naked. Awesome.

"You ready?" he asked.

She was ready to do many things with him. But first, she needed that bath. "Yes."

He held out his hand for her and she stepped into the tub, settling into the water, which was hot and steamy and oh so perfect.

Nathan stepped in after her, and she was grateful she'd opted for the town house with the oversized soaker tub, because he was a big guy. He settled in behind her and pulled her against his chest. And even though it was a good-sized tub, he still had to sit with his knees bent.

"Feeling cramped?" she asked.

"I'm good. I have you—naked—leaning against me. Trust me, I'm really good."

He reached for her sponge and dipped it in the water, then ran it over her breasts and shoulders. He repeated the action over and over again. Mia closed her eyes and let the warm water and Nathan's attention melt the last of the day's tensions away.

She opened her eyes and smoothed her hands over his knees, the crisp hairs on his legs tickling her palms. His thighs were massive compared to hers, and she pictured the way he looked in his uniform, those powerful legs used to dash away from defensive linemen as he positioned himself to throw the ball.

When he wrapped his arms around her, she used her fingers to map his forearms. So much muscle there, too.

She shifted in the tub to turn around, straddling his thighs.

Nathan arched a brow. "Shouldn't you be under the water, relaxing?"

"I am relaxed. I want to ogle you."

He cracked a smile. "Ogle? This is relaxing to you?"

"In ways I couldn't possibly explain." She traced a finger over his stomach, though it was somewhat covered by the water. Rippling, taut abs—a wall of solid muscle. "You have an amazing body, Nathan. So well-muscled. It speaks to the hard work you put into it."

He grasped her hips and dragged her against his now-hard cock. "Whereas your body is all soft curves and these sweet angles I love to look at. But underneath that softness is muscle. You work hard at it, too. Did I mention how much I love your legs?"

She liked that he appreciated more than her tits and ass. Not that she had much in the breasts department anyway. She liked that he appreciated that, too.

"I believe you've stated that before."

"You have great legs. I know you dig that yoga stuff, and I've watched people contort themselves into positions I could never get into."

She squeezed her thighs against his. "Oh, I don't know. I'll bet you could if you tried."

"Not sure I want to even try. I'd probably just embarrass myself. But you, you're all grace and beauty and elegant lines. I could see you standing on your head and making it look sexy."

As he talked to her, he was dragging her sex back and forth

across his shaft, creating agonizing pleasure sparks that made it damn hard to pay attention to the conversation.

"Nathan."

"Stand up, Mia."

She pushed off his shoulders and stood, her body dripping water all over him.

"Now kneel against my shoulders."

She shuddered as she realized what he had in mind, but she needed this, wanted it more than she could vocalize.

She braced her hands on the wall, and pressed her knees against his shoulders, spreading her legs for him. He cupped her butt and put his mouth on her.

His lips felt like hot melted butter spreading over her sex. She moaned and leaned into the delicious feel of his tongue lapping at her clit, lost in the heady sensations. She was intoxicated by the rush of heat and tingling pleasure. Her knees went weak and she was thankful she had the wall and Nathan to hold her up.

Nathan was relentless in his pursuit of her orgasm, and it didn't take long. It stirred within her, quivering and vibrating with each lap of his tongue over her flesh. And when she came she shook all over, shuddering against him in forceful quakes that seemed to go on and on until she could barely stand anymore.

She finally sank into the water and wrapped herself around Nathan, kissing him with a deep passion that still quivered within her. He stood, taking her with him out of the tub. He laid her on the bathroom rug and left only long enough to get a condom. Then he was back, his body dripping over her as he opened the condom wrapper and put it on. He laid on top of her, spread her legs and thrust into her.

She was still quivering inside from that orgasm, her body tightening around him as he seated himself fully inside of her.

"Fuck," was all he said as he grabbed hold of her butt and pushed himself deeper.

"Yes." She wanted more. She wanted all of him.

And he gave it, pounding into her with hard, punishing thrusts that took her ever higher. She lifted her hips and wrapped her legs around him, needing that deeper contact.

She was going to come again, her pussy tightening around him like a vise.

"Yeah. That's it, give it to me," he said, tunneling with renewed force.

She went first, spiraling out of control with a wild cry as sweet pulses of orgasm flew through her.

Nathan went with her, taking her mouth in a deep kiss that made each sensation that much more pleasurable. It was like being sucked into a vortex of unimaginable sensation, so incredible she could hardly breathe. All she could do was hold on to him and ride it out.

After, she was spent and exhausted, like a limp noodle barely able to even move a limb.

Nathan rolled off of her and lay next to her.

"I might sleep here on the bathroom floor tonight," she said.

He looked over at her. "Damned uncomfortable. Besides, now I'm thirsty."

She sighed. "Demanding bastard. Fine, we'll get up."

He stood and helped her up. They got dressed, went downstairs and she fixed ice water for both of them. They ended up watching the rest of the baseball game, then Nathan said he had to leave.

He looked down at her. "Unless you want me to stay."

She didn't even hesitate. "Of course I want you to stay. I've missed you the past couple of weeks."

"I have an early practice tomorrow. I was just thinking about you. I didn't want to wake you."

She crawled onto his lap. "I have a meeting in the morning. And if you wake me early . . ."

He cupped her butt and dragged her against his hard cock. "So many benefits to me spending the night."

She grinned and dug her nails into his shoulder. "So many."

TWENTY-NINE

IT WAS GAME DAY—THE FIRST PRESEASON GAME. Nathan had a lump of anxiety the size of Texas in his stomach. He really wished his dad was here, but he understood Dad's reasons for not coming to the game. He had told him that showing up for the game would shift focus from Nathan and the team onto him, and he didn't want that. So despite wanting to be there for Nathan, his mom and dad told him they'd watch every second of the game on TV.

He sucked in a breath as he listened to the raucous chatter of his teammates in the locker room. He couldn't even focus on their talking, and fortunately it wasn't directed at him anyway. But he was going to have to get his head straight before game time.

He didn't have this much of a feeling of dread last year when he was a rookie, probably because he knew he wouldn't be playing. Oh sure, he got playing time during the preseason. Everyone did.

But otherwise he knew he'd spend the entire season warming the bench on the sidelines. So . . . zero stress.

Unlike today, when all eyes would be on him. The fans and all the media would be watching him to see if he was half the quarterback his father had been. The coaches would be checking him out, too.

He'd likely only play the first quarter, since the starters didn't play much early in the preseason. Coaches had a roster to cut down and they had to evaluate all the players, which meant his playing time would be limited. He wasn't sure if he was happy about that or not.

If he did great in the first quarter, then he'd be happy. If he sucked, then everyone would judge him based on that limited amount of playing time.

Fuck. Even more to stress about.

Jamal came and sat next to him.

"You stressed?" Jamal asked.

"Like crazy." The only person Nathan would say that to was his best friend.

"Relax, man. You're the best I've ever seen at quarterback, besides your dad. You got this. You just have to believe in yourself."

He knew Jamal was right. He wouldn't be in this position right now if the team and the coaches didn't believe he could do the job. He just had to believe he could do it.

He looked over and nodded. "Thanks."

Jamal nudged him with his shoulder. "Always gonna have your back, buddy."

"How about you?" he asked Jamal. "You ready for this?"

Jamal gave him his signature grin. "I'm easy. Ready to rock and roll this thing."

That's what he liked about Jamal. He was always low-key and no tension.

Nathan nodded. "All right, then."

"Now let's go kick Detroit's ass."

Coach met them in the locker room and the entire team huddled around him.

"I know we've made some changes in several key positions this year," coach said. "Most notably in our QB position. I want you all to give your support to Riley here, because he's given all he's got to this team and I know he's the leader to take the Sabers right to the playoffs this season."

Nathan winced. *No pressure there, Coach.*

"So let's rally behind him and all our new players and rookies and let's get this done."

They all put their hands in the center of the circle, then shouted, "Go Sabers!"

Then it was time to take the field.

Nathan wanted to believe this giant boulder in his stomach would go away and be replaced by exhilaration. After all, this was his debut as the starting quarterback for the Sabers.

But as they took the field and the sold-out home stadium crowd got to their feet with a roar and applause, that boulder suddenly felt like he'd ingested an entire mountain.

"Use the crowd to energize you," Jamal said as they moved to the sidelines.

Nathan nodded and tried to remember all these people wanted him to succeed. He'd gotten an early morning text from Mia, who had wished him luck and told him she'd be at the game today. So she was somewhere in this crowd. He had no idea where but he looked around the entire stadium, letting the sounds and the cheers fill him with adrenaline instead of scare the shit out of him.

Detroit won the coin toss and they elected to receive the ball, which meant Nathan would have to wait it out while the Sabers' defense took the field first. Pent up with nervous energy, Nathan couldn't sit. He wandered the sidelines and watched the defense as they stuffed Detroit on first down for no gain.

On second down, Detroit's quarterback threw a short pass for five yards.

It was third down. The quarterback dropped back, intending to pass. Flynn skirted past the offensive lineman and the quarterback barely got past him, and with no receivers open, had to throw the ball away.

Oh, hell yeah. Flynn had been a beast on that play.

Nathan fought a smile, not knowing when he'd be on camera. And now it was the offense's turn. So while Detroit punted, he took his last-minute instructions from the offensive coordinator and put on his helmet.

Then it was time to take the field. He hoped to God he didn't pass out on his way out there.

But the funny thing was, as soon as he stepped out onto the field with his offense, that boulder disappeared, and all that tension was gone. He was focused, his vision was clear and he knew exactly what he was supposed to do.

Until he took the first snap from center, threw a pass and it was an incompletion. Because he'd overthrown the receiver. Like by about ten fucking yards.

Shit. That didn't go well. He went back to the huddle and reorganized his thoughts for the next play, which he managed to get off without screwing it up, mainly because it was a run. Their running back gained six yards, which meant they were at third and four.

Since it was short yardage, the offensive coordinator called for a run on third down. Nathan handed the ball off to Anthony Weston, their running back, who took the ball seven yards for a first down.

He breathed a sigh of relief as he listened to the crowd's cheers. At least they were still on the field.

The next play was a pass play, and he had to get it right. He huddled up with the offense and gave them the play.

But he threw another incompletion, overthrowing the receiver again.

Sonofabitch. It was like he'd forgotten how to throw an accurate pass. What the hell was wrong with him anyway?

His gut tightened as the next play called was another pass. Why would they do that? Couldn't they see he didn't know what he was doing? He hoped like hell they were warming up his backup.

As they broke the huddle, Jamal took a second to walk with him.

"You know what you're doing. Breathe, brother."

Nathan nodded and took his position under center.

Yeah, he knew what he was doing. This was second nature to him. Every game, no matter where it was played, was the same. As he worked his count, he remembered he'd done this hundreds of times before.

Pull it together, Riley. And just fucking play football.

He took the snap, dropped back and searched out Jamal fifteen yards down the left side. He launched the ball in the air, watching it as it landed right in Jamal's hands for a perfect catch.

Fuck yes, that felt good.

The crowd roared its approval.

After making that first successful throw, he got into a groove. They moved down the field, alternating running and passing plays. It was working.

When they found themselves in the red zone, that pressure feeling returned, but Nathan used it to his advantage. And when he hit Jamal right in the numbers in the end zone, he raised his arms in triumph and ran to meet him.

"You were right there every time I threw to you," he said to Jamal.

Jamal handed him the ball as they jogged back to the sidelines. "Your first pro touchdown, bro. So damn proud of you."

That's right. It had been his first touchdown. Sonofabitch, it had felt good. He grinned. "Thanks."

Hopefully, this feeling of euphoria would never go away.

MIA SAT IN THE STANDS WITH AMELIA. MOSTLY, THEY stood, because the Sabers were kicking ass in this game. They were either driving their way down the field and scoring, or pushing Detroit back with outstanding defense.

Both her brother and Nathan had done well. They'd both played first quarter only, and had come out of the game after that. But it had still been an outstanding game.

"I don't know how the coaches decide who to cut," Amelia said as they sat in the stands about fifteen rows up. Flynn had offered to get them seats in one of the private clubs, but they had told him the weather was supposed to be nice, so they got great seats close to the action.

"At least we're not drunk today," Amelia said, referring to one of the games they'd come to and ended up toasted by the end of it.

Mia grinned. "I remember nothing about that game. Other than the amazing wine we consumed."

"Flynn said we sang in the car on the way home."

Mia gave her a look. "We sang?"

"Yes. And talked about our periods."

Mia threw her head back and laughed. "That is awesome."

After the game, they headed down to the player entrance since they had passes. They had to wait out media interviews, so they chatted up player family members while they waited.

"I remember seeing you here a while back," Tiffany La Salle, one of the players' wives, said to Mia. "You're here for your brother Flynn, right?"

Mia nodded right away. "Yes. How are you, Tiffany? And congratulations." Tiffany was sporting a healthy looking baby belly.

She rubbed her stomach and grinned. "Thank you. It's our second baby and pretty soon I'll have a three-year-old and an infant. Lord help me."

Amelia laughed. "I can't even imagine. But you're smart and capable and I know you're going to wrangle Randy to help you."

"You know it. He was great with Tyrone, our first. I know he's going to be just as good with this one. It's a girl. I can't wait to see how she wraps her daddy around her tiny baby finger."

"Aww, that's so wonderful," Mia said. "I'll bet you're so excited."

"We are."

The doors opened and the reporters poured out. Soon enough, the players followed. Flynn came over and wrapped his arms around Amelia.

"It was such a good game," Amelia said. "You were amazing."

"You really were, Flynn," Mia said. "Defense looks solid."

Flynn turned to her, keeping his arm around Amelia. "Thanks. It's just preseason so positions aren't fully set yet, but I liked the way the defense felt in that game against a damn good opponent."

Amelia laid her hand on his chest and looked up at him. "Building blocks, right?"

He smiled down at her. "Right, babe."

Nathan came out then, and Mia made sure to keep her distance as he stopped to chat. Since journalists were still wandering around, she didn't want to give them any gossip fodder, plus she was still on the lookout for that photographer who'd been stalking them. She didn't see him here, though.

"Hey, great game, Nathan," she said.

He smiled. "Thanks."

"You looked amazing out there, Nathan," Amelia said.

"I appreciate that."

"Don't go giving him a swelled head," Flynn said. "He was just okay."

Nathan laughed. "That's Flynn, always keeping my feet solidly on the ground."

Flynn slapped him on the back. "That's what I'm here for, man."

Jamal came out and stood next to Nathan. "Hey, Mia. How's it going?"

"Good. Is Wendy here?"

He shook his head. "She was disappointed she couldn't make it, but she had to take an early flight out today. She has a client meeting in New York first thing in the morning."

"Next home game, then."

Jamal nodded. "For sure. Which is in two weeks since we fly to Tampa next."

"Oh, that's right. You and Barrett get to beat up on each other in the preseason," Mia asked.

Flynn grinned. "Yup. That's always fun. We'll plan on plenty of trash talk."

"I guess I'll have to get in the middle of that since I'm the one who'll be scoring on Barrett," Nathan said.

Flynn arched a brow. "Score one touchdown and suddenly you're a superstar, huh?"

Nathan laughed. "So you *don't* want me to score against Tampa?"

Flynn frowned. "Careful, kid, or you might find yourself crammed into one of the lockers at the stadium."

"Yeah, I'll mention that to my offensive linemen."

Jamal laughed hard. "He got you, Cassidy."

Mia grinned at Flynn. "I don't think you're going to win this one."

"I don't know. I think me and my defense can take the kid and his offense."

"Bring it, Flynn," Nathan said.

Flynn shook his head. "Kid. You're cocky. I kind of like this new side to you. But don't push it."

Nathan laughed.

Mia knew they were all joking, so she blew it off, and when Amelia suggested they all go grab a bite to eat, she thought that sounded like a great idea. But she let them walk off ahead of her and said she was going to stop in the restroom first and she'd meet them at the restaurant. Mainly, not to be seen with Nathan. Even though Jamal was with them and it wasn't like they would look coupled up, she was still sensitive about it.

Probably oversensitive, but it was better to be cautious.

So she showed up at the restaurant ten minutes later than everyone else, then sat next to Amelia instead of Nathan. She saw the look Nathan gave her, and she knew he'd ask her about it later.

They decided to stay local and eat closer to the stadium rather than fighting traffic to get back into the city. The Fish Market was crowded with people from the game, which meant that Flynn, Nathan and Jamal were recognized. They smiled and took some pics and signed a few autographs, but then people left them alone.

Mia was glad she'd made sure to arrive separately. And since Nathan was huddled with Jamal and Flynn, it gave her an opportunity to chat with Amelia.

"Does it feel good to have a Sunday off from Ninety-Two?"

"I never mind being at the restaurant. It's relaxing for me to cook. I often do that on my days off anyway."

"True. I hear cookbook sales are going well. Flynn told me they often sell out at the restaurant."

"Which surprises me all the time. I'd originally planned to write the book and maybe self-publish it in digital format just for fun. I had no idea it would end up in print. Or be reprinted. It's amazing. And now to be working on another cookbook is a dream come true."

"I'm so glad you get to do something you love so much."

"Me, too. And now, so do you."

"Thank you. I'm pretty happy about it. At first it was all on paper, but now that it's a reality it's become more than I could have ever imagined. Still a bit scary."

Amelia nodded. "Of course it is. Nothing worth fighting for is ever going to be easy. If it is, then you're doing it wrong."

Their waiter brought the drinks they'd ordered. After they looked at the menu, Mia decided on the linguine with clams. They all decided on oysters for an appetizer.

She hadn't eaten during the game, so she was starving. By the time the oysters arrived, she was more than ready to down several, along with the delicious bread they offered.

Since she'd driven down to the game today, she wasn't having any wine, which was a shame because a nice pinot grigio would have gone well with the oysters, but she was content with a sparkling water and the view of a hot man who continued to give her questioning looks from across the table.

She gave him a smile back and arched her brow.

"Excuse me, I'll be right back." She got up from the table to use the restroom. When she came out, Nathan was waiting.

She leaned against the wall. "I don't know if you noticed, but this is the ladies' room."

"Funny," he said. "How come you didn't leave the stadium with us? And why aren't you sitting next to me?"

She'd expected to have this conversation with him—later—not now, outside the ladies' room.

"Because the media was loitering outside the locker room and I didn't want to give them any reason to think you and I are together. And same reason here."

He rolled his eyes. "Come on, Mia. We are together."

"I know that and you know that, but the press doesn't need to know it."

He palmed the wall, caging her between the hallway and the corner. "The press isn't here right now."

She couldn't deny her reaction to having his body so close to hers. But she pressed her hand against his chest to move him away. "Nathan. You have a lot of fans in this restaurant, so we shouldn't be seen together."

"Oh come on. Now you're being paranoid."

"Maybe you should be *more* paranoid. Your season is just kicking off and the last thing you need is some fan taking a pic of the two of us hanging out in a restaurant hallway together and posting it on social media."

He lingered, his gaze connected to hers. Sure, she wanted to be with him all the time. But the timing on this wouldn't be good—for either of them.

She pushed at his arm and he dropped it.

"This conversation isn't over, Mia."

"Whatever you say."

She went back to the table, feeling irritated and out of sorts. She took her seat and grabbed her glass, taking a long drink of her water.

A few minutes later, Nathan returned to his seat, giving her a pointed stare.

She decided to ignore him.

"What is going on with you two?" Amelia asked in a whisper.

Mia turned to her. "With who? Nathan and me? Nothing."

"Please. The vibes are obvious."

"What kind of vibes?"

"Angry hot ones. Do you have a thing with Nathan?"

Mia noticed Flynn was deep in conversation with Jamal and Nathan had joined in, which was good. "Define thing."

Amelia laughed. "So that's how it is. Nothing serious, then?"

"No." Mia took a sip of her water to cool down her wayward emotions. "We're just friends."

How many times had she said that to someone? How often had she said it to herself? She was lying to her friends and her family about her relationship with Nathan.

Why? Who was she protecting? Was she doing the right thing?

She didn't know the answers to any of those questions anymore and it made her feel even more out of sorts.

It was clear that Nathan wasn't happy about her not sitting next to him. Frankly, she wasn't happy about it, either. And what difference would it have made if they had hung out together? They might be in a relationship, but first and foremost they were fr—

That word again. That word was beginning to annoy her. And it pissed her off that she was becoming annoyed with it.

"Seems to me it's more than friends, Mia," Amelia said.

Mia picked up her water, needing the cool glass surrounding her hands to ward off the heat boiling inside of her.

"Honestly, I don't know what it is anymore. But whatever it is, it's confusing the hell out of me."

She was going to have to figure it all out soon.

THIRTY

NATHAN HAD PUT ALL HIS FRUSTRATIONS AND ANXIeties into the game against Tampa, which worked in their favor. They'd won the game twenty-eight to seven, which meant they were two wins up in the preseason, and his confidence level was rising. In that department, at least, he was feeling pretty good.

He'd played a little more in the game. Getting more reps was important and he looked forward to the next home game this weekend against Kansas City.

Right now, though, he was glad to be home and to have a day off. The first thing he wanted to do was see Mia. She'd dashed out of the restaurant after dinner last weekend, and she'd claimed she was swamped with work after that, so he hadn't been able to talk to her or see her. Her text replies had been pretty much one-line answers and he realized she was busy so he didn't want to bother her.

But he also knew she was avoiding him. So he drove to her office and parked in the garage, then took the elevator to her floor.

He'd purposely waited until close to the end of the workday. That way, maybe most of her business would be finished, the office would be virtually empty, and he could talk her into going out for a drink so they could talk.

The elevator doors opened and there was a slam of people hustling back and forth past the front desk.

What the hell were all these people doing at four thirty on a Monday? Didn't they ever wind down? Didn't anyone cut out early? Christ.

"Hi, can I help you?"

He noticed the young, sharply dressed woman at the front desk had directed the question at him, so he walked forward.

"I'm here to see Mia Cassidy."

She smiled at him. "Do you have an appointment?"

"No, I don't. Can you tell her Nathan Riley is here to see her?"

The woman blinked. "You're the Nathan Riley? The quarterback?"

His lips curved. That was the first time he'd heard that one, since the "the" part was usually reserved for his dad. "Just Nathan Riley."

She picked up her phone. "I'll ring Ms. Cassidy and let her know you're here. Please, take a seat."

"Okay, thanks."

He grabbed a chair and took out his phone to answer a few text messages and e-mails.

"Would you like something to drink, Mr. Riley?" the receptionist asked.

He looked up from his phone. "No, thanks, I'm good."

Mia walked out, looking gorgeous in a purple dress that hugged her body. The dress had tiny white buttons down the front and all he could think about was undoing those buttons one by one and unveiling what she wore underneath.

Yeah, probably not a good thing to think about. Or the fact that she wore sky-high heels that accentuated her beautiful legs.

He stood and cleared his throat.

"Nathan. What are you doing here?"

"I was in the neighborhood. Thought I'd drop by and see your office. But if you're busy, I can come back some other time."

"Of course not. Come on, I'll give you a tour."

He followed her as she turned right.

"To the right here is the conference room," Mia said. "For example, if you were interested in working with MHC, we'd do a presentation to you here."

The conference room was big, with glass walls on one side, windows on the other and several oversized comfy chairs. A long table centered the room. There was a projection screen on one side of the room and a whiteboard on the other.

"Over here is where our tech staff is housed," she said. "They handle making sure everything's in working order in the conference room so our presentations go off without a hitch. They're in charge of all our software as well as our hardware, so we kind of worship them."

Nathan's lips curved. "Understandable."

She made a turn around the corner. "Lunchroom is over here."

He stuck his head in the lunchroom. Of course Mia would make sure they had a good-sized spot for everyone to kick back and relax, with a full-sized refrigerator, microwave and even a stove, along with several tables, chairs and a sofa.

They made their way down the hall. "Individual offices here and there for our finance and marketing staff, along with mini conference rooms for department meetings."

He could see this office had been well thought out and planned for everyone's needs.

They turned the corner. "Marketing and PR is in this section.

They, too, have their own small conference room over here for meetings."

She led the way to the other side of the office.

"This is administration, where my staff is housed."

They walked past a few other offices. "Monique is in here."

Monique was on the phone and waved at Nathan as they walked by.

Finally they made their way to the end of the hall.

"And this is my office."

It was a big office, nicely painted in a soft gray with a large white desk, a couple of chairs, and a sofa nestled against the far wall. The décor was definitely Mia. Bookshelves, an antique clock, and a few watercolor paintings. Colorful, but not ostentatious.

"I like it."

She closed the door behind them. "Would you like a water or a soft drink?"

"Water would be good."

She went to the mini fridge and pulled out a couple of cold waters, handing him one and opening one for herself.

"I'm sorry I've been unavailable," she said as she took a seat on the sofa.

Nathan sat next to her. "I figured you were avoiding me."

Her eyes widened. "I was not avoiding you. We had a couple of very complex presentations the past week or so and it's occupied all my time. I think I told you I was busy."

He leaned against the back of the sofa and stretched out his legs. "Busy could mean a lot of things, Mia. Including 'I don't want to talk to you.'"

"Nathan. If I didn't want to see you or talk to you, I'd just tell you that. You should know me well enough by now to know I don't play those kinds of games."

"Okay, fine. But it sure felt like a brush-off, especially after last home game when we went out to eat. You practically ran out of there before we could talk."

She took a sip of water and laid the bottle on the table. "That night was confusing for me. I'll admit I retreated."

"What confused you?"

"You. Me. My feelings about what was happening between us."

He leaned forward. "Talk to me about how you feel. What's bothering you?"

She shook her head, then looked down at her hands. "I don't know."

"Is it us?"

Her head shot up. "No. It's not that at all. I think I was just in a weird mood that night. I'm sorry. A lot of it is the job. There's so much pressure, you know?"

He smoothed his hand down her arm. "Babe, I know. I'm sorry you're feeling that way, but you know you can talk to me about anything."

"I know. Thank you. That means a lot."

She was staring down at her hands and he could tell there was something more on her mind. He wished he could get her to open up to him. She'd always told him what she was thinking, what was bothering her. So what had changed between them that she couldn't talk to him now?

He reached over and grasped her hand. "Mia."

She lifted her head and looked over at him. "Nothing's wrong, Nathan. Actually, things between us are fine. It really is just work that has me tense."

He wasn't sure that was true, but if she didn't want to talk about the two of them, he wouldn't push her on it. "What's going on with work?"

"*Women in Business* magazine wants to do a profile interview on me."

His lips curved. "Really? That's not a bad thing, is it?"

"Well, no. But it's giving me the worst anxiety."

"Come on, Mia. You'll sail right through that interview. You know your business inside and out, and you can sell it with a smile and confidence."

She inhaled, then let it out. "Maybe you can do it for me. With a smile and confidence."

He laughed. "Not my area. But I'll be happy to be the practice interviewer for you. When are they coming?"

"Wednesday. Which means I have two days to prepare for it."

"Okay. So tell me why you decided to start up a sports management company, Ms. Cassidy."

She arched a brow. "Oh, we're doing this now?"

"Why not?"

She placed her hands in her lap. "I've always loved sports. My family is a dynasty of professional athletes, including my father. I know everything there is to know about sports."

"Is that right? Who won the football championship the year you were born?"

"That's easy. Dallas."

His lips curved. "Somehow I knew you'd know that. Okay, who won the year after that?"

"Dallas. Again."

"Oh, you're good, Ms. Cassidy."

"Thank you."

He questioned her for about forty-five minutes on all kinds of trivia, from baseball to basketball to hockey and even on golf and the Olympics. Her knowledge was impressive. Of course, they'd always talked sports in college so he was aware of her knowledge, but he quizzed her as if he didn't know her, asking her how she had prepared to launch a start-up, what her goals were. She did well.

He finally took a break and finished off his water. "I think you've got this. You come off knowledgeable and passionate, but not arrogant. It's clear you love what you do and you care about athletes and their careers."

"I hope so."

"Then relax."

She stood, smoothing her hands down her skirt. "Easier said than done."

"Maybe you need a drink, ease some of that tension."

She walked over to her desk. "And maybe you're just trying to get me drunk so you can get into my pants."

"Ha. You're not wearing pants. And I really did come by today just to talk. Which we've been doing."

"I appreciate you coming by. And I was happy to show you the office. You know I've wanted to do that ever since we opened."

"You've done great for yourself, Mia. I'm impressed as hell."

Her smile was like a beam of sunlight. It always made him happy when she smiled like that.

"Thank you. That means a lot to me."

"Now let's go get a drink. Drag some of your coworkers with us."

"Okay. Hang on."

She left the office, so he got up and looked out her windows. It was well after office hours, so he looked down at the street level. There were still a lot of people rushing to BART or buses or just walking somewhere. Downtown was always busy this time of day. One of his favorite things to do as a kid had always been to watch people, to wonder where they were headed. He'd always loved going into the city. The noise and rush of people had always energized him.

Maybe that's why he loved standing in the center of a filled-to-capacity football stadium. He drew strength from that crush of a noisy stadium. It fueled him.

"So . . . the office is empty."

He turned to see Mia leaning against the doorway.

"Is that right?"

"Yes. I checked everywhere and no one's here. I guess everyone left for the day. I hadn't realized it was after six."

"It was nearly five when I showed up here."

"Really. Time got away from me today. I told you we've been busy."

He got up and closed her door, then pushed the button to lock it. "You need some relaxation time. Maybe you should consider putting in a spa."

She laughed. "Oh, right. That's exactly what we need in here."

He shrugged. "Might as well. You have everything else."

He took her by the hands and led her over to her desk, leaning her butt up against it. "So while we've been in here, I've been thinking about having you on your desk."

"And by having me, you mean fucking me on my desk?"

Just hearing her say the words made his dick harden. "Yeah."

"You have a dirty mind, Nathan Riley."

"I know. That's why you like me."

"No, that's not why I like you."

When he gave her a direct look, she said, "Okay, it's not the only reason I like you."

He closed her laptop and shifted it to the side of her desk, along with a few pens and her planner. Then he stepped in between her legs, wrapping his arm around her.

"You can't deny it'd be hot to fuck on your desk. Then, every time you're sitting here at work, you'd think about us having sex here."

She kicked off her shoes and wrapped a leg around his hip. "That could be a distraction. I'm not sure I need any distractions."

He cupped the side of her neck, coming in closer to brush his lips across hers. "This is a good distraction."

As he talked to her, he listened to the way her breathing changed, going from even breathing to short gasps, signaling her desire. Yeah, she wanted this as much as he did. Her leg was wrapped around him and her pelvis hitched up against his cock so she could rub her pussy against him. He was already hard as steel and he wanted nothing more than to release his cock and plunge inside of her. The scent of sex filled the air around them.

"So is that a yes?" he asked.

She tilted her head back, and raw desire was reflected in her beautiful blue eyes.

"Put your cock where your words are, Nathan, and fuck me. Right here on the desk."

He laid her back on her desk and lifted her dress, revealing hot purple underwear that matched her dress.

"You are so fucking sexy, Mia."

He pulled her underwear down and off, laying it on her office chair, then dragged her forward so her butt rested on the edge of her desk. Then he pulled a condom out of his pocket.

Mia eyed the condom, then turned her attention to him. "Did you come in here today with plans to seduce me?"

He unzipped his jeans and shoved them, along with his boxer briefs, over his hips. "I always have plans to seduce you." He put the condom on and stepped between her legs, lifting them as he fit himself inside of her. Damn it felt good to ease into her, to feel the way they fit together. It was always perfect.

"After being caught in the coat closet together without a condom, I swore that was never going to happen again."

Her lips curved and she arched upward against him. "I'm glad you were prepared today."

"Me, too. Because I needed to be inside of you, to feel your pussy tightening around my cock and to listen to those sounds you make when I move inside of you."

She made those sounds as he thrust, the sweetest moans and gasps that made his cock spasm.

Not yet. Not when those little white buttons on her dress needed to be undone.

"When I first came into the office and saw you, these things caught my attention."

He leaned over and laid one palm on the desk, still moving inside of her while he used the other hand to pop the first button on her dress.

She watched him, her breathing deep and fast.

"You wanna know what I was thinking?" he asked.

"What?"

"That I wanted to undo every one of these buttons to find out what you were wearing underneath this dress." He undid the second button, then the third.

"Is that right?"

"Yeah." The fourth and fifth button went next, and he made his way down all the buttons until he pulled the dress apart to reveal the sexy matching purple bra. He decided right then that purple was his favorite color.

"This is pretty." He skimmed his fingers over the swells of her breasts, then flipped the front clasp to open the bra, releasing her breasts. He used his thumbs to draw circles around her nipples.

Mia gasped and he felt the tightening around his cock.

"Do you have any idea what you do to me?" he asked. "What it does to me seeing you half-naked and sprawled on your desk with my cock buried inside of you?"

Mia reached out and skimmed her nails over his forearms. "I can feel what you're doing to me, feel your cock swelling inside of me, grinding against me every time you thrust. It makes me want to come."

She moved her hand to her sex and began to rub her fingers back and forth.

Hell, he was going to come so hard if she kept doing that. Just watching her work her body, the scent of sex filling the air around them, and watching his dick pumping in and out of her pussy, it was all he could do not to come. It was taking every bit of restraint he had to hold on.

But he would, because he was waiting for Mia to come first.

"That's it," he said, needing to coax that orgasm out of her. He gripped her hip and drove deeper. "Make yourself come. I love watching you touch yourself."

"I'm going to come, Nathan."

"Fuck yeah. Do it." He felt her pussy tighten around his cock, felt the spasms grow stronger.

And when she began to buck against him, when she cried out with her orgasm, he cupped his hand around her butt to draw her close. He leaned over her to kiss her, to take her mouth in a deep kiss as he came, too, groaning against her lips and shuddering with his own orgasm.

He softened the kiss, taking them both down from that euphoric high. His fingers were cramping under her butt so he eased them out and raised Mia from the desk.

She blinked, then traced her fingers over his jaw. "That was . . . exceptional."

He grinned. "I thought so, too."

She had a restroom connected to her office, so they went in there to clean up. Mia glanced over at him and smiled as she buttoned up her dress.

"What?" he asked.

"Who knew little white buttons were such a turn-on for you?"

He shrugged. "What can I say?"

"I'm filing that away for future reference."

He laughed, then pulled her against him for a deep kiss. When he let her go, he said, "I'm hungry. How about you?"

"Ravenous."

"Good. Let's have dinner."

He waited while Mia packed up her things into her bag, then they headed out.

"You want to talk about what was bothering you earlier?"

She looked over at him while they waited for the elevator. "Nope. Not at all."

"Okay, then."

But at some point, they were going to talk. Mia had something on her mind, and it had to do with him. And he was going to make sure they discussed it.

THIRTY-ONE

MIA SWALLOWED PAST THE GIANT LUMP IN HER THROAT and tried her best to appear calm, even though she was anything but.

"You look like you're about to attend an execution," Monique said.

"I do?"

"Yes. And you're pale. Their makeup team did a stellar job on you, and you still look like you have the flu. Here, let me touch you up a little."

They were in Monique's office while the magazine team set up in Mia's office for the interview and photo shoot. Mia would have preferred to just dive in and get this over with, but apparently these things took time. And while she waited, she grew more and more nervous.

Monique applied blush to her face, then squinted as she surveyed the results. "A little better, but try to avoid appearing as if you might vomit at any second, okay?"

"I'll try."

Zelda, the magazine's production assistant, stuck her head in the door. "We're ready for you, Ms. Cassidy."

"Thank you. I'll be right there."

Mia shot a helpless look at Monique, who gave her two thumbs-up in reply. "You can do this."

She went into her office, which had been transformed into something that didn't look like her office anymore. It was filled with a lot more color, with orange and purple pillows on the sofa, a rug on the floor and different chairs.

They'd told her they were going to have to accessorize the office to photograph well. She'd said she was fine with that.

She was fine with whatever. She just needed to get through this. She could get through anything.

Andrea, the editor who was going to interview her today, came over and smiled at her. "Are you ready?"

Mia nodded.

"How about we sit on the sofa to start?"

"Sure."

She took a seat on the sofa and Andrea sat with her. Mia folded her hands together in her lap so Andrea wouldn't notice her hands were shaking.

Get a freakin' grip, Mia. This isn't your first interview.

She'd done an interview with one of the San Francisco newspapers when MHC first opened. She'd been totally together. So what was the big deal here?

Andrea started out with a few innocuous questions about Mia's educational background and where she'd grown up, no doubt icebreakers to keep Mia relaxed. Which was good because it was working. They gradually made their way into the reasons for Mia starting her business, and how things were going. They discussed the athletes MHC had signed so far, and what the company's plans were for the first year and going forward.

Once Mia settled in and started talking business, she relaxed. Andrea was an engaging interviewer, and Mia found a rapport with her.

"And what about your personal life?" Andrea asked. "Any boyfriends? Girlfriends?"

"Oh." That question hit her like a ton of bricks. "Not really."

"Surely someone as successful as you knows it's important to have a social life. I mean, it can't be all about work all the time, right?"

"Of course. I date. But no special guy in my life right now."

She wanted to take the words back as soon as she'd said them.

"That's understandable. It's good to be social, but of course you're building a company from the ground up. I can totally relate to not wanting any heavy involvements in your life at the moment."

"Yes. Right. That's it, exactly." She so wanted this interview to be over with.

"Okay, I think that's enough for now. Let's take a few photographs."

They took some photos of her leaning against her desk, and sitting at her desk, and brought in a few of her staff, Monique included, to mimic her doing some meeting-type work. That didn't take too long. Andrea thanked her and told her they'd have the article up on the magazine's website within a week, and in next month's print magazine.

The staff returned her office to its previous state, décor wise, in short order.

She thanked Andrea and the entire staff for their time, and walked them all to the elevators.

Then she exhaled and leaned against the wall, feeling incredibly drained. She could drink an entire bottle of wine right now.

With a straw.

Monique came down the hall.

"How did it go?"

Mia pushed off the wall. "Fine, I guess."

"You guess? It was either good or bad. Was it bad? How was it bad?"

"I don't know." She turned to head down the hall to her office.

Monique followed. "There's something you're not telling me. What are you not telling me?"

When they got back to Mia's office, she went to the mini fridge and grabbed a water, opened it and took a long swallow, then headed over to one of the chairs in front of her desk and slumped in it.

Monique slid into the chair across from Mia's desk.

"Okay, spill," Monique said.

"The front end of the interview was fine. We talked about my early life, my education, my motivation for starting the company. I was enthusiastic and on point about MHC. I killed it there."

"Okay, that's awesome. Tell me the downside."

"She got into my personal life, asked questions about who I was dating."

Monique wrinkled her nose. "I hate that. It's so intrusive. What the hell does that have to do with you and MHC?"

"Nothing. I told her there was no special guy in my life right now. I wanted to take the words back as soon as I said them."

"I see. You're upset that you indirectly dissed Nathan."

"Yes."

"Honey, the interviewer put you on the spot. Don't worry about it. He won't take offense. Besides, you've been keeping this relationship on the down low. Neither one of you wants it in the spotlight."

She sighed. "I know. But still, I feel like I insulted him, like he doesn't matter to me."

"And he does matter to you."

"Yes. He's my friend."

Monique cocked her head to the side. "He's more than that, though, isn't he?"

"Yes." She rubbed her temple, already feeling the headache starting to form.

"Have you talked to him about how you feel?"

"No. I've been trying to avoid talking to him about how I feel."

"Why?"

"I don't know. I'm still afraid of upsetting the status quo between us."

"Which is ridiculous. You two are getting along great. The sex hasn't changed anything between you, right?"

"I guess not."

"So what's worrying you?"

"I don't know. Some gut feeling that what's happening between us is going to end. That our friendship will end. I always feel like I'm standing on a cliff just waiting to fall over, and when I do, I'll be falling by myself. Does that even make any sense?"

Monique looked at her. "It does to you and that's all that matters. Talk to Nathan. Tell him how you feel."

"I don't want to talk to Nathan. There's not even anything to talk about. Things are going well between us, so why upset that?"

Monique went over to the mini fridge and grabbed a green tea, holding it up for Mia, who nodded, so she grabbed two. She came over and handed one to Mia, then took her seat, unscrewed the lid and took a sip. "So you're going to live in denial?"

"That's preferable, yes."

"You realize you can't live in denial land forever."

"Why not? It's nice here."

Monique laughed. "You're the most realistic person I've ever known, Mia. And you've never been afraid to face anything head-on.

So maybe whatever it is you're feeling for Nathan that has you running scared might be love."

Mia wrinkled her nose. "I can't be in love. I don't want to be in love. Love will ruin us."

Monique rolled her eyes. "How will love ruin you?"

"If I thought sex was bad for our friendship? Falling in love could destroy us."

"Sometimes your sense of logic is utterly mind-boggling. Falling in love might be the best thing that could ever happen to you and Nathan."

She shook her head, gripping the bottle of tea she had yet to open. "I don't see it that way."

"Maybe you should think about it. And for God's sake, talk to Nathan instead of keeping your thoughts to yourself."

"I'll . . . think about it."

Instead, when she went home after work that night, she changed into shorts and a tank top, grabbed a glass of wine, got her planner out and made herself comfortable on the sofa to work on her Pros and Cons list.

Love versus Friendship

The Friendship list was easy. On the Pro side, she listed fun, trust, sharing all her secrets, being able to keep him as her best friend and no emotional attachments. But if she moved him back over to the Friendship side, she'd pull sex out of the equation. That's just how it would have to be. So the con of friendship would be no more sex.

She leaned back on the sofa and thought about the no more sex thing. In college they'd had sex one time before she'd crossed it off the list. This time it was different. They'd been sexing it up on a pretty regular basis. She had to admit she'd grown accustomed to his body, to his touch, to occasionally sleeping with his body wrapped around hers.

She'd miss that. With sex came intimacy, and being closer to Nathan these past couple of months had been everything.

Enough to risk losing Nathan's friendship, though?

No. She'd live without the sex before she'd lose Nathan.

She moved over to the Love side.

She listed warmth, tenderness, emotional gratification, his touch, the way he looked at her and the way he touched her. Definitely the sex, too, which had been growing in intensity every time they were together. It was passionate, definitely, but there was a depth to their lovemaking now that hadn't been there before.

She wanted to be with Nathan more and more. She felt part of him, so she added that to the Love side.

On the Con side of Love was commitment. Not that commitment was a con. But she didn't think either of them was ready for that big a step in their relationship. They were both early in their careers. Having fun was one thing. Sex was one thing. Falling in love? That was a big deal.

She also added risk to the Con list. Their friendship was solid and always had been. But with love came risk and if it didn't work out, it could end them forever. That scared her. She would never want to put her friendship with Nathan at risk.

In addition, she still didn't know how Nathan felt about her. He might still think of their relationship as all fun and games. So what if she threw the Love card out there and he didn't love her back?

She didn't even want to think about that.

She put her planner to the side and laid her head back against the sofa.

Everything had been much simpler when they were just friends. Why were sex and love so confusing?

Her doorbell rang. She closed her planner and went to the door, looking out the peephole to see Nathan.

She was surprised since she wasn't expecting him. She opened the door to see him holding a bag.

"I brought Thai food. I hope you're hungry."

"What are you doing here?"

"Bringing you dinner. Are you gonna let me in?"

"Sorry. Yes, of course." She pulled the door all the way open and he walked in. She shut the door behind him and followed him into the kitchen.

"I suppose you still don't have paper plates."

She opened the cabinet and pulled out plates. "No. These are fine."

She was happy to see he'd brought crab Rangoon and chicken satay, along with pad Thai chicken and Thai fried rice. She spooned out a little of everything onto her plate.

She hadn't thought she was hungry, but the food smelled delicious. She fixed large ice waters for both of them and they sat in the living room to eat while they watched a movie on TV.

Though she wasn't really focused on the movie. Her thoughts kept straying to the pro/con list she'd been working on before Nathan showed up.

Which, by the way . . .

"So, it was a surprise to see you at my door."

He scooped up a forkful of rice, chewed, then swallowed. "Monique texted me."

Mia arched a brow. "She did? Why?"

He shrugged. "She said you needed me."

Leave it to her friends to think she needed rescuing when she didn't.

"Do you?"

She glanced over at him. "Not really."

"She said you had a shit day. Did the interview with the magazine go badly?"

"No, it was fine. Though I might have said something that will piss you off."

"In the interview?" He laid his fork down.

"Yes. Everything was going well when we were talking business. Then all of a sudden the interview shifted to my personal life."

He grimaced. "I hate when interviewers get personal. What did she ask?"

"She asked if I was seeing someone. I panicked and said there was no one special in my life."

"Oh." He shrugged. "Good answer."

Just like that? "And you're not mad?"

"Why would I be mad about that? Did you think I'd want you to declare your undying love for me in a magazine interview?"

"Well, I guess not."

"Come on, Mia. She was out of bounds and you gave a professional answer without coming right out and telling her your personal life was none of her damn business. Which it isn't."

Her entire body relaxed in relief. "Thank you. I was so worried you'd be angry."

"Why? I don't give the media any information about my personal life because it's not for them to know. They can have all the information they want about what I do on the field. Off the field? Not their business. The same has to hold true for you. I mean, they're always going to dig up something here and there because that's the nature of the business these days. But you sure as hell don't have to be the one to feed it to them, ya know?"

She nodded. "You're right. She just caught me off guard because I didn't expect the question."

"Even the most reputable journalists will sometimes dig into your personal business. Now that you know that, you'll be better equipped to handle it the next time."

"You're right. I will." With a renewed sense of relief, she finished up her meal, then cuddled up with Nathan to watch the movie.

At least one issue had been resolved tonight. The other one she decided to table for the moment. She felt such ease right now she didn't want to build up the tension again with a "Hey, how do we feel about love?" conversation.

That could definitely wait for another time. It was enough that he wasn't mad at her about what she'd said during her interview. She didn't even know why she'd worried about it. She knew him well enough to know he wouldn't take it seriously.

Would he ever take anything seriously, including her? Including them?

As they watched the movie, she chewed on a hangnail that had been giving her grief all day. Which was probably some ridiculous metaphor for leaving things hanging.

She blew out a breath.

Nathan rubbed her arm. "You okay?"

"Fine. Still trying to blow off the remnants of the day."

He brought his hand up to her neck, teasing her skin with the lightest touch of his fingers. "Hard to get rid of that tension sometimes, isn't it?"

"Yes." She straightened, then turned to face him, crossing her legs over each other. "And I just realized I never asked about your day, which makes me a terrible friend."

"Girlfriend."

"What?"

"We're more than friends, Mia, aren't we?"

Yet another thing she couldn't get right. "Yes, of course we are. So anyway, that makes me a terrible girlfriend."

He laughed. "Hey, it's okay for you to be all about you sometimes."

"No, it's not." She took his hand and entwined her fingers with his. His hands were so much larger than hers, his fingers rough and calloused. She could feel the amount of strength in his hands, and yet he was always so gentle with her.

"How did practice go?"

"It went well. We're focused, offensive line and receivers look good. The cuts were tough this week, but it only makes the team stronger."

"And you'll get more playing time in the game this weekend."

"Yeah. A shorter week since we play on Saturday, but that's okay. I'm more than ready for it."

"I'll for sure be there."

He moved his hand to her leg, snaking his fingers along her knee and up toward her thighs.

"To watch your brother play, right?"

Her next breath hitched as he slipped his fingers inside one leg of her shorts.

"Please do not mention my brother while your fingers are inching their way up toward my pussy."

He pushed her back onto the sofa, then tucked his fingers inside her underwear.

"Slick, hot pussy, too," he said, moving to lean over her, not once stopping his movements across her sex.

He painted her with her own moisture, teasing her clit with broad, circular strokes.

The tension she'd felt earlier dissolved, replaced with a new form of tension, this one taut with needy desire. She raised her arms above her head and arched her hips to search out more of that heady sensation.

Give up sex with Nathan? What was she thinking? She made a mental note to underline at least three or four times in her planner how awesome the sex was. With her favorite purple pen. Because damn he was good at this.

And when he slipped a finger inside of her and began to pump, she moaned her pleasure. He used his finger to slowly and steadily thrust in and out of her, his knuckles brushing against her clit in an agonizingly sweet way that made her climb ever higher toward orgasm.

He added another finger inside her, then swirled his thumb over the bud.

"Oh, yes," she said. "Oh, I'm going to come."

"That's it," he said. "Come on, babe. Feel me fucking you with my fingers. Come on my fingers, Mia."

His voice was soft, coaxing the orgasm from her.

The double sensation was more than she could bear. She released with an incredible climax that left her breathless, yet still wanting more.

Nathan did, too, because with his fingers still moving within her, he leaned over and kissed her, a soft kiss that sparked her passions to a fevered pitch.

She smoothed her hand over his jaw. "Let's get naked."

His lips curved. "Thought you'd never ask. Want to go upstairs?"

She shook her head. "No. Right here."

"I'll go grab a condom. Get to taking off those clothes."

She smiled at him, and he disappeared upstairs. She stood, pulled off her tank top and discarded her bra, then shimmied out of her shorts and underwear.

Nathan returned and shed his T-shirt, jeans and underwear, put on the condom and took a seat on the sofa.

"Come here, babe," he said, holding his hands out for her. "I want you to wrap those beautiful legs around me."

She settled in on his thighs, easing down over his rigid cock. The sensation was amazing as he filled her. When she was fully seated on him, she wrapped her legs around his back and her arms around his neck.

"This is good," he said, cupping her butt in his hands. "You and me, close together like this. I can touch you everywhere."

He demonstrated by using one hand to brush across her nipples.

"And I can kiss you."

He put his lips on hers, and then he thrust into her. She felt a flash of heat and sensation unlike anything she'd ever felt before. Maybe it was being so connected to him, being filled by him, while he kissed her and touched her at the same time.

The way he looked at her, as if he was looking deep into her while he moved within her, made her feel that connection between them like never before. Maybe it was the rush of her emotions, her head and her heart adding to the feelings of her body. She had no idea, but this felt like a first.

She wrapped herself around the feeling and soaked it in, letting every wondrous sensation rain down over her as he moved within her.

She brushed her palm over his jaw, his beard sending tingles of pleasure straight to her sex.

She leaned back, bracing her palms on the sofa. He shifted, falling on top of her but balancing his weight.

She'd had her eyes closed, falling on that blissful cloud of sensation, reveling in every nuanced feeling.

Until Nathan said, "Mia, look at me."

She opened her eyes and Nathan locked gazes with her. The intensity of it doubled her emotional reaction. She wasn't sure if he felt what she felt, but it seemed as if there was something different about the way he looked at her.

Or maybe it was just her, projecting her own feelings.

He reached up and locked fingers with her, then put his lips on hers in a kiss that spoke more of love than of sex, that said more of emotion than of just fucking.

She knew it wasn't just her imagination.

She felt cocooned within his big body and the sofa, and once again wrapped her legs around him to pull him within her. He thrust, hard, using his body to grind against her until she splintered with her orgasm, crying out his name as she came.

He had a death grip on her hip as he shuddered with his own orgasm, which only served to deepen the intensity of her climax that rolled on and on, a timeless fall into blissful oblivion.

And throughout it all they remained locked on each other's gaze, a naked reveal of their emotions as they came. Nathan kissed her lips, her neck, and ran his hands over her body. She felt as if she were suspended on a cloud, so euphoric she never wanted to come down. And maybe he did feel the same way because he didn't move for a very long time, just shifted slightly so they nestled against each other.

She might have fallen asleep. She wasn't sure because she was in a groggy state when Nathan finally got up and left the sofa. He came back a few minutes later.

"Come on," he said. "Let's go upstairs."

He took her hands and pulled her up to stand. They got into bed together and, just as they had been on the sofa, he wrapped his arms around her, his chest against her back.

"Better now?" he asked.

She smiled. "Much better."

As she lay there with him, she wasn't shocked at all to realize that she was in love with him. This emotional connection she'd felt earlier, the passion she felt for him, the way he was always there for her to listen to her—that was all love.

But she didn't know how he felt and she didn't want to upset the balance in their relationship. She knew she had to talk to him about how she felt, to figure out where they stood.

But not tonight. Tonight had been perfect and they could talk another time.

You're a coward, Mia Cassidy.

She mentally shushed her inner voice and closed her eyes.

THIRTY-TWO

IT WAS GOING TO BE A GOOD GAME TODAY. NATHAN could feel it. He had the home field advantage, his parents had flown in for the game, and he felt more prepared than he ever had before.

He actually just felt really fucking awesome about life in general. He was stoked for the season to start, the team was healthy and he knew this was going to be a good year for the Sabers, and all that nervousness he felt before the preseason started was gone.

He was confident and he knew he could lead this team.

As he got dressed for the game, he thought about Mia. Something monumental changed between them the other night when they were together. At first he couldn't put his finger on what it was, if he had fed into Mia's mood or what. But it had been intense and emotional and he sure as hell never got emotional about sex.

Until then.

He finally had to come to the realization that he might be in love with Mia.

He considered that further as he finished getting dressed in the locker room, his thoughts drowning out all the chatter going on around him.

Or maybe there was no "might" about it. Because you either were or you weren't in love with a woman.

She frustrated him more times than not. She challenged him, for sure. The sex was amazing. He trusted her like he'd never trusted another woman before. She was his friend. She'd been his friend from the moment they'd met in college. She knew more about him than anyone ever had.

He couldn't imagine not having Mia in his life. In his bed. In his future.

Yeah, he was in love with her. No maybe about it.

He grinned.

"Thinking about the game today?" Jamal asked.

He pulled himself out of his thoughts and turned to face his teammate and friend.

His feelings were new, and he sure as hell wasn't going to talk about them with anyone else until he talked to Mia first. "Yeah. Ready to win this one."

Jamal bumped fists with him. "Hell, yeah."

By the time the team took the field, he'd tucked away thoughts of Mia, but he was happy to know she was at the stadium. As soon as the game was over, he intended to talk to her, so he could tell her how he felt. But for now, he was going to use that knowledge and this sudden feeling of euphoria to fuel the team to victory today.

Kansas City won the coin toss and they deferred, so Nathan and the Sabers had the ball first. After the kickoff, he went out there with his offense. Kansas City had a solid defense this season, so this wasn't going to be a cakewalk for them.

Nathan took the snap from center, rolled back, looked to his left to find no open receivers, so scrambled to his right and hit Randy La Salle, the wide receiver, on a post play for a twelve yard gain.

Great start. The next play was a run, and they gained six yards, giving them a short second down. They used a running play on second down and gained five yards for a first down.

So far, so good. They went for a pass on the next first down, but Kansas City blitzed around their offensive line and Nathan was in trouble. He scrambled and ended up having to throw the ball away.

That was a close call. In the huddle, he talked to his offensive linemen about keeping their heads up and watching for the blitz.

On second down, they ran the ball for three yards, which meant they had a long third down and Nathan would have to pass. Defense would know they were passing and would no doubt blitz again. He'd have to be fast on his feet and get the ball out of his hands in a hurry.

They got in formation, the ball was snapped and Nathan had his eye on his receivers, who were trying to get open. He finally found his tight end up the middle for nine yards and a first down.

He blew out a sigh of relief. Things were going their way, but this wasn't going to be easy.

After several plays, they finally made their way into the red zone on the nine yard line. Nathan dropped back and threw a pass to Jamal, who was wide open in the end zone.

Yes! Touchdown.

Nathan smiled and nodded. That had felt damn good. The entire offense worked hard for that one.

They moved over to the sidelines and Nathan congratulated Jamal for the touchdown, and his offensive line, who had toughed it out against a stellar defense.

He got a drink and talked with his quarterback coach about the series, then focused on watching the Sabers' defense play.

Kansas City's offense was just as good as their defense.

The Sabers' defense was better. They gave Kansas City a good push back on all their plays. They gained no ground and had to punt after two first down series.

After that it was the offense's turn again.

Time to turn the heat up and get in the end zone again.

MIA SAT IN THE CLUBHOUSE WITH AMELIA AND WENDY, along with Mick and Tara Riley and several other players' wives, girlfriends and families.

She was stoked to be here, and excited because this game was kicking serious ass. They were deep into the third quarter and the Sabers were up twenty-four to ten. Both offense and defense looked solid today.

Nathan and Flynn were still playing and Mia was on the edge of her seat. Amelia sat on one side of her and Tara on the other. Defense had finished a solid series and Kansas City had just punted the ball, so there was a break in the action. She sat back and took a sip of her drink.

"Are you going to take Sundays off to come to the home games?" she asked Amelia.

Amelia nodded. "Yes. I'll probably go ahead and work when Flynn is on the road and give my assistant chef a chance to take those days off. That way we can swap."

"That's a great idea."

"I do like to be around when Flynn isn't on the road, so we've made the schedule flexible. And my cooks are awesome in that they don't mind working when I need to be off."

"It makes a world of difference to have good people working for you, doesn't it?"

"It does. How's work going for you, by the way?"

"Good days and some not so good days, which is pretty much what I expected when I decided to start up this business. But we've stayed pretty busy, so I'm happy about that."

"Great. I'm so glad to hear it's going well for you. I knew you'd make a success of it, Mia."

"Thanks, Amelia."

"What about you, Tara?" Amelia asked. "I know running an event planning business can't be easy. When Mick was still playing, you had to have events on the weekends."

Tara nodded. "We had several events on Sundays, so I missed a few games. Fortunately, I hired great staff, so on occasion I could shift events to some of my staff and go to a few home games. And Mick understood the nature of my business, so he certainly didn't expect me to be watching or attending every one of his games."

"Of course," Amelia said. "Same here. I do have to work some Sundays, and Flynn knows that. We're businesswomen and our jobs always come first."

"I'm sure you've set Nathan straight about that, haven't you, Mia?" Tara asked.

Mia blinked. "What?"

Tara gave her a knowing smile. "About you not being at his beck and call during game days."

She tried to play dumb. "Why would Nathan care whether I'm at the game or not?"

"Oh, honey, it's just us here. And surely you realize I know how you feel about my son."

A giant mental neon Uh-Oh sign flashed in her head. "Yes. We're friends."

"More than that, we think," Amelia said. "All of us have eyes, Mia."

Had they been that obvious? She thought they'd hid it well.

"Oh. Uh. I didn't know everyone knew."

Amelia shrugged. "I don't know about everyone. But the way you look at each other? To me it's obvious."

Wendy gave her a knowing smile. "We all know, honey."

Tara nodded. "Agreed. There's been a lot more than friendship going on for a while now. No need to hide it. And no need to be afraid I'm going to say anything to anyone."

"Neither will I," Amelia said. "That's between you and Nathan and it's no one's business. Until the two of you are ready to come out in public with your relationship, anyway."

Mia sighed. "Thanks. We've been dating and having a wonderful time with each other. But that's really as far as it's gone. We need to talk to each other about how we feel first. I mean, we know we're dating and in a relationship, but as far as talking about those deeper feelings . . . "

"Oh," Tara said. "So that part hasn't happened yet?"

Mia shook her head. "Not exactly."

"Sometimes it's hard to have that conversation," Wendy said. "When you know you have feelings for each other, but you don't know how to sit down and talk about them."

Mia nodded. "Yes. We haven't gotten there just yet."

Tara patted her hand. "Then we'll just mind our own business."

Mick came over and put his hand on Tara's shoulder. "What are we minding our own business about?"

Tara laughed. "Something that's none of your business."

"I see how it is," Mick said with a grin. "Must be a woman thing."

"Definitely."

Mick slid into the seat next to Tara. "Then let's watch some football."

Fortunately football resumed, which gave Mia a reprieve from talking about her relationship with Nathan. With Nathan's mother, of all people.

She'd had no idea they'd been so obvious about their feelings toward each other. She thought they'd hid the passionate part of their relationship well. Clearly, not so much. Maybe feelings couldn't be hidden.

And if how she felt had been so obvious to those around her, she wondered if Nathan was aware of them as well? She supposed it was time for that long overdue conversation after the game.

She wished she had brought her planner so she could organize her thoughts before she talked to Nathan.

Passion was one thing. Sure, the sex had been great, and maybe the amazing chemistry between them had been what Tara and Amelia had seen. That didn't necessarily mean Nathan felt the same way as she did. Fun and great sex was one thing. Love was something entirely different.

She rubbed her temple, feeling that stress headache bubble to the surface.

Go away. I don't want to deal with you now.

Why did relationships have to be so damn complicated? Her relationship with Nathan had been so much simpler when they'd been just friends.

But, oh, she'd have missed out on the sex.

"Did you see that catch?" Amelia asked as everyone jumped up and clapped.

She stood, too, and clapped, though she'd had no idea what just happened, because she'd been all wrapped up in her thoughts. She mentally shoved all thoughts of Nathan her boyfriend aside to concentrate only on Nathan the quarterback for now.

They watched the rest of the game unfold.

Nathan played well and so did Flynn. The starters were pulled after the third quarter, which meant Mia could relax a little. She got up and wandered around to chat with some of the players' wives and girlfriends, and noshed on some snacks.

"They look good," Wendy said. "Jamal's going to be happy about this game."

Mia nodded. "I think they're all going to be happy heading into the start of the season. The Sabers look strong."

"Which means we all need to celebrate after this game."

Mia grinned. "I'm game for that."

Tara came up to them. "I thought we might all want to meet up at our house after the game. It's close to the stadium, we can whip up some snacks and just chill. Sam's in St. Louis with his grandparents this time so I'd love to have some grown-up time."

"That sounds like a wonderful idea," Amelia said.

"I'd love to," Wendy said. "And I know Jamal would be thrilled."

"Mia?" Tara asked.

"Absolutely." Her conversation with Nathan could wait. There was no rush.

But she couldn't wait too much longer. She had a lot to tell him.

THIRTY-THREE

MAN, THAT HAD BEEN A GOOD GAME. THE TEAM HAD been firing on all cylinders today. Sure it was still preseason, but Nathan couldn't help but feel like it was a precursor for what was to come.

They still had one preseason game to go, and it was a road game, but he was beginning to sink into his role. And with every game he felt more and more ready to lead the team. He didn't want to be overconfident because that could be the kiss of death, so he knew he had to rein in his enthusiasm. But damn was he ever fired up after today's win.

He took his shower and did his interviews, then headed out of the media center to find his family there. He hugged his dad and his mom.

"What did you think?" he asked his dad.

"You look damn good out there. As good as I ever did."

He knew that statement was just his dad trying to pump up his confidence, but still, it felt great to hear it.

"Thanks. I don't think I'm anywhere near as good as you were, but everything felt right today. Team was overall in good shape on both sides of the ball, don't you think?"

"If I'd been playing I'd have had no complaints, so you're right about that."

"We're all going to the house to eat and celebrate," his mom said after she hugged him.

"Sounds good." Nathan looked over at Mia. "Are you coming?"

"I wouldn't miss it. And you had a great game." She came over to him and hugged him.

When she went to pull away, he held her there with his arm around her. "I'm glad."

Reporters were filtering out through the hallways, and they stopped to get some sound bites from Nathan's dad.

"What did you think of Nathan's play today, Mick?"

His dad looked over at Nathan and smiled. "He looked like a pro quarterback today. He's at ease in the pocket. He hit all his targets. I'd say he knows what he's doing out there. I have every confidence he'll lead the Sabers as well as, or even better than, I ever did."

They took photos and that's when Mia realized Nathan still had his arm around her. She started to ease away but Nathan held firm to her.

"What's the status here, Nathan?" one of the reporters asked, referring to Mia. "Are you and Mia Cassidy dating?"

"Right now? We're hungry. We're all headed out to eat, so I know you won't mind excusing us."

But as they walked away, Mia heard *Riley* and *Cassidy* and *a couple* buzzed about by the reporters. She winced.

She should have tried harder to extricate herself from Nathan's embrace. Now, instead of reporting on Nathan's great performance in the game, all they were going to talk about was the two of them. She could already imagine the headlines tonight and tomorrow.

Dammit.

They all headed down the hall toward the parking lot. Nathan walked her to her car.

"See you at my parents' house?" he asked.

"Yes."

"I want to talk to you tonight." He looked around, then reached down to entwine his fingers with hers. Just his touch was a calming balm to her nerves.

"Yes, me, too."

He inhaled deeply. "I really want to kiss you right now."

"That would be such a bad idea." For so many reasons.

"Would it?"

"You saw the reporters in there, didn't you?"

"I did. So what?"

She tilted her head to the side. "They could still be lurking."

"In the parking lot?" He looked around. "I don't think so."

"You have a lot to learn about the media, Nathan."

He laughed. "Whatever you say. I'll see you in a few."

They made their way over to Tara and Mick's house. On the way there, Mia couldn't empty her head of all those reporters. Of their whispers and all the cameras focusing on the two of them.

Why did it have to be such a big deal who Nathan dated? Or if he dated anyone? And why did the thought of the reporters and what they were going to write consume her with dread?

She pulled up in front of the house and pulled up social media. And she had her answer.

Some of the sports feeds had already picked up the story—with pictures.

Is Nathan Riley dating Mia Cassidy?

Riley + Cassidy. A New Dynasty in the Making?

How Will Nathan's Love Life Affect His Game Play?

As if those weren't bad enough, there were worse ones. *Is Mia Cassidy Courting Nathan Riley for Her New Sports Management Company?* And *Mia Cassidy Building Her Sports Management Brand by Getting Close to Nathan Cassidy.*

Shit.

Mia gripped the steering wheel. Shit, shit, shit. One innocuous photo of Nathan with his arm around her and suddenly there were multiple headlines about his love life. And even worse, accusations of her getting close to Nathan in order to build her business. Nothing on his stats, or how well he was playing for the Sabers, but on his love life. And on her using Nathan.

Goddammit.

She could handle herself just fine, could diffuse talk about her using him for her company. But she couldn't let the focus shift from Nathan's play onto the two of them. Publicity of any kind that wasn't game related, especially now, was not good for Nathan's career. Nothing should pull focus from football.

She looked over at the house. Everyone was there.

If Nathan had been one of her clients, she'd tell him to take a step back from the relationship, to focus on football.

The season was about to start and that's where his head had to be—where all his attention needed to be.

She knew what she had to do.

She pulled out her phone and sent him a text message.

Have a headache. Going home. Tell everyone I'm sorry I can't make it.

She put her car in gear and started for home.

Her phone pinged on the way but of course she couldn't answer when she was driving.

She didn't answer her phone after she got home, either, not even when it rang. Instead, she changed into shorts and a T-shirt, poured herself a glass of cabernet and settled in on the sofa with her planner and her laptop, working out her plan for next week.

It was time she focus on work, too. She had to put her attention on her job and not on the man she . . .

Well, it was time to concentrate on other things.

She was deeply into planning the week when her doorbell rang. She sighed, knowing who it was.

Dammit, Nathan.

She got up and opened the door. He didn't even wait for an invite, just walked inside.

"You don't have a headache."

She closed the door. "How do you know I don't have a headache?"

He turned to her. "First, you look amazing. Second, you squint when you have a headache and you're not squinting. Third, you have red wine on the table over there and you always drink white when you have a headache."

Damn the man for knowing her so well. "Fine, I don't have a headache."

She went over to the sofa and sat down. He followed, sitting next to her on the sofa. Or as close to her as he could since she had her paperwork spread out everywhere.

And she wasn't going to move it, because she needed the barrier.

"So why did you blow off the party?"

She shrugged. "I had work to do."

"You could have said that. But I still don't think that's the reason. Something's bothering you."

"I just needed to be alone."

"Why?"

Break it off, Mia. Be quick and brutal about it and break it off.

Just the thought of it cut her sharply. But she knew she had to do it. "I don't know, Nathan. I've been doing a lot of thinking. You're busy, I'm busy. You're about to start your season and I have so much going on. I just don't think this is working between us."

The shock and hurt on his face was evident. And she hated it. She wanted to take it all back, but she wouldn't.

"Wait? What? What are you talking about?"

"I'm talking about us. I need a break."

No, no. Not a break. She needed to make it more final. A break indicated that they might get back together. She needed to remember the press. She didn't want any more of that. It wasn't good for Nathan's career. "I mean, not a break. I just need . . . I'm sorry. I need to not see you anymore."

He just stared at her as if she were some alien that had crawled out of a human body. Which was exactly what she felt like.

Because she was lying. To him and to herself. And the hurt look on Nathan's face made her want to crawl onto his lap and cry and tell him she was lying, that she didn't mean any of what she'd just said. She wanted to tell him she loved him. Instead, she was breaking up with him.

"You are so full of shit," he said.

"Excuse me?"

"What's really going on, Mia?"

"I just told you."

"No, you didn't. You made up some bullshit story about work."

"It is not bullshit."

"When did you stop trusting me, Mia?"

His words shocked her. "I've never stopped trusting you."

"Haven't you? Because it seems to me the closer we get, the further you pull away from me. You used to tell me everything. Every thought you had, every feeling you felt. Hell, even shit I didn't want to hear sometimes. And now you're feeling a lot of things but you're telling me nothing. You're holding back. So why don't you trust me anymore?"

His words hurt like a knife going through her heart. Because he was right. She had always told him how she felt. And now, when she really needed to tell him everything, she couldn't. Because in order to protect him she had to lie to him.

"I do trust you. And I am telling you the truth, Nathan. I need you to take a step away. This is all too much for me. Being with you is pulling my focus away from my work and I just can't do it. I mean, look at all of this."

She waved her hands over her file folders and her planner and her laptop. "I have so much work and I'm neglecting it because I'm spending all of my time with you. And I just can't do that. I have to put all my attention on my company. I'm afraid I'll fail because I'm not giving it the focus that it needs. I just don't have the time for a relationship right now. I'm sorry."

Again he gave her that look of disbelief. For a few seconds she thought he was going to push at her again, to tell her she was lying to him.

She'd continue to fight him, because even though he didn't know it, she was fighting *for* him. For his career and for his future.

And for her own.

"Tell me the damn truth, Mia. What's going on?"

She knew he wouldn't walk away from her so easily. She decided to use what the media said about them to get him to leave her.

She stood. "Fine. You want the truth? I warned you about the reporters. But you refused to listen. And now they're targeting me, saying that I'm using you to benefit my business. I can't have that, Nathan."

He frowned. "What?"

"I can't be seen with you anymore. It's hurting my company."

She showed him social media, but only pulled up the ones that mentioned her using Nathan to grow MHC.

"Well, that's a load of shit."

"You know that and I know that, but optics is everything. And I can't have anything negative affect MHC."

"I can deny it."

She rolled her eyes. "Like that will do any good. I can't afford negative press right now. My company is more important to me than anything. Even you."

She saw the hurt on his face and it nearly buckled her legs. It took everything in her to stand firm and stare him down.

"Really," he said.

"Yes, really. I'm sorry, Nathan, but I can't do this with you anymore. It could spell disaster for me."

"This is really what you want. You're not willing to fight for us."

She gave him a curt nod. "No. I can't. Maybe sometime down the road things will be different."

She wanted to cry because the pain on his face destroyed her. But she held her chin up and met his gaze.

"Sometime down the road? Do you even hear yourself, Mia? This doesn't even sound like you. I've never known you to be so fucking cold."

She wrapped her arms around herself, feeling as cold as the words she spit at him. "I'm sorry. I really am. This hurts me, too, Nathan."

"Does it? Because it's like I don't even know the woman standing in front of me."

She shrugged, afraid if she said anything more the tears would fall and she'd end up blurting out that everything she'd said was a lie.

"Okay. If that's the way you want it, fine. We're done."

He turned around and walked out the door, shutting it behind him.

She waited a full fifteen minutes, making sure he didn't come back—part of her hoping he would. But when she was sure he was gone for good, she set her laptop aside, placed her folders and planner into a neat pile on top of it, then brought her knees up to her chest and let the tears come.

THIRTY-FOUR

THEY'D LOST THEIR LAST PRESEASON GAME BY ONLY four points. It was only a preseason game, but Nathan hadn't felt like himself. He'd been off. Coach had told him they'd all been off their game that day and for him to shake it off.

Whatever. He knew the loss of that game was on him. He'd lost his focus and he hadn't been able to rally his team to victory.

Jamal had told him to shake off whatever it was because the regular season was starting and he needed to look forward, not back.

Jamal was so right about that, in so many ways.

Today was the first official game of the season and he had to get his head right. He'd worked hard this week to put his mind-set where it belonged—on football. They'd finalized the roster, the rookies all looked ready and the offensive line was mean. His receivers were sharp and Nathan knew the playbook like his own personal bible. He should be charged up and ready for this.

Except he wasn't. His gut was tight and it felt like rocks sat in his stomach.

He missed Mia, and no amount of attempting to push her out of his head the past two weeks had helped get her out of his system. Or his heart.

He'd replayed their conversation over and over and it still made no sense. He knew the media thing had been worrying her, but they'd always worked things out together. Plus, she was a shrewd businesswoman with a great PR team. His team had one as well and they could have figured out a way to spin this in their favor.

She'd never even given them a chance. It was like she'd turned into someone he didn't even know. So what the hell was it that had flipped her switch so suddenly, that made her push him away?

"You ready, kid?"

He jerked his head up to see his coach standing over him, which meant his thoughts about Mia were going to have to be pushed away until after the game.

Nathan stood. "Hell yes I'm ready."

Coach grinned and slapped him on the shoulder pad. "Let's go."

The team waited in the tunnel and, when it was time, came running out to the earsplitting sounds of the sold-out stadium. Nathan felt fortunate to have a home game to start the season. They'd follow up this one with two road games, but at least he'd have the home crowd support on his side to start things off.

He'd like to say he was confident as fuck, but that would be a lie. He was as nervous as he'd been at the start of his first preseason game. But he hid that from his teammates because they needed to be able to rely on him.

This was the real deal. This game counted. And he wasn't going to let them down. So he sucked up all that nervous energy, determined to use it to his benefit.

And hopefully, he wouldn't screw up. Because he wasn't going to get a second chance at this.

He had to wait it out a bit because the Sabers won the toss and deferred, so Arizona had the ball first. He went over the offensive game plan with his coach and tried to keep his nerves in check. Fortunately, and thanks to Flynn and the defense, Arizona went three and out and offense was up.

Jamal came over to him and shoved into his shoulder. "You got this."

Nathan gave him a quick nod. "I know."

He'd gotten nothing but positive remarks and vibes from his offense all week. They believed in him.

Now he just had to believe in himself.

MIA HADN'T WANTED TO MISS OPENING DAY. SHE'D wanted to be there, at the stadium, but for now it was best if she stayed out of the spotlight. Once things died down and the media found something else to talk about, she could go to the games again.

There had been a few more articles about Nathan and her, but there had been no facts, only supposition based on a few photos of the two of them together. They'd even interviewed Mick Riley, who'd told them how Nathan and Mia had been friends since college. He'd left it at that, so there'd been nothing for the press to chew on.

For the past two weeks there'd been nothing but football for Nathan, and for her, work. And those two had been separate. Which was a very good thing for both of them.

Except her heart hurt so badly she could barely draw a breath.

She knew she'd hurt Flynn's feelings when he'd asked her if she was going to be there today and she'd told him no. And he hadn't

believed her when she'd told him she had work to do. But there was
nothing she could do about that. He'd just have to deal with it.

She was hurt, too. For so many reasons. She wanted to be at the
game, cheering on her brother.

Cheering for Nathan.

Instead, she was in her raggedy old shorts from college, her favorite Sabers T-shirt, sitting with her feet cross-legged on the
couch watching the game on TV while eating cheese and drinking
wine.

She was so miserable and lonely she wanted to cry. Instead, she
ate more cheese, then got up and poured herself another glass of
wine, determined to suck it up for Nathan's sake.

God, she was so pathetic.

The first series went amazing. Nathan didn't look at all nervous as he threw the ball to his receivers. A couple of dropped
passes and missed connections, but that was to be expected in his
first game of the season. Once he settled into the pocket, she could
see his confidence grow and he connected solidly with Jamal on a
twenty-three yard pass.

She pumped her fist in the air, trying to feel as if she was part
of the stadium crowd.

Another pass in the next series of downs for twelve yards. Then
another for sixteen.

Now they were rolling. The running game looked solid as well,
and when Nathan skirted around a defensive lineman and threw a
pass to the tight end for a touchdown, she nearly spilled her wine
when she leaped off the couch and cheered. She had to set her wineglass down to do her own touchdown dance. Her heart was racing
and she wanted to hug and high-five someone.

Only she was alone. She didn't have Amelia or the other players' wives or Tara or anyone with her.

This sucked.

She shook her head. "No, this is fine. I'm doing the right thing."

She sat and picked up her planner, making some notes for next week's meetings while she watched the game. It was time to calm down.

The game progressed well. The opposing team didn't score on them until well into the second quarter, and then, only a field goal.

Mia grinned. That would make Flynn happy. And the Sabers had scored another touchdown, which was even better.

By halftime they were up fourteen to three. Mia got up to stretch and make herself a salad. She decided before she ate she'd head upstairs to do some yoga, which might help alleviate some of her tension. She did a few light stretches, working on her breathing and clearing her head. She felt much better after and settled in with her salad to watch the second half of the game.

She picked up her phone to see a text message from Amelia.

Miss you. Wish you were here at the game.

And another one from Wendy.

Girl. Why aren't you here? Work can wait!

She sighed.

She texted them both that she missed them, and that she'd be there next time.

Maybe. Maybe not. It would all depend on how the media handled Nathan after the game. Nathan might not realize why she'd broken up with him, but when he did his presser after the game and they focused only on the game and not on the chick in the stands who'd been rooting for him, he'd thank her.

Nathan was a superstar in the making, and that's where all the attention should be. If he had a good management company supporting him, that's exactly what they'd tell him. No girlfriends, no PR about girlfriends, nothing to take the focus away from his career.

This just wasn't the right time for them. She knew that, and he'd come to realize it as well.

Even if she didn't sleep well at night anymore. Even if her heart hurt every day. Even if she did still love him, and probably always would.

She was tough. She'd get over it.

THIRTY-FIVE

THEY'D WON. BY THE TIME HE'D FINISHED THE FIRST series with a touchdown, Nathan had known they were going to win this game. He'd felt the confidence rushing through him. His team had felt solid on both sides of the ball.

He felt great. Now he just had to get through media interviews, which so far were going well.

"How did you feel going into your first regular game of the season?"

"Confident. Coach has put together a talented team on offense. Defense held Arizona to two field goals, making it easier for us to do our jobs. All in all, I thought it was a great start to the season for the Sabers."

"Any concerns about the team at any level?"

"None at all. Everyone's healthy and as you could see from the game play today, everyone's pulling their weight at every position. I'd say we're in fine shape for the start of the season."

"So you feel focused and ready to roll?"

Nathan smiled. "Yup."

"What about your personal life? Are you still seeing Mia Cassidy?"

He'd expected the question. "My personal life isn't up for discussion. Let's stick to football."

"Was she at the game today?"

"I'm not discussing my personal life, today or any day." He got up. "Thanks, everyone."

When he left the media room, his coach came over to him. "Sorry about that."

"It's okay, Coach. They can keep asking the questions, but they won't get an answer from me."

"You did good, kid. And in the future I'll take care of those questions. They won't like my answer."

Nathan could well imagine how his coach would handle reporters asking personal questions. His coach was a nice guy—until you pissed him off.

"Thanks. I appreciate it."

"Hey, I agree with you. What you do when you're not on the field is no one's business but your own. So now go relax and we'll see you at practice."

"Thanks, Coach."

He went to his locker. Jamal was just finishing up, so he smiled at Nathan.

"Wendy and I are headed out to celebrate. You in?"

"Not today, but thanks. You two enjoy."

Jamal laid his hand on Nathan's shoulder. "You okay, buddy?"

Nathan laid his hand over Jamal's. "I'm good. And hey, great game today. You were always right where I needed you to be."

"Always will be. On the field and off."

Nathan grinned. He knew he could always count on his best friend.

At least there was one person he knew he could always count on.

"What the hell did you do to my sister?"

He turned to see Flynn standing in front of him, arms crossed, a fierce expression on his face.

"What?"

"Mia."

"I know who your sister is, Flynn. I just don't know what you're talking about. I didn't do anything to her."

"Didn't you? She's upset."

"Oh, is she? Well I didn't cause that."

"Didn't you? She didn't come to the game today. And when I asked her why she just said she was busy with work. Which sounds like a bullshit reason to me and could only mean she's upset with you."

Nathan shrugged and grabbed his bag to leave. "If she didn't want to come to the game, that's her decision."

"Did you two break up?"

"No, Flynn. *We* didn't break up. She dumped me. Two weeks ago."

Flynn frowned. "She did? What the hell did she do that for?"

"Hell if I know. Maybe you should ask her, because as far as I know everything was going great between us, and suddenly she decided her career was all important, and our relationship was getting in the way of that."

Flynn's stance softened. "That doesn't sound like Mia."

"Apparently it is, because she gave me the boot right out the door, and I haven't heard from her since."

Flynn was silent for a few seconds. "Hey, I'm sorry, man. I didn't know."

"No reason you would unless Mia wanted to tell you about it." Which, apparently, she hadn't.

"So you two didn't have a fight or anything?"

"No."

"Huh. I need to go talk to my sister."

"Yeah, you do that. I'm outta here."

"Okay. Later, Nathan."

Nathan walked out the door, mixing in with several of his teammates who were greeted by wives and girlfriends and family members.

His mom and dad weren't there today, which meant there was no one to greet him.

He walked down the long hallway toward the parking lot.

Alone.

THIRTY-SIX

MIA HAD JUST FINISHED A MEETING WITH A PROSPEC-
tive client and was on her way back to her office when Monique
flagged her down.

"Your brother is here."

"Flynn?"

"Yes."

Curious, she went to the reception area. Flynn was alone, wearing dark jeans and a button-down shirt and currently being ogled
by her receptionist. She remembered Lina telling her about her
crush on Flynn when she interviewed her, even though she'd in-
formed Lina that Flynn was taken.

She smiled at the memory. "I wasn't expecting you."

"I know. Do you have time for lunch?"

She looked at her phone. It was still early, and her staff meeting
wasn't until two. "Sure. Let me grab my purse."

They ended up walking to the Plant Café Organic, and got a table outside since it was a warm day.

They both ordered water and the shitake spring rolls for an appetizer.

"Where's Amelia?" Mia asked.

"At home making both a chocolate and a lemon tart."

"Now I'm really hungry."

Flynn laughed. "Yeah, it smelled pretty good in there when I left her place."

The waitress brought their appetizer, so they dug in, and also ordered lunch.

"So what brings you out here?"

"I missed you at the game yesterday."

"I missed being there. It was lonely cheering for you at the house all by myself. I mean, the game was awesome, of course, but not the same as being there."

"So why didn't you come?"

"I had work."

He took a large bite of spring roll, swallowed, then took a drink of water before answering with, "That's a load of crap, Mia. You can't keep hiding behind work."

She sighed. "Nathan told you."

"Yeah, but only after I accused him of hurting you."

She frowned. "Oh, you didn't."

"I did."

"It was me, Flynn. I broke up with him."

"You can tell me it's none of my business, but you know I'm always here for you if you want to talk."

She knew that was true. And Flynn of all people would understand.

"Two weeks ago after the game we were all gathered outside the locker room and Nathan had his arm around me. The press was out there, too. That was the day we were all headed over to Mick and Tara's for a postgame celebration."

"I remember that. You decided not to come."

"I surfed some social media sites after that, and they had linked Nathan and me together. I got scared."

"Because you don't want to be linked to Nathan? Why? Because of MHC?"

"No. Okay, partly yes because some articles implied I was using Nathan to benefit my company."

"Assholes."

"True. But I can handle that. It was mainly because of Nathan's career. Because I didn't want the press to focus on the whole Cassidy/Riley dynasty thing to the detriment of his career. One photo of the two of us together and that's all the media covered. Not how well Nathan played that day, but how Nathan Riley and Mia Cassidy were a couple."

Flynn took a sip of water and looked at her. "I see. So you broke up with him because of that."

"Yes."

"And you think that would matter to Nathan?"

"It matters to me. As someone who manages athletes, it matters how they're perceived, and what the press focuses on. Nathan's just starting out and the attention should be on his performance on the field. Not on what he's doing off of it."

Their lunch arrived, so Flynn didn't say anything else for a while. Mia tried to enjoy her miso soup, but she wanted to know what was on her brother's mind, so she ended up leaving half of it.

"Well?" she finally asked.

"Well, what?"

"What do you think?"

"I think you should talk to Nathan. Tell him the truth, and then the two of you should decide what's best for both of you.

I don't think it's up to you to make a decision about his career, Mia."

She sighed. "I was afraid you'd say that. But I did what I thought was right."

"So you don't really care about him."

She threw her napkin on the table. "How can you say that? I broke up with him because I love him."

Flynn laughed. "Yeah. That's how you tell someone you love them. By telling them you don't want to see them anymore."

"Screw you, Flynn."

Their waitress came over to refill their water glasses, so that silenced her for a few minutes, which was probably a good thing, because she was about to blow up at her brother in a public restaurant. Instead, she took a couple of deep breaths and a few sips of water to calm herself down.

"How is Nathan?" she asked.

"He seems a little pissed."

She nodded. "Okay."

Flynn reached over and grabbed her hand. "I know you think you did the right thing. But you didn't give him a chance to be a part of this decision you made. And knowing Nathan, I don't think he would have been on board with your idea."

"But—"

"But nothing, Mia. If he cares about you like I think he does, it won't matter. And honestly? The media is hot on a topic one week, and the next week they're on to something else. It might not be as big a deal as you think it is."

"Of course it shouldn't matter. But the timing of it sucked. Nathan's career is a priority right now."

"Nathan might think you're just as important a priority. Don't you think you should give him the chance to prove that to you?"

"I guess." She was kind of surprised by Flynn taking Nathan's side. She'd worried for so long about how her brothers would react to her dating Nathan. Flynn didn't seem surprised—or even bothered by it. In fact, he seemed pissed that she'd broken up with Nathan.

"So talk to him."

"I will."

They walked back to her office and she hugged him outside. "Thank you for lunch, and for listening. And I guess for the lecture."

He laughed and gave her a tight squeeze. "That's what big brothers are for. To give you all that unwanted advice you need."

"I love you, Flynn."

"Love you, too, Mia. Now go talk to Nathan."

After Flynn left, she rode the elevator back up to her office, and realized Flynn was right.

She'd made unilateral decisions without discussing her thoughts or her feelings with Nathan. And without taking his feelings into consideration.

She'd made a colossal mistake, and she needed to talk to Nathan.

If he even wanted to speak to her anymore.

But she loved him, she missed him and she was going to make him listen to her. After that, it was up to him.

THIRTY-SEVEN

NATHAN WAS SLUGGISH DURING PRACTICE. ALL DUR-
ing drills today he'd felt like he was dragging a Chevy through the
turf. Even his coach had noticed and told him more than once to
pick up his own ass and run.

He'd never been happier to see the end of a practice. He'd stood
under the running water in the shower for what seemed like an
eternity, hoping it would wash away the tons of turf he'd eaten
when his defense had knocked him down over and over again.

There wasn't a part of his body that didn't hurt like hell. What
he wanted right now was a damn beer and a cheeseburger.

"You look like you've been run over by a truck," Flynn said as
he passed by his locker.

"Feel like it, too."

"I've had rough practices like these before. Some days are just
like that. You need to shake it off."

"I plan to. With a beer and a cheeseburger."

"Ninety-Two makes the best cheeseburgers in the city. Let me treat you to one."

He wasn't in the mood to socialize. He'd planned to grab something on the way home and nurse his aches and pains on the sofa, but Flynn was a veteran and he could probably use some insight into why he'd been dragging ass on the field today. So he nodded. "Sure. That sounds great. Thanks."

"Okay. Meet you there."

Flynn left and Nathan sat there for several minutes, trying to summon the energy to get dressed.

He had to start getting his shit together. They had a tough game coming up this weekend against Dallas and he had to get his mind-set right.

Last night he'd stayed up way too late thinking about calling Mia. Or going over to Mia's place and making her talk to him.

God, he missed her. He thought by now he'd be over her. It had been three weeks. He always got over women fast.

But he'd never loved a woman before. Not the real love kind of love. This really fucking hurt. Getting over her wasn't going to be easy.

Maybe he needed to text her, to ask her to meet with him so they could talk things out, so she could make him understand what the fuck had happened.

Closure. What he needed was that mystical closure thing people talked about when relationships ended. He'd always laughed about that when his friends talked about it or he saw it portrayed on TV. What the fuck was closure anyway?

Whatever it was, he needed it so he could move the hell on with his life.

He got dressed and drove into the city, parking in the lot at

Ninety-Two. By the time he got there, he decided that the closure thing was overrated. What he needed was a beer and a cheeseburger and an awesome game on Sunday.

Those were all the things he needed to be happy. He needed to stay away from women and relationships, because those two things screwed with his head. All he needed in his life was football. If he just concentrated on football, everything would be perfect.

Then he walked in the door of the restaurant and saw Mia sitting at the bar, and his newly constructed life plan went totally to shit.

MIA SAW THE LOOK ON NATHAN'S FACE WHEN HE WALKED in. He was not happy to see her. She half expected him to turn around and walk out. In fact, she found herself holding her breath for that fraction of a second as their gazes met, waiting for him to do exactly that.

When he didn't, when he walked toward her, she exhaled in relief. He could be mad as hell at her, he could even yell at her. But what she couldn't handle was him walking away.

Though that's what she'd done, wasn't it? She'd walked away from him—from them, without even giving him a truthful explanation about why. She owed him that, so she really hoped he'd stay to hear her out.

"I'm here to see Flynn," he said.

She swallowed, her throat gone dry. "He's not here."

Nathan frowned. "Okay. I'll wait for him."

"I mean, he's not going to be here. I asked him to ask you to come."

"Why?"

"Because I figured if I asked you to come you wouldn't."

"You're right. This is a waste of time."

He started to walk away but she laid her hand on his forearm. "Please stay."

"I don't need closure, Mia."

"Closure? I'm not— I don't want that, Nathan. I want to talk to you."

He looked around and so did she. The restaurant wasn't crowded. It was still early so the dinner crowd hadn't arrived yet.

"Fine."

She felt such relief at that one word. "Let's get a table somewhere private in the corner where we can talk. Would you like something to drink?"

He told the bartender he wanted a beer. Once he got that, they went to a table in the far corner of the restaurant.

Mia took a sip of her wine while Nathan took several long swallows of his beer, then set it down on the table.

"What's this all about, Mia?"

Now was the time to lay the truth out on the table. She hoped he didn't bolt when she did, but she owed him that. She owed him the truth—and her feelings.

"I lied to you."

"When?"

"When I broke up with you. It wasn't about my company or me. It was about you."

He didn't respond to that, so she continued.

"That afternoon of the preseason game, you put your arm around me and the media was there. They took photos and those photos showed up online. I sat outside Mick and Tara's house. You remember we were supposed to meet there."

"Yeah, I remember. You cancelled."

"Right. I saw those photos and what the reporters were saying about you and me. They focused on the two of us together. They asked if we were a dynasty in the making. They accused me of using you to benefit my company. And suddenly it wasn't about your game that day, Nathan. It was about us."

"So?"

She sighed. "How can you be so nonchalant about that? You know how the press focuses on an athlete and his personal life. I didn't want that for you. Not at such a critical juncture in your career."

Nathan took a sip of his beer. "Oh, I get it. So you decided it would be best to end things between us to save me. How noble of you."

She knew he'd be mad about it. "I'm sorry. I thought what I was doing was for the best. For you."

"Without talking to me about it. Without asking how I felt about it. Because Mia Cassidy knows best."

She shook her head. "It wasn't like that. I was scared for you, Nathan. I was worried how you'd be perceived, that the focus would be about the two of us instead of your performance on the field."

"So instead of treating me like someone you care about, you treated me like a client. Hell, Mia, for that, I should sign with MHC, because you handled me beautifully, didn't you? Your instincts were right on. Tell the client that personal life and entanglements come second to career. Right?"

This was not going like she thought it would. Couldn't he see what she'd done for him? Couldn't he see how much her heart was hurting? "That's exactly the way I thought. I sacrificed us for you. Don't you see that?"

His gaze narrowed. "Oh, I see it perfectly. Only I was in love with you, Mia. So while you were thinking all about business you ripped my goddamn heart out."

He was in love with her? It was the first time he'd said it and she should be elated.

But she could only watch him as he stood, tossed money on the table for his beer and, without another word, walked out of the restaurant.

Mia stared at the empty chair where he'd sat.

Oh, God. She'd hurt him so much, even more than she'd thought.

Because she'd had to be the one in control. So instead of loving him and talking to him about her fears and concerns, she'd managed him. He was so right. Instead of talking it over with the man she loved, she'd treated him like a client.

It really was over between them. And she couldn't fix it. What she'd feared the most had happened.

She'd lost Nathan. Only it wasn't the sex or falling in love that had driven the wedge between them.

It was her. She'd ruined them. And she totally deserved this feeling of utter loss and devastation.

NATHAN THREW HIS KEYS ON THE TABLE AND PACED the confines of his condo. He raked his fingers through his hair, still hot after the long drive home.

"Fuck."

Mia had manipulated him, treated him no better than she'd treat any one of her clients.

He'd loved her. Hell, he still loved her, goddammit. And she didn't care at all about him. How could she shred him like that without a thought to how he felt?

His phone buzzed in his pocket. He pulled it out and saw that it was Mia. He gripped the phone so tight it made his hand cramp, so he threw the damn thing on the sofa.

She'd made all the decisions and never once thought to ask him how he felt. Because in Mia's world, business was everything. Business came first.

Well, no more. He was done with having his heart stomped on. And he was done with Mia for good.

THIRTY-EIGHT

THE VISIT FROM HER MOTHER HAD BEEN A SURPRISE. Maybe it was the tone in Mia's voice the past couple of weeks during their phone calls, or maybe Flynn had said something to her, but when her mom showed up on her doorstep three days ago, Mia had stepped into her mother's arms and cried. And cried some more. And then even more.

She'd taken a couple of days off work, which she hadn't wanted to do but they had no presentations and Monique had insisted they had everything under control. Monique told her she was tired of seeing her moping around the office, so she should spend some time with her mom.

Mia needed it.

They'd cuddled and talked and cooked and drank wine together. And Mia had poured out her story about what happened with Nathan.

"So, you screwed up," her mother said.

Leave it to her mother to pull no punches.

Mia had reached for a tissue and blew her nose. "Yes, I screwed up."

"What are you going to do about it?"

"Nothing. I tried explaining it to him and I only made it worse. He hates me now." That made the tears spring forth anew so she had to grab for another tissue.

She was so tired of crying.

Her mom gave her a decidedly unsympathetic look. "I did not raise a daughter who gives up. You'll have to find another way."

She sighed. "I don't know what to do. I thought I was doing the right thing. How could I have been so wrong, Mom?"

"Oh. You mean you're not perfect and you don't always make the right decisions? That's called life, Mia."

Mia frowned. "This is not helping."

"Sorry. But you got yourself into this mess by not being open and communicative with the man you love. What were you thinking?"

"I . . . don't know. A total collapse in common sense, I guess."

"You know what you have to do. Apologize to Nathan. And keep apologizing to him. Tell him you love him. You've told him you love him, haven't you?"

She wiped her nose. "Well, no."

Her mother rolled her eyes. "Tell him you love him. That you're sorry. And keep telling him until he listens to you. Until he believes you."

She sighed. "I hate being wrong."

Her mother laughed. "I know. But it's good for your character. Think of it as part of growing up."

"Being a grown-up sucks."

Her mother put her arms around her and cuddled her close. "Don't I know it. Every time I've had to apologize to your father, I've thought much the same thing."

Mia laughed.

Once she finally got over crying and feeling sorry for herself, Mom made her shower and get dressed. They went out for lunch and went shopping, and by the second day she felt a bit more like herself.

She was still sad and felt awful, but she had renewed hope. Because her mother was correct. She was going to have to find a way to make amends with Nathan. She might not ever get him back, but she had to make things right between them.

She was smart.

She'd figure out how.

THIRTY-NINE

THREE GAMES INTO THE SEASON AND THE SABERS were three and oh. Nathan was a goddamn machine on the field and he felt incredible about it.

As long as he could play football and not have to think about anything else, life was damn good.

"Feel like celebrating tonight?" Jamal asked.

"Nah, my parents are in town so I'm heading over to hang out with them."

"Oh, great."

"But thanks for the invite. And great game again. You rocked those two touchdowns today."

"Hey, only because of you and your rocket arm, my man."

He finished up his interviews and packed it up. His parents were in town for the home game today so he was meeting them at the house for dinner. They had Sam with them and he was looking forward to catching up with his little brother.

"Nathan!" Sam flew into his legs as soon as his dad opened the door.

"Sammy!" Nathan scooped him up and twirled him around. "Hey, you're heavy."

"That's because I'm big now."

His dad laughed. "It's always the same with you two. Hey, Nathan."

"Hey, Dad."

"I saw you play football today." Sam plucked at his football jersey. "I'm wearin' your number."

"I see that. It's probably why we won today."

Sam's eyes widened. "You think so?"

"I know so, buddy."

He played with Sam for a while, until his little brother decided to go hang out with his friend next door. Then Nathan sat down with his parents while his mom fixed dinner.

"You're looking solid out there on the field, Nathan," his dad said. "Press coverage says you're like a machine."

Nathan laughed and took a sip of the soda his mom had given him. "Thanks, Dad. Things seem to be gelling well for the team. It helps to have a lot of great weapons to throw to."

"Don't I know it."

"How's Mia?" his mom asked. "I didn't see her at the game today."

"No idea. We aren't seeing each other anymore."

Her mom looked shocked. "Oh, no. What happened?"

"Tara," his dad said. "That's not our business."

"But you two were so close. I thought it was love."

"Yeah, well, it wasn't."

"Mick, go grab Sam from the Millers'," his mom said. "It's time to eat."

"Okay."

After his dad left, his mom sat next to him. "What happened?"

When his mother asked, you didn't get to dodge the question. So he told her everything.

"You know she did that to protect you."

"I didn't need protecting. And I didn't need to be treated like one of her clients."

His mother took his hand. "I can understand how you might see it that way. But I think Mia was genuinely frightened for you. And maybe you could see it her way. You do realize she's in love with you, and she sacrificed the relationship for the good of your career?"

Nathan shook his head. "Nah. She didn't care enough to save it."

His mother sighed. "Men and their pride. It's always so black and white with you. If you take some time to really think things over, maybe you'll think differently."

"I don't want to think differently."

She smiled at him. "That's because you're hurt. But you love her, don't you?"

He didn't want to answer that.

"You don't have to tell me. But search your heart, Nathan. Because a true love like the one I think you have with Mia only comes around once in a lifetime." She brushed his hair away from his face and it reminded him of being a kid again. "I'm always here for you. Anytime you need to talk. You know you'll never be too old to need your mom."

He squeezed her hand, then leaned over and kissed her cheek. "Thanks, Mom. I love you."

"I love you, too, Nathan."

After dinner, he drove back to his condo. He had plenty of time to think about what his mother had said.

Had he just reacted to what Mia said without thinking about her motivation?

They'd been friends forever. She had never done anything to hurt him. And she'd always been in his corner where his career was concerned. She'd never been callous or thoughtless. Hell, that just wasn't her.

Until she'd dumped him, of course. And that's all he'd been thinking about lately.

But they'd been growing closer and closer, and he'd known he was in love with her. He could have sworn her feelings were the same. Which was why it had been such a shock when she'd dumped him. If he was honest with himself, thinking back now, she'd looked as hurt about it as he had. But he'd only thought about his own feelings.

Had she really sacrificed their relationship for him?

There was only one way to find out, and that was to talk to her.

He wasn't ready yet. And maybe that was his ego talking, but he needed to sound out his feelings with someone he trusted, someone who'd understand what he was going through. Right now he needed to talk to one of his boys.

He texted Jamal. He was free, so he went over to his place.

He lived in a condo similar to Nathan's. It had been a while since he'd been here, and Nathan could see Wendy's influence. There were flowerpots and some trendy new art on the wall along with decorative pillows. And was that a new couch?

"Added some new shit to the place, huh?"

Jamal cracked a smile. "Wendy. Did I tell you she's moving in?"

"You didn't." He followed Jamal into the kitchen.

"Beer, energy drink or water?" Jamal asked.

"Water's good, thanks."

Jamal fixed him a glass of ice water and they went back into the living room. Nathan pulled up a chair and Jamal sat on the sofa.

"So things are getting serious between you two, huh?" Nathan asked.

Jamal nodded. "Yeah. I'm in love with her. She's good for me."

"That's great, man. I'm happy for you."

"Thanks. So what's up with you?"

"It's Mia. She's got my head all screwed up."

Jamal leaned back against the sofa. "Talk to me."

He told Jamal everything that went down between Mia and him, what she'd done, how the breakup happened and why.

"Huh." Jamal took a long swallow of his energy drink. "That's messed up."

"Yeah."

"I don't blame you for kicking her to the curb for good. She's trash."

Nathan frowned. "I wouldn't go that far. I mean, she messed up, definitely."

"Come on, man. She fucked you over. She's a piece of shit. Dump her for good and move on. She's not worth your time."

Nathan looked down at his hands. They were clasped tight and he felt the stirrings of anger. Nathan being mad at Mia was one thing. Hearing Jamal talk shit about her didn't sit right with him. "She did it because she cares about me."

Jamal's lips curved. "So you love her."

Then it dawned on him. "You were testing me. Fucker."

Jamal laughed. "Hey, it worked, didn't it? You don't want things to be over with her, do you? If you were really done with her, you'd have joined in the trash talk. Instead, you defended her."

"You're right."

"So, she made a mistake and your ego got bruised. Man, I've been there. It's hard to admit to ourselves when that happens. Hell, wasn't that long ago Wendy and I had a big-ass blowup. She walked out and I swore we were done."

"So what happened?"

"I cooled down and we talked and we both realized we were

two stubborn people who liked things our own way. But we talked to each other, man. We figured it out. That's what you and Mia have to do."

Nathan dragged in a deep breath. "You're right. Thanks, Jamal."

"Hey, that's what friends are for. You know I'm always here for you."

He didn't know what he'd do without his best friend.

Now he had to go and get his other best friend back.

FORTY

MIA WAS SHOCKED TO HER TOES WHEN SHE GOT THE text message from Nathan while she was at work.

Can you come over to my place tonight?

She didn't know what it meant, but she was more than open to it. She quickly sent back a reply.

Yes. Anytime.

He replied with: How about 6:30?

There was nothing in his message to indicate whether he wanted to yell at her some more or whether he was in a good mood. But she wanted to be prepared either way. After work, she stopped and bought something for him. Then she took a shower, dried her hair and put on makeup, then slipped into a black-and-white sundress and her sandals. She wanted to keep it casual, but she wanted to look good, too.

She drove over to his place and took out the bag and carried it to his door, her heart pounding the entire time. She rang the bell, hoping she didn't pass out from the stress while she waited.

Nathan pulled the door open. He was wearing relaxed jeans and a tight dark T-shirt. His hair was thick and long and if they'd still been friends she would have teased him about needing a haircut.

But she didn't have that right anymore.

He looked so good and all she wanted to do was smother him with kisses and wrap herself around him and never let him go.

She resisted.

"Hi," he said. "Come on in."

"Thanks."

She walked in and he shut the door behind her. She felt awkward and nervous and hated every second of how she felt around him.

She really missed her best friend.

"I have wine. Would you like a glass?"

She'd like about four glasses.

"Yes. Thank you."

He sounded just as nervous and awkward as she was. That made her feel a little better.

"I'll be right back." He stopped and turned around. "Uh, you can sit down if you'd like. I also have snacks. You hungry?"

"Not right now."

"Okay."

She took a seat on his sofa and looked around. His place was still as she remembered. Very chrome and black and gray. Nicely furnished, but . . . stark.

He came back in with a glass of white wine and handed it to her.

"Thank you."

She noticed he took a seat on the chair, not on the sofa with her.

"Nice dress," he said.

"Thanks."

She was going to die if they continued to talk to each other like they were acquaintances instead of friends. Lovers.

"My mom was here visiting last week. I got the dress when I was out shopping with her."

His brows raised. "Your mom came to visit?"

"Yes. Unexpectedly."

"Oh, yeah?" He frowned. "Everything okay? With your parents? Your brothers?"

"Yes. Everything's fine." She wasn't about to tell him her mother came because she'd utterly fallen apart after their last encounter. "Just an impromptu visit."

"I'm sure that was nice."

"It was."

"My parents were here with Sam after the game last weekend."

"Oh, great. I'm sure you had a wonderful time visiting with them. And with Sam."

"Yeah, it was good."

"And your game was exceptional."

"Thanks."

He took a swallow of beer and set it down on the table. "Mia, I—"

"I love you, Nathan."

He stared at her. She couldn't believe she'd just blurted it out. "What?"

"I realized I'd never said it to you. And I'm sorry. I should have said it before. And I meant to. It was my main motivation for—for what I did. Because I loved you. I mean, not past tense. It's not like I don't love you now, because I do." She set her wineglass on the table. "God, I'm screwing this up."

He slanted a look at her, one that spoke of the same confusion she felt. "We're weird around each other now. It sucks."

She inhaled deeply, then blew it out. "Yes. I hate it. We've never been weird around each other and I hate that we are now. And it's all my fault and I'm sorry about that. I made such a mistake, Nathan. I was trying to do the right thing for you and I ended up screwing up. I screwed us up right when things were going so well."

"Yeah, you did. But I didn't help things by not coming out and asking you what was going on. You know how pushy I am. But my pride got in the way."

"None of this is your fault. It's entirely mine."

"And I loved you, too. Love you, too. Still, present tense."

She blinked. "You still love me?"

"You're kind of hard to fall out of love with, Mia. God knows I've tried. But I can't. I think I've loved you since college. I'll probably love you forever."

Tears pricked her eyes. "I love you, too. So, so much. I've cried buckets over you the past few weeks, Nathan Riley. And I have never once cried over a guy. I cried so much it forced my mother to get on a plane and come out here to babysit me."

"Oh, so that's why she was here."

Tears streamed down her face. "Yes. Days and buckets of tears. I was wrecked over losing you. And I don't cry. You know this about me. And if that isn't love, I don't know what is."

He gave her a half smile. "So loving me makes you cry?"

She got off the sofa and came over to him, dropping to her knees in front of him. "No, Nathan. Losing you made me cry. You've been my best friend forever. And then I fell in love with you and I did something so stupid that I lost you. And I knew I'd never get over losing you. That's what made me cry. Please forgive me."

He swept his hand over her hair. "I love you, Mia. As long as you trust me with your heart, you'll always have mine."

"I love you, too. You have my heart, and my trust. Always and forever."

He took her hands and helped her up, then put her on his lap. And then he kissed her, and her heart swelled with such joy she thought it might explode. Just feeling his body against hers again made the tears spring forth. But when Nathan swiped his thumb over her cheek and murmured, "No more tears," against her lips, she shuddered.

He was right. It was time to celebrate. Because she thought for sure this day would never come. Though she should know better, because she was in love with a man who had the most generous, most forgiving heart.

"Oh, I got you something," she said.

"You did?"

"Yes."

She slid off his lap and went to get the bag she'd brought. She came back and sat on his lap again and handed him the bag.

He opened it and pulled out two pillows. One was lavender and gray, the other was a darker purple and yellow.

His lips curved. "Some color for the living room?"

She sniffed and swiped away residual tears. "Yes. God, you need some color in here, Nathan."

He laughed. "Thank you. They're perfect."

He set the pillows back in the bag, then kissed her. "You're perfect."

"I'm so not."

"Then you're perfect for me."

She felt serious for a moment. "I promise to always trust you with what's on my mind. Even if they're stupid nonsense thoughts."

He rubbed her back. "That's my girl. And I promise to always listen to you, and to tell you what's on my mind, too. Even if it's football."

She laughed. "I love you, Nathan."

"I love you, too, Mia."

He kissed her, a deep soulful kiss. She felt the love in his kiss and she knew they were going to be all right.

LOOK FOR THE NEXT PLAY-BY-PLAY NOVEL
COMING FROM BERKLEY
FEBRUARY 2018

Jaci Burton is the *USA Today* and *New York Times* bestselling author of the Play-by-Play series, including *The Final Score, Rules of Contact, Unexpected Rush, All Wound Up, Quarterback Draw, Straddling the Line, Melting the Ice* and *One Sweet Ride,* and the Hope series, including *Love Me Again, Don't Let Go, Make Me Stay, Love After All, Hope Burns, Hope Ignites* and *Hope Flames.* Visit Jaci online at jaciburton.com, facebook .com/authorjaciburton and twitter.com/jaciburton.